Books by James Patterson
for Young Adult Readers

For previews of upcoming books in these series and other information, visit confessionsofamurdersuspect.com, maximumride.com, and witchandwizard.com.

For more information about the author, visit jamespatterson.com.

WITCH & WIZARD

THE LOST

JAMES PATTERSON

and Emily Raymond

LITTLE, BROWN AND COMPANY
NEW YORK   BOSTON

Copyright © 2014 by James Patterson
Witch & Wizard® is a trademark of JBP Business, LLC.
Excerpt from *Maximum Ride Forever* copyright © 2014 by James Patterson

Little, Brown and Company

Hachette Book Group
1290 Avenue of the Americas, New York, NY 10104
Visit us at lb-teens.com

Little, Brown and Company is a division of Hachette Book Group, Inc. The Little, Brown name and logo are trademarks of Hachette Book Group, Inc.

The publisher is not responsible for websites (or their content) that are not owned by the publisher.

First Edition: December 2014
First International Edition: November 2014

Library of Congress Cataloging-in-Publication Data
Patterson, James, 1947– author.
   The Lost / James Patterson and Emily Raymond. — First edition.
      pages cm. — (Witch & wizard)
   Summary: "Magical teen siblings Whit and Wisty Allgood struggle against a mounting public opposition to magic and a brutal crime wave led by a powerful wizard intent on ruling the City"— Provided by publisher.
   ISBN 978-0-316-20770-6 (hardcover) — ISBN 978-0-316-24002-4 (large print hardcover) — ISBN 978-0-316-20773-7 (ebook) — ISBN 978-0-316-24234-9 (library edition ebook) — ISBN 978-0-316-24266-0 (international)   [1. Brothers and sisters—Fiction.   2. Witches—Fiction. 3. Wizards—Fiction.   4. Totalitarianism—Fiction.   5. Government, Resistance to—Fiction.   6. Magic—Fiction.]   I. Raymond, Emily, 1972– author.   II. Title.
   PZ7.P27653Lo 2014   [Fic]—dc23   2014007349

10 9 8 7 6 5 4 3 2 1
RRD-H
Printed in the United States of America

BOOK ONE

DEMON, BEGONÉ

Chapter 1

Whit

THERE'S BLOOD EVERYWHERE. Bright red pools of it on the gurney, and still there's more gushing out, running in rivulets to the floor. It seems impossible that there could be a single drop left inside the little girl. Her face is obscured by a tangle of dark hair, but the skin I can see has gone gray and her breath comes in harsh, wet gasps.

I rush to her side as the rookie attendant who brought her in retches in the corner. "Stabbed," he heaves, barely getting out the words. "Multiple times."

"Who—" I begin.

"The Family," he spits.

I rip away the girl's shirt to reveal the worst of the damage as Janine, a newly trained trauma nurse at City Hospital, presses her fingers to the thin little wrist.

"There's no peripheral pulse," Janine barks. "We've got to hurry."

"Tell me something I don't know," I growl. I put my

hands on the girl's punctured abdomen and begin to recite a healing spell.

Unfortunately I'm getting used to this kind of work. And I owe it to the Family, a secretive, savage cult that's been terrifying the City for weeks. Every day there's a new robbery or assault, a new reason to fear. I'm no stranger to the criminal element—hell, *I* was a wanted criminal under the New Order—but members of the Family make the average robber look like a puppy swiping a treat. They live to steal, and they don't care who they hurt. Even if it's a little kid.

The girl gives a weak cough. My fingers tingle as I feel my powers beginning to build. I picture being inside her body, following the paths of her blood, searching out the wounds and binding them back together with magic.

Janine brushes the girl's black hair away from her face, and that's when I nearly fall backward in shock. This isn't some random street kid who was in the wrong place at the wrong time.

It's Pearl Marie Neederman.

Lying near death on a cold metal table is the girl who once snatched my sister and me away from The One's zombie wolves. The kid who helped nurse Wisty back from the brink of death from the Blood Plague. The fierce little survivor who now looked more dead than alive. I let out a strangled cry. *"Pearl!"*

Janine gasps. "Oh, Whit," she cries. "Can we save her?"

It's not looking good. "I don't know," I say.

My fingers flex as they aim their healing magic, and Pearl's breath steadies. But then suddenly the electricity of the M starts to feel weird. Unbalanced. Instead of a tingle, it's a prickle, then a sting. An intense ache begins spreading from my fingertips, radiating up my arms and into my head.

"Something's wrong," Janine yells.

I don't understand what's happening, but it's *bad*. I close my eyes and try to beat back the surging pain.

A nurse appears at my elbow, screaming. "What do you think you're doing?" she yells. She tries to shove me aside so she can pack Pearl's wounds with gauze.

"Voodoo," snarls another. "The girl needs donor blood, not spells."

She's wrong. Even through my rising panic, I'm sure of it. I've been working at the hospital ever since we formed the new Council, and I've seen enough to know that magic is Pearl's only hope.

But Janine is the only one on my side. The only person in the entire room who believes in me, that what I'm doing is right.

The door bursts open and the Neederman family rushes in. Hewitt's shirt is on inside out and the look on his wife's face nearly tears my heart out.

"Oh, my baby," Mama May cries. "My little baby—"

"Those barbarians!" Hewitt spits out vehemently.

I'm giving it every ounce of strength I've got, but I'm feeling exactly what Pearl's feeling: my heart spasming, my lungs filling with blood, choking off my oxygen. My brain shooting off electric charges of terror.

I'm capable of thinking two things. The first: *I faced down the evil Mountain King to rescue this kid, and I am* not *going to give up now.*

And the second: *how awful it is to die.*

"Her blood's going acidic—" Janine calls.

My eyes fly open and I see Wisty blaze in and skid to a stop, her eyes sparking in fear.

"Whit," she cries. "You're *bleeding!*" She stumbles toward me and a nurse grabs her, holding her back. Wisty pushes her off, but another nurse snatches her other arm, and now they've got her pinned.

"Let her go," I gasp through intense throbbing, trying to keep focus on Pearl. *I can't let this little girl die. She's like another sister to me.*

The staff is no match for a determined Wisty, who shakes them off like gnats. Then she's at my side, yelling.

"Whit, you have to stop. It's killing you—"

Her voice sounds like it's a million miles away. When she hits me, hard, on the arm, I can barely feel it.

"*Blood!*" Wisty screams. "Blood is pouring out of your *ears!*"

Chapter 2

Whit

I'M BLEEDING out of my *ears*? That might explain the agonizing pain in my head, like something's inside my brain and chopping at it with an *axe*.

"More time," I gasp. My hands are sticky with gore and the spells are gone. Pearl and I are racing together to the gates of Shadowland.

Then Wisty's grabbing at my shirt, pulling me away. She's screaming my name. *No!* I want to shout. *I can't leave Pearl now. Not ever.* But Wisty's using magic now, too—on me. She yanks me back against the wall.

Pearl's eyes fly open, silver and unseeing. They roll back in her head. Then her body shudders—and goes still.

Wisty wraps her arms around me. "It's over," she whispers. "We lost her."

I slide out of Wisty's embrace and sink to the floor. "Exsanguination": bleeding to death. A terrible word for an even more terrible fate. "No, *I* lost her," I moan.

Wisty crouches down by my side. "It was too late," she says gently. "No one could have saved her. Not even you." Tears glitter in her eyes and she tries to blink them away. Behind her, I can see Mama May and Hewitt holding each other, rocking back and forth in their grief. I'm too wrecked to cry.

"Don't listen to them," Wisty urges.

I don't know what she's talking about. I'm numb. "Don't listen to who?" I say flatly.

That's when I start to hear them: all the nurses and doctors who watched the battle I lost to Death.

"Freak," one of them says.

"No one should have such unholy powers," says another.

And I realize they're talking about *me*.

Janine's voice cuts through the noise, pleading. "Please," she says. "Be reasonable—he's saved so many lives—"

But no one's listening to her. The angry clamor builds until I want to cover my ears.

"He's a *monster.*"

"He might have helped kill that little girl."

I clench my fists until my nails cut gashes into my palms. Those people have no idea how much Pearl gave to me, to my family. How much she suffered, too.

"He needs to submit," says a tall, sour-faced doctor.

Wisty stiffens and her cheeks flush red. "Don't even say that word around me," she yells.

The doctor's face contorts into a cruel grimace. "*Submit*," he says again. "Give up your dark magic. Both of you."

He doesn't care that Wisty and I stopped General Matthias Bloom from surrendering our City to the wicked Mountain King. Or that we defeated The One Who Is The One and ended his totalitarian reign of terror. No: all that matters to this man is how much he hates our powers.

Our powers—the phrase taunts me. How could I save an entire City but not one little girl's life?

"Abomination," says a nurse.

"Speak for yourself," Wisty says defiantly. "I didn't see any of *you* saving Pearl's life." Then she reaches out and grabs my bloodstained hands. "Get up, Whit. You need to show me you're okay."

I hear the fear in her voice, and I struggle to stand. As Wisty hurries me away, Janine catches my eye. But Mama May and Hewitt don't look at me as they clutch each other in their overwhelming grief. I will never be able to make up for this loss.

When we get outside, the sunlight feels like a slap in the face. Pearl is dead, and everyone in the hospital thinks I'm a demon. Maybe even the Needermans do, too.

The sobs come now in a wretched-sounding torrent. "How could the Family *do* that to a little girl?" I croak.

Wisty's face goes dark. "Actually," she says, and then stops and shakes her head.

"Actually what?"

"The Family didn't kill Pearl, Whit." She swallows. "She was a *member* of the Family."

I don't think I heard Wisty right. I shake my head. "No. That's impossible."

"You know there was a robbery this morning," Wisty goes on. She takes a deep breath. "And now you need to know that Pearl wasn't the victim of the crime. She was the one committing it."

I'm too stunned to speak.

"She robbed that store with a gang of kids. But unlike the rest of them, she didn't get away."

Pearl, a knife-wielding outlaw? My brain just can't comprehend it. And then, whether it's exhaustion or grief or shock, I don't know—everything goes dark.

Chapter 3

Wisty

THE ALERT COMES IN seconds after I've helped a barely conscious Whit into his bed. There's been another break-in, this one at a theater down by Industry Row.

I pull the covers up to my brother's chin. "Be safe," I whisper, "I've got to run."

Whit's proud of me for signing on as a consultant to the police force—he says I'll be *way* better at it than I was as a member of the Council—but right now he clutches my hand. Hard.

"*You* be safe," he gasps, and then slips back into his fever dream. It's a little unnerving.

A dirty kid on the street corner stares in wonder as I climb onto my chromed-out motorcycle and pull back on the throttle. His gray eyes remind me of Pearl's, and my throat constricts in a flash of pain. I hope the hospital staff lets the Needermans light a candle for her, but after that nasty scene in the operating room, I kind of doubt they will.

I peel out into the street and tear down the main thorough-fare, going way too fast. I want everything that's bad—Pearl's death, my brother's collapse, and the voices demanding that we *submit*—to get blown away by the wind.

I don't know why people have started talking about magic like it's a weapon to be confiscated. Yes, the City's suffered through more than its share of evil magic: from The One, and the Mountain King, and loathsome Pearce, just to name a few. But who, in the end, stopped the villains? People with *good* magic. People like my brother and me.

It doesn't matter to the Normals, though. Supposedly they've even developed a procedure that sucks the power out of you like a vacuum. Surrender your gift, they say, and you'll live a life of peace and quiet and contentment.

Honestly, I can't imagine anything worse.

I race down a tree-lined avenue, alongside the newly reopened art museum. A half mile past that is the almost-finished new aqueduct, still crawling with workers as busy as ants. But then I careen around a corner and have to screech to a halt, seconds before ramming into an old man carrying a squawking chicken under his arm. It's market day: the town square is jam-packed with vendors, selling everything from fruit and vegetables to resoled shoes and jerry-rigged bicycles.

I take a deep breath, downshift, and begin to weave my way through the throngs. It's proof that under the new Council, life's returning to normal. Our City is healing. The kids kidnapped by the Mountain King are back with their families, and General Bloom, that dough-faced trai-tor, is in exile.

We had to learn the hard way that adults couldn't be trusted with City leadership: power corrupted them too easily. By unanimous vote, we banned anyone over nine-teen from serving on the Council.

And so far, so good. The market's hopping, and the nearby central stadium—where we can host everything from foolball matches to rock concerts to benefits for new schools and health centers—is back in business.

Take that, you middle-aged cynics!

A stray dog skitters in front of me, and I swerve to the right, knocking a basket of oranges onto the ground. I don't have time to stop, so I snap my fingers and the oranges float up, spin around, and deposit themselves back into a neat stack.

The surly vendor shoots me a black look, then makes the sign I've seen all too much of lately: two fingers crossed in an X in front of her chest, like she's warding me off. It's an ancient gesture, left over from the days when people believed in man-eating goblins and bloodthirsty bogeymen. It means, basically, *Demon, begone.*

Some people are so rude!

A guard stationed by the fountain raises his baton at me. "Walk the bike," he hollers.

I pretend not to hear him. It's not a *bicycle*—it's the fast-est machine in the entire City, and I'm definitely not going to walk it. But then he plants himself in front of me.

"Turn off the motor," he says. His eyes are narrow and mean.

"I'm in a hurry," I tell him. "Police business."

"Turn off the motor, witch."

The way he says that word makes it sound like a curse. My skin begins to tingle and flush. *No one* talks to me like that. Not today—or *any* day.

"I said turn off—" he begins.

But tongues of fire are licking out of my fingertips.

His eyes widen and he takes an involuntary step back, knocking over the same basket of oranges. The vendor curses, but she can pick up her own damn oranges this time.

"Oh dear, what's this?" I say, faking total confusion. The ends of my hair have combusted, the red curls turning into the delicious heat of curling flames. "Could I maybe just...scoot by you? *Sir?* I, uh, seem to be on *fire....*"

The guard reaches into his belt—maybe he's going to call for backup, or maybe he's going to actually try to hand-cuff me (as if!)—but I *seriously* don't have time for this. So I close my eyes in concentration, and then—*fwoop*—my bike and I have rematerialized on the other side of him. Still in neutral, I gun the engine until it roars like a mythic beast.

The guard whirls around, reaching out to grab me, but I shift into gear and pull back on the throttle. I focus my power, and, using my own magic and the motorcycle's absolutely kick-ass engine, I rocket into the sky, shooting over the final six market stalls before landing on the other side of the square, flames following me like the tail of a comet.

Over the engine, I can hear the crowd gasp in awe—or maybe horror. Then I launch a white-hot fireball high over the street, and it explodes into a shower of multicolored sparks.

Submit? Never. I live to *burn*.

Chapter 4

Wisty

OUT ON THE WESTERN EDGE of town, the Academy Theater is wrapped in brightly colored police ribbon, like a present you don't want to open. The big front windows are smashed to pieces, and broken glass litters the sidewalk.

A pigeon flaps away as I step through the door that hangs crookedly from one hinge. Inside, it looks like someone picked up the lobby lamps and used them as baseball bats, knocking over trash cans, bashing up the popcorn machine, and clobbering the frames of the velvet couches.

"Hello?" I call. But it's dark and dead silent under the soaring ceiling. And even though I'm still hot from my flames, I shiver. "Hello?" I try again.

Then a figure in a black leather police jacket rounds the corner, playing a flashlight around the walls. His back is to me, his shoulders hunched in concentration.

"Glad you could make it, Wisty," a male voice says.

He doesn't turn around, but I'd recognize that voice

anywhere. It's Byron Swain, one of my biggest nemeses and also one of my best friends, depending on the day. And, okay, maybe I've kissed him once or twice. But in this dark, godforsaken place, that feels like a million years ago.

I'm both reassured and annoyed that it's him. "Give me a break, Swain," I grumble. "I practically flew over the entire market to get here. Pissed off a guard, too."

"Typical," he says.

His voice is lower than it used to be, and I swear he's even grown an inch or two. Either his new job as a police investigator has matured him, or else he's finally hit full-on puberty.

He turns around to look at me then, shining the flashlight slowly up my body. I can't help but remember how he used to gaze at me for minutes on end, like he was memorizing every inch of my figure. Now he probably does that with his new girlfriend, Whatshername McWhatshername. She's a redhead, too. I guess he has a thing for those.

"Wisteria Allgood," he says smoothly. "Show-off extraordinaire."

I'm not in the mood for Byron's cocky new attitude. I take a step closer to him, my fingers flexing. "You want to check out the crime scene from the viewpoint of a weasel, Byron? Or a cockroach? Because I can make that happen. *Just. Like. This.*" My index finger points threateningly at his chest.

Unsurprisingly, Byron backs down. He always was

kind of a chicken. "Very funny, Wisty," he says. He sighs. "I'm just saying you should be careful. Try not to put your powers on display. People don't like it."

"I don't care what people like," I retort. I give his sternum a poke.

Again, he sighs. "Come on. We're wasting time here."

I drop my hand. "Fine. Truce. Although I would have enjoyed turning you into something small and squishable." I squint around the dim room. "What do we know about the robbery?"

"The cash box is gone," Byron says. "And the movies."

"Can't imagine why they'd want to steal *Agent Zero IV*," I quip. "That movie sucked."

Byron ignores me. "I've pulled some fingerprints from the counter, and it seems like one of the perps left his hat." He points to a filthy brown knit cap. "I haven't checked the storeroom or the crawl space or the—"

"I get it," I say. "We've got a lot of ground to cover."

Part of the problem is that we need more good cops in the City. Byron is a natural, but there are too many officers who pledged allegiance to the New Order or General Bloom (or both), and it's tough to trust them. But the Council is training new forces every day. They know we need to stop the current crime wave. If we don't, say the newspapers, we risk the City falling into irreversible chaos.

"Do you think it's the Family?" I ask.

Byron shakes his head. "I don't know."

He hands me a spare flashlight and we search the main

theater and the bathrooms. There's nothing but old ticket stubs and more spilled popcorn.

Then we walk back toward the storeroom—and we see the foot.

I stop short, my breath catching in my throat. I desperately want to believe that we'll turn the corner and find some lazy kid asleep on the job.

But I'd have to be pretty stupid to think that, and I am not stupid.

Byron strides forward and rounds the corner, and reluctantly I follow him. On the floor is a girl, probably fifteen or sixteen. Her arms are covered in lacerations, and her neck is bent at a strange angle. She's lying halfway through the door of the storeroom. The stack of napkins she'd gone back to get is scattered around her. Many are red with her blood.

I feel like I'm going to be sick. I grab Byron's arm to steady myself.

"DOA," he says softly, almost to himself.

"They could have just shut the door," I cry. "Locked her in so she couldn't call for help. They didn't need to kill her."

Byron says nothing. He points to the graffiti on the wall. The letters are a dark, violent purple, and almost as big as he is. "No, they didn't need to kill her," he finally says. "But they wanted to."

Take what you want, the spray-painted letters read. *It belongs to you—the Family.*

A chill shivers up my spine. "It's one thing to take money—but the life of an innocent girl? *Why?*" I whisper.

Byron's tone is matter-of-fact. "To provoke terror," he says.

Two gruesome deaths in one day, and a heinous message scrawled for everyone to see. My heart is pounding hard in my chest, and adrenaline sparks in my limbs.

"Well, it's working."

Chapter 5

Darrius

THE LITTLE BOY expertly juggles a soccer ball with his knees: sixty-eight, sixty-nine, seventy times without letting it touch the ground once. But his black eyes keep darting over to the Academy Theater. He's waiting for the girl to come out.

Not the one who worked there—she's never coming out again.

Well, not alive anyway, he thinks, unable to suppress a snicker.

Sure, it was too bad she had to die. She'd seemed nice, and she wore such pretty dresses, and she'd begged so fervently for her life. But orders were orders, and the Family *always* followed their orders.

Orders, of course, which he had given to them.

No, the boy is waiting to see the *other* girl. Wisteria Allgood: the one with the name of a flower and the heat of a bonfire. The one they call witch.

He's getting impatient, though. He kicks at his stupid ball and it turns, instantly, to dust. It's time to shift things around a little bit. His outline shivers, then fades.

A moment later, there's no boy. Instead there's a homeless woman, dressed head to toe in filthy rags. She shuffles back and forth in front of the theater, muttering to herself. She pulls at her long, rank hair. She's no more patient than the boy.

"Such incompetence," she grunts through a nearly toothless mouth. She could tell that smarmy police investigator anything he needed to know, if he'd only step outside. And then she could see the fire girl, too. She'd like to whisper things into that pale, delicate ear.

But... perhaps not in this form. The old woman's *smell* might be a bit of a turnoff.

Around her, a crowd has begun to gather. People are nervous, and rumors swirl in the air. "It was just kids, breaking windows," says someone. "No," says someone else. "It was the Family."

Bingo! she thinks gleefully.

Then she scoots toward the back of the crowd, and they give her a wide berth—she really *does* stink—then she vanishes in a tiny burst of light.

When she reappears, in her true form, it's as a handsome young man with cold, pitiless golden eyes. He is Darrius Z: the father, so to speak, of the Family.

He sidles up behind a pretty girl with a long gold braid. Smooth and light as air, his hand slips into her purse and withdraws her wallet. He grazes her hip with his fingers. "Finders keepers," he whispers.

Then he's gone, and the girl has a smile on her face.

Yes, Darrius can make being robbed feel *nice*.

He straightens his broad shoulders, and muscles ripple down his long, lean torso. He looks like an athlete, but games don't interest him, unless the consequences are life-and-death.

Such are the games he plans on playing with Wisteria, once they finally meet.

Chapter 6

Wisty

IT'S A TOTAL mosh pit of people outside the Academy, except that no one's dancing: they're just milling around like a bunch of frightened sheep. They want to know what happened, why the police have cordoned off the theater.

They don't know about the dead girl yet. When they do, things are going to get a lot nastier. These people think the new government's too young, too inexperienced, and too soft on crime—and they're going to want to take their fear and frustration out on someone.

Personally, I think Byron's as good a target as any. So, it's time for yours truly to split.

I give him a quick pat on the shoulder and wave. "Sayonara, Swain," I say. "Make some new friends, why don't ya?"

His eyes flash nervously, but he's too proud to ask me to stay.

The only problem with my quick exit, though? My motorcycle is gone.

That's right: *gone.*

I shove my way through the throngs in the street, scanning madly in all directions for a glimpse of it. I strain to hear the roar of its engine. My fingers begin to tingle in fiery anticipation—I'm probably about to erupt in flames of rage—but then, from far away, I hear the sound of a horn. *My* bike's horn.

Instantly I'm sprinting toward the sound, down a narrow alley lined with trinket shops and toy boutiques, most of them still shuttered. My feet slam on the old cobblestones as I dodge rain barrels and trash cans and skinny stray cats.

I know the thief can't be too far away. This part of the City is old and labyrinthine, full of blind alleys and pathways that suddenly get so narrow only a street rat could slip through. I push myself to go faster, and my lungs scream in pain.

When I race around the next corner, nearly losing my footing on a pile of gravel, I see my motorcycle in the lane ahead. On top of it is a hunched, unfamiliar figure in black.

As the bike slows to navigate around a crater in the road—an ugly reminder of The One's bombing campaign—the driver wobbles and the engine almost stalls. I grit my teeth as I speed up.

If that thief wrecks my motorcycle, today is his LAST day on earth.

"Police business!" I shout, just in case anyone's watching as I leap onto an old dirt bike parked in front of a grocery store. I fire an ignition spark from the tip of my finger straight into the engine. The bike coughs, rattles, and then sputters to life. I yank the throttle back and peel out, tires screeching.

By now the thief's made it to open ground, as the buildings give way to the wide streets and concrete lots of the old industrial side of town. Steering with one hand, I make a fireball with the other. It shoots into the sky and arcs down, exploding just ahead of the thief. He swerves, nearly losing control again.

Okay, that was a bad idea. While I wouldn't mind seeing him smash his face into a brick wall, I want my bike back unscathed. I realize I'm going to have to get ahead of him—and cut him off.

Up ahead the road splits, and I follow the thief through the high stone gates of a cemetery. I swerve off the road and tear over the grass, dodging angel statues, obelisks, and bunches of fake flowers. I'm gaining on the thief, but the dirt bike's rattling like its wheels are going to fall off, and my headlamp's not working.

If you've ever wanted to ride a motorcycle fast and blind, here's some advice: *don't.*

I send another jolt of magic into the engine. The bike shudders, then shoots forward like a rocket. I brake and pull a hard right, skidding to a stop in the road—

To see the thief barreling toward me.

He's not going to stop.

I raise my hands over my head, and lightning shoots out in crackling stars. A ball of fire condenses in front of me. It grows lighter, brighter, until it blazes so hot he's got to feel like he's driving into the sun.

At the last possible moment, he spins out. My bike tilts—it's falling—it's going to crash—

Quickly I use my powers to right it, but I let the thief land hard. Then I lower my incandescent hands.

I look closer at the dark form crumpled on the ground. Holy M: the thief is a *girl*. "Are you insane?" I yell.

Her eyes spark dangerously as she stands up. "Take what you want," she intones. "It belongs to you."

I see the glint of a knife in her hand, but she could have a cannon for all I care. "Yeah, I've heard your stupid motto before," I spit. "And since this *does* belong to me, I'll be taking it."

She cocks her arm and flings the knife. The blade grazes my cheek, and I feel a gash open up. If she does something like that again, I'm going to charbroil her like a shish kebab.

And sure enough, she's whipped out another little dagger. I feint left, then whirl to face her. My flames burn higher. Hotter.

She begins to cower in the light. I can see the tattoo on her wrist in sharp relief: the cursive *F*s circling her wrist like a daisy chain, or like handcuffs. *F*, for Family.

But suddenly I see her tense, then charge. *Some people never learn!*

I lob a fireball at her. It explodes right at her chest, and she's beating at her shirt and screaming like she's been struck by a comet. It takes her a minute to realize that there was no heat, no burn. It was only light: a trick.

She collapses in sobs on the ground.

"Don't steal. And *especially* not from a witch," I hiss, and then I sling my leg over the back of my motorcycle and roar away into the dark.

Chapter 7

Whit

JANINE IS YANKING me down the street toward the Government Towers, where the Council is holding some kind of special nighttime session. "Hurry up, Whit," she's saying. "We're going to be late."

"I'd rather play spin the bottle with the Lost Ones than go to a Council meeting right now," I grumble. "Or give a bunch of zombie wolves a flea bath."

Janine laughs. "It's not going to be *that* bad."

"So you say." I don't care what the meeting's about. All I can think about is what happened this morning at the hospital. My mind swirls with brutal, heartbreaking images. Every time I blink, I see Pearl again: gasping, bleeding out, dying.

What if Wisty was wrong? What if someone else—like a *doctor* instead of a wizard—could have saved her?

I'll never know the answer to that question, and I feel like it's going to haunt me until the day I die.

"Earth to Whit," Janine says, interrupting my dark thoughts. "I don't think you've heard a word I said."

"I'm sorry," I say. I put my arm around her shoulders and pull her close, breathing in the sweet, lilac scent of her hair. "What were you saying?"

She smiles sadly. "You're thinking about Pearl, aren't you?"

"I can't stop," I admit. "What if using magic was the wrong choice?"

Janine leans her head against my chest. "You can't think that way," she says. "You did what you believed was right." Then she gazes up at me, her green eyes serious. "And just in case you have any doubts, I think it was right, too."

I realize I've been holding my breath. I had no idea how much I needed to hear those words.

We enter the meeting room hand in hand. The benches are full of Council members and spectators, all whispering excitedly. The air is hot and close.

A moment later, the gavel raps against the marble podium, and all eyes turn to our new Speaker, seventeen-year-old Terrence Rino. He's small and pale—he sort of looks like a grubworm, if you ask me—but his power of speech is already legendary.

"Good evening, citizens," Terrence says. He brushes a piece of lank blond hair away from his brow. "Thank you for coming out on this fine evening. I realize the hour is late, but I have an extremely important announcement." He pauses and lets his eyes slowly scan the room. He's purposely building the suspense.

Sure enough, everyone leans forward in their seats. They're desperate to know what he has to say, and pretty soon they're going to start panting for it like dogs do for scraps.

"Like a phoenix, our new Council rose from the ashes of old despotic powers. Together we began to rebuild," Terrence says. "And now, in these days of growing turmoil, we must recommit to our common cause and our fundamental equality."

Everyone's nodding, and a few people clap. *Yes, we're united!* But Terrence is far from done.

"Seared by the memory of all we have lost, we know too well the cost of unchecked powers," he cries. "It is time to take steps we consider both necessary and legitimate to preserve peace and order. We must all be equal."

Equality's great—so why are the hairs rising on the back of my neck? Something is coming, and I'm not going to like it.

"Which is why I have the pleasure of announcing the development of a new, cutting-edge scientific process." Terrence pauses dramatically. "We call it," he finally says, "Excision."

Behind him, a short kid in an argyle sweater nods approvingly. But no one else reacts, because they have no idea what he's talking about.

"It is a precise and methodical process whereby unnatural powers are extracted from their host," Terrence declares. He looks around the room expectantly.

It takes everyone—including me—a minute to realize what he means. He's talking about *submission*.

I feel my stomach lurch as the room erupts. Suddenly everyone's jabbering, calling out, demanding more information. Me, though, I'm stunned into silence.

I guess I had hoped that submission was just a rumor. But it's a *reality*. And the Council wants us to do it.

"We have seen the damage that magic can do," Terrence cries. "And *is doing this very minute*, as the Family and its anonymous wizard leader threaten the safety of our fair City." Terrence is flushed now. He's loving his moment in the spotlight. "Magic, my fellow citizens, too often leads to madness and thirst for power. It is time to *minimize its risks*."

I swear I'm having déjà vu. Terrence sounds like General Bloom did, back when he declared acts of magic forbidden and made everyone with powers register them with the Council.

Janine reaches for my hand. Her fingers seem small and cold. Little Sarah Thompson shoots me a worried glance from across the room. So does her brother, Tommy. These kids can levitate a little, and their cousin Hank can shapeshift. But he can only ever become a dog, and who wants to go around peeing on tree trunks and sniffing strangers' butts? What kind of threat do these kids pose?

Of course, not all of us are harmless. My sister, Wisty, for example. But she uses her powers for *good*.

Mostly.

"You know the phrase—*power corrupts, and absolute power corrupts absolutely*," Terrence shouts. "It is time for us all to be equal, and to build our community on traditional *human* strengths."

The room is in an uproar, and I feel like my head's going to explode. Then the door gets flung open, and a bright blaze of light nearly blinds us all. The flames advance into the Council chamber, and people start to panic, tripping over one another to get out of the way.

Then, from inside the light, comes a familiar voice.

"So," Wisty calls out, "what'd I miss?"

Chapter 8

Wisty

I HAVE A SUPERGOOD EXCUSE for being late (hello, *grand theft motorcycle*), so I don't know why Terrence Rino is looking at me like I'm some dead piece of rodent flesh that a stray cat dragged in.

I'm wearing a clean dress and a pair of cute sling-back shoes—not to mention a little spritz of perfume so I don't smell like gasoline and singed thief. And hey, I used to *be* on this Council, so I think I deserve a slightly warmer welcome at its tedious meeting.

"Take a seat," commands the secretary, a girl with weird, unflattering purple glasses.

My flames (little ones—just decorative, really) sizzle out, and I slide into a seat next to Whit and Janine. Whit glances over at my cheek with an alarmed look on his face.

"Oh, it's nothing," I say, wiping away a smear of blood. "Just looks bad. It doesn't actually hurt."

Whit frowns. "No offense, sis," he says quietly, "but it's not you I'm worried about."

"Oh, really?" I say. "Well, see if I care the next time you nearly amputate a finger trying to cut carrots for a salad. See if I care when you—"

"Wisty, just *listen*," Janine interrupts.

I'm so surprised by her tone (Janine's nothing if not nice) that I shut up. And right away, I understand why my brother is *freaking out*.

They're talking about *Excision*. The technical term, apparently, for submission.

I can barely believe it. That pompous blond maggot we elected Speaker of the Council is up there on the dais, calmly betraying everything I've ever believed in and counted on.

I don't want to hear another word. I shoot up from my seat. "You mean *submission*," I yell. "Don't make it sound like you're doing surgery on something malignant, like a *tumor*. What you're talking about is stealing the essence of who we are."

"Ms. Allgood—"

"Don't Ms. Allgood me, *Terry*. And don't you dare suggest I give up my powers. I saved this City with them!" I point my finger at him, and he flinches.

"Had you arrived on time, you might have heard the reasons—"

"Oh, I've heard all I need to hear of your so-called reasons. Assuming that I might use my powers wrongly is biased, bigoted, prejudiced, and illogical."

"Also small-minded and unfair!" pipes up the kid who can turn into a dog.

"Right on, Fido," I yell. By now I'm hovering six inches off the ground and giving off waves of heat. "Are you going to put us in ghettos the way Bloom did, Terrence?"

He offers me a smug, excruciating smile. "If you agree to Excision, Wisteria, then we won't have to."

People are shouting, but I'm not done. "Your job is to follow the will of the people, and people like me aren't interested in submitting!"

Then, above the fray, I hear a familiar voice, and I turn to see Whit standing on the bench. Not hovering, like me. Just... *standing*. Like a regular person.

"I would like to say," he yells. And when the room quiets, he lowers his voice. He always hated speaking in front of a crowd. Right now he's strangely calm, though. Almost cold. He sets his jaw. "I would like to say that I will consider anything that serves the cause of uniting and strengthening our City."

I feel like I've been punched in the gut.

The room stays silent for another moment. And Whit slowly sits down.

"What?" I hiss, dropping down next to him. "What are you talking about?"

"Just what I said," Whit says flatly. "I'll consider it."

I shove my finger into his chest. Hard. "Whit, I love you, but you're talking like a perfect idiot."

He gazes at me with exhausted eyes. "Am I, though?

Isn't it the *opposite* of idiotic to try to see both sides of an argument?"

"No," I bark. "It's not. Because you are a wizard. It's the soul and spirit of you, Whit. Without your powers, you're just another ex-jock! A former prom king whose best years are already behind him!" He flinches like I've just hit him.

I realize, belatedly, that everyone in the room is watching our little sibling spat. "Who brought down The One Who Is The One?" I yell. I'm not arguing with Whit now, I'm arguing with the whole room. "I did—*with magic.*"

Terrence's voice lifts. "He was a wizard who wasn't stopped in time. Excision, citizens, is a process that prevents crime before it happens."

"He's right," someone calls.

"No," I yell. "It prevents that which is extraordinary and wonderful. What makes life inspiring is energy, creativity, and magic—a bit of healthy, delightful chaos!"

I'm expecting to get a few hoots and cheers. But the room is strangely hushed.

"Chaos," Terrence utters through clenched teeth, "is never *delightful.*"

"Oh, really?" I holler. "Are you sure?" And with that, I wave my arms above my head, close my eyes—

And turn everyone in the room into kittens.

It's totally, completely hilarious to watch them pouncing on one another, chasing their tails, and leaping up to catch dust motes. Tell me they're not having some nice, chaotic fun!

After an extremely satisfying minute of watching Kitty Terrence trip over his big white paws and then lick his own rear end, I turn them back into people.

"Tell me that wasn't *delightful*," I pronounce as I head for the door.

But before I exit, I turn around and look every member of the Council in the eye. "Think about it. If you had powers like mine, would *you* ever give them up?"

No one answers. They just gaze at me coldly.

"I didn't think so."

Someone grabs my arm as I leave, and I whirl around, ready to fight. But standing before me is a tall and unbelievably gorgeous stranger, a guy with dark hair and pale, almost golden eyes.

His full lips part to show perfect white teeth. "You're the only one with any guts around here," he says. His voice is almost a purr.

But I'm so mad I don't care if he's the hottest thing since the center of the earth. I yank my arm away and hiss, "You're damn right."

Chapter 9

Whit

BACK AT HOME, Janine unpins her hair so it falls in dark curls past her shoulders. On any other night, I'd steal up behind her, brush it away, and cover the back of her neck with a thousand kisses.

But I'm too upset now; I can't stop thinking about what Terrence said. How he twisted his words to make magic sound as dangerous as a loaded gun. And how Wisty didn't help matters by nearly setting the room on fire and turning everyone into kittens.

Janine pats the couch next to her. "Come sit," she says. She props her feet on the old traveler's trunk that serves as our coffee table. It's battered and covered in old bumper stickers, but she claims to love it—maybe because it was my one contribution to the household. When we moved in together six months ago, the only other thing I brought was a suitcase of wrinkled clothes.

Oh, and the ghost of my dead first love, who still visits

me sometimes from Shadowland. It takes a special girl-friend, like Janine, to be okay with that.

So I flop down next to her, and I try hard to be still. A moment later, though, I get up again in agitation. Sit down, get up, repeat. I'm like a human pogo stick.

Our powers are being demonized: how could this be happening—*again*?

"Talk to me, Whit," Janine urges.

I'm pacing the room now, clenching and unclenching my fists. "I want to be a good citizen. But do I have to be *Excised* to do it?"

"It seems like a lot of people think so," Janine says.

"Wisty said I'd be nothing without my powers."

Janine frowns. "That's not true."

I meet her lovely sage-green eyes. "But who am I *with* them? A demon? A menace?" I slam my hand against the wall in frustration. "I don't want to be looked at like I'm some kind of *enemy*."

"People fear what they don't understand," Janine says.

"But is it *my* fault they don't get it? Am I supposed to suffer because of their ignorance?" I ask bitterly.

Janine bites her lip. She doesn't answer. Maybe because she's never felt the thrilling, electric surge of magic—or the crushing despair when it doesn't work. She doesn't know what it's like to be awed by your own power.

She and I have been through so much evil together: we've dodged bombs, we've seen our friends murdered—and we've witnessed the triumph of good, too. *Twice.*

40

Basically, we've been through the best and worst moments in our City's history together.

So why does it feel like a gulf has opened up between us? Is it just me, or are magic folk and nonmagic folk suddenly on two different teams?

Then I shake my head, hard, like I can rattle these disturbing thoughts away. I'm being crazy. Of course Janine and I are on the same side. We always have been, ever since we met in Resistance headquarters a few years ago.

I'm still pacing, and Janine is watching me with concern. She lets me do this for a few more minutes, and then she holds out her arms. "Come here," she says. "*Stay here.*"

I finally collapse, exhausted by everything, onto the cushions. She traces her fingers along the palm of my hand, then kisses it. Her lips are as silky as rose petals.

Now her hands are running through my hair. Her touch is tender, thrilling.

"Poor Whit," Janine says. "You look so beat. But I think I know what might help you."

Considering I just heard my stomach rumble, I'm sure she's going to say a bowl of chicken soup or something.

I start to tell her I'm not hungry. But she's already standing up and pulling me into the hallway.

Not to the kitchen, though. To the bedroom.

"Trust me," she says. "I'm a medical professional."

And suddenly I'm ravenous. It's just an appetite of an entirely different sort.

Chapter 10

Wisty

MAYBE I SHOULD have expected something like the whole Council fiasco. I mean, when has life ever been simple? Honestly I can hardly remember. Must have been when I was twelve or something—before I knew I was a witch, or my brother a wizard.

I decide to take a walk to blow off some steam. My cats come with me, meowing and waving their tails like furry flags. (They're a lot better behaved than the Council kittens I created earlier tonight.) As much as I hate to admit it, I'm basically on my way to becoming a crazy cat lady these days. It wasn't on purpose. But then again, does any woman wake up one morning and say to herself, *Today I'm going to guarantee eternal singledom by acquiring five hundred cats?*

I only have six cats, though, so maybe there's still hope for me. First I rescued three kittens from a bombed-out apartment building, then a three-legged stray showed up on my doorstep, and then my parents' cats, Pancho and Lefty, decided they wanted to move in, too. (My mom's still not over it.)

"Hey, that's her," someone murmurs.

I don't pay any attention, because I assume they're talking about Nevada Manning, an actress who lives in this neighborhood with her sister, Belle.

"I saw her at the market," says someone else. "She, like, *flew*. On a *motorcycle*. It was insane."

Oh, wait: they're talking about *me*? I pick up my pace. I can't believe I'm being recognized. Being famous (or infamous, more like it) is definitely not something I bargained for when I made my first fumbling attempts at magic.

"Excuse me, uh, Wisteria?" the first girl calls.

But instead of answering her, I smile, wave, and quickly duck down a side street. I'm not sure if they were going to ask me for my autograph or call me a demon, but I guess I don't really want to know.

Mittens, Puff, Tink, and Tux go crazy sniffing all the trash cans and stoops, while Pancho and Lefty, who are older and grumpier, hang back by my heels. I watch Mittens take a flying leap at a moth, and suddenly I'm struck by how much fun being a cat looks.

I wonder . . . *Could I . . . ?*

The fact is, I've rarely used my powers for a romp. That's probably because I'm usually trying to *save* someone with them (often, as it turns out, myself).

The urge is too strong to resist. I imagine my body

shrinking, my fingers curling into tiny fuzzy toes, and whiskers sprouting from my nose. Immediately, I experience an uncomfortable feeling of contraction, of shriveling—and then the weird, prickling tingle of fur growing out of my skin.

A second later, I'm a cat. A black one, of course.

I dash away, and my own, real cats take up the playful chase. Together we cross the neighborhood by scooting along the tops of fences. My balance is perfect. And suddenly I can see all the degrees of darkness—how black is not one single color, but instead has a million subtle shades.

I spy a mouse in a clump of grass, a tiny quivering thing, and part of me wants to pounce on it. But I'm still Wisty—a human, a *girl*—and I don't want to be picking fur out of my teeth.

Also: considering I don't even like sushi, I'm definitely not going to dig raw mouse.

I skitter up a tree while my pets keep going down the sidewalk (they know their way home). I pause to think. *What do I do next? What things come naturally to cats?* Napping, shedding, sneaking into places they don't belong...

And that's when it comes to me. *Sneaking into places they don't belong:* I'm going to creep my way into Terrence Rino's apartment, and I'm going to shred his couch to pieces.

The idea's so perfect that I don't pause to consider the potential problems, such as: what happens if he's home, or what if he has a cat-devouring dog, or what I should do if my spell suddenly wears off and I find myself scratching at a sofa with sorry, bitten-down fingernails that haven't had a manicure since before time began.

Nope, I'm off and running, and I'm slipping in through Terrence's door and unsheathing my needle-pointed claws before you can say "hairball."

The first scratch is delicious. The soft fabric catches in my claws, and when I pull back, I can feel the threads breaking, one by one. Pulling harder, the weave begins to unravel and shred. In ten minutes I'll have mutilated this couch beyond recognition.

I'm having so much fun with my art project that I don't even hear Terrence come into the room.

"Aaaaagh!" he screams, and every single hair on my body stands straight up like I've been shocked.

I skitter toward the front door, but he blocks my way, his normally pale face purple with rage. He lunges at me, and the broom in his hands slams down an inch from my head.

The only way to escape is up the stairs. I make a mad dash up two twisting flights to the attic, and I leap to the nearest window ledge as I hear Terrence sprinting up behind me.

I slip through the gap between window and sill. Ten feet away is an elm tree, its branches offering shelter and safety.

I'm pretty sure I can make it.

I leap.

I feel my paws touch green leaves, and my claws come out. I'm scrabbling madly to catch the branch, to keep from plummeting—

Cats always land on their feet. Right?

Right?

That's my only thought as I fall spinning through the air.

Chapter 11

Darrius

LAUGHTER, HE BELIEVES, is a sign of a feeble mind. But when Wisty, in the form of a cat, falls onto a pile of trash bags under the Council Speaker's window, bounces off, and then zips away—well, he laughs for a long time about that.

Which for him is about five seconds.

He's enjoyed spying on her today. Getting to know her. He likes what he's seen very much. If he believed in having friends, Wisty could be one of them.

Barring, of course, their very different opinions on stealing, assault, and murder.

Invisible, he follows Wisty as she begins walking home. Returned to her human form, she's got a slight limp from her fall. He can tell that she's annoyed, that she hates to feel vulnerable. He understands: he used to feel the same way, before he became, for all intents and purposes, indestructible.

Darrius escorts Wisty all the way to her stoop, an unseen gentleman. Who says chivalry is dead?

He notes that she has four dead bolts on her front door. A nice attempt at safety, but when he wants in, he'll get in.

He follows her up the steps. He's so close to her now, he could reach out and touch her fragile white neck.

Suddenly she whips around, and he has to leap back. "Hello? Is someone there? If you are, come out and show yourself!"

It's a very tempting invitation, but it's time for him to go. After another moment, lovely Wisty goes inside and shuts the door.

Click, click, click, click go her useless locks.

An instant later, Darrius is all the way on the north end of town, where most of the buildings are still bombed-out and vacant. Becoming visible again, he strides through the door of the Family's headquarters.

It's in an abandoned toy factory, still full of old assembly-line machines gathering dust. The décor is decidedly macabre: severed doll heads line the windowsills, and dismembered arms and legs—from dolls, teddy bears, and vintage superheroes—dangle from pieces of wire, like Holiday garlands in hell.

The factory floor is dotted with tents, makeshift walls, and pallets nailed together to make sheltering cubes. It's a chaotic, indoor shantytown. Darrius could have housed his gang of thieves in an abandoned hotel, but this way everything's visible to him at once: Sean, his deputy, berating a kid for coming home with empty pockets. Sam, the one who killed the theater girl, dozing on an ancient beanbag. Ellie cooking on a camp stove. Jake hanging up laundry.

The room suddenly hushes: they've realized Darrius is back. The kids, who range in age from seven to nearly twenty, all stop what they're doing to press a fist to their sternums. It's the Family greeting.

Darrius puts his fist to his chest and nods curtly. "As you were," he says.

And then, rising from her place on a stolen couch, Sybil comes gliding toward him. She's his...well, he wouldn't go so far as to say *girlfriend*. Perhaps "companion" would be the best word. Or maybe "plaything." She's wearing a green silk dress, and her gold hair is coiled in an elaborate, twisting braid.

Sybil presses herself against his arm. "I missed you," she says. "Where have you been all day?"

Instead of answering, he takes a drink of home-brewed wine that Sean offers him. It tastes bitter. Someone's going to pay for that.

Sybil's eyes narrow. Beauty is her primary magic, but she has supernaturally acute senses, too. "You've been with a girl," she says sharply.

Still he says nothing.

"There's someone else," Sybil insists. "I can smell her on you."

Darrius throws the wine to the ground. He pulls Sybil

toward him and wraps his arms around her waist, kissing her deeply. Their lips generate heat, and she melts into his embrace. His hands caress the silkiness of her dress and skin.

"Oh, Darrius," she says, breaking their kiss and gazing up at him adoringly. "Where did you go? Who did you see? Why do you torture me?"

These inquiries *bother* him: the answers are none of her business. Hasn't he taught his followers—even his favorites—not to question anything he does?

So he kisses her again, harder this time. Then even harder. She tries to pull away, but he only grips her tighter. Her fingers flutter, her body trembles and shudders—

Then Darrius steps back, and Sybil simply *crumbles*. Her beautiful face dissolves; her skin turns gray and shrivels into cinders. In a matter of seconds, there's nothing left of her but a small, silvery pile of ash.

The entire room goes deathly silent—no one's even breathing. The Family members have just witnessed their first spontaneous cremation.

Darrius allows himself a tiny smile. "I'm a very bad boy, Sybil," he whispers. "I trust you know that by now."

Then he calls to the fat kid nearby, the one staring at him in awe and terror. "Simon," he says, "get over here and clean up this mess."

Chapter 12

Whit

I THOUGHT I KNEW every inch of this City—and unlike Wisty, I've got a pretty good sense of direction. But here I am, shivering on a dark street I couldn't name if my life depended on it. There's no one else around. There isn't even a light in a window.

I shiver and pull my jacket tighter around my shoulders. My footsteps sound like gunshots.

I've got to get home.

Where is home?

I walk in confused circles for what feels like hours, but then suddenly, I catch a whiff of a familiar scent—of flowers and spring and warmth. My heart skips a beat.

"Celia?" I whisper. "Celes, is that you?"

A gust of wind makes the scent grow stronger, and a dull ache blooms in my chest. My first love was killed—*murdered*—a long time ago, but I guess some wounds don't ever fully heal.

"Are you there?"

I hold my breath until she flickers into view, just as I remember her: the bright blue of her eyes, the dark soft curls of her hair. But she's so faint—fainter than she used to be.

"Hey, you," she whispers.

"Hey, you, back," I say. I smile and hold out my arms, as if I could hug her, but I know that I can't. She's a Half-light, a ghost. Trying to hold her is like trying to hold a wisp of fog.

I wait to see that perfect smile that lights up her whole face—but it doesn't come. The cold, creeping dread I felt moments ago returns in a rush. "Celia, what's wrong?"

Maybe it's Janine, I think. *Maybe Celia doesn't want me to move on after all.*

She reaches out to touch me, and I feel the slightest breeze—but nothing else. "You're in terrible danger," she whispers. "You and your sister and the whole City."

"What else is new?" I joke, although I grimace instead of smile. And I can't help but blurt out, "When are you going to show up with *good* news, Celes?" Because she has a habit of turning up in my dreams as the harbinger of doom.

But she ignores my jab, and the words come faster now. Frantically. "Powers of darkness and evil. They're coming. Their strength is building every second."

She gathers herself, trying to go on, but she's so faint.

I can see that the effort to say even these few words has cost her, that she wants to say so much more. "I see... great movements of people. I hear screaming." She pauses for a breath. "I see an army of horses. They're coming, Whit."

"Horses?" I repeat incredulously.

Her eyes are so genuinely terrified, their blue seems almost black. She reaches out to me again, and her ghostly hand passes through mine. "I want to protect you, but I can't. You see how faint I've become. You have to be prepared, Whit." She begins to dissolve, her hand still trying to hold mine.

"Celia, wait!" I whisper urgently, but she's already just a glimmer—and then she's gone.

I wake with a start, shivering from head to toe. Janine's arms are tight around my chest.

"I'm right here," she whispers. "It's okay."

"Janine," I say. I grip the sheet in my fists. "Something terrible—"

"It was a dream, Whit." She kisses me on the cheeks, the lips. "Take it easy. You were just talking in your sleep." She tucks the covers around me and snuggles her head against my shoulder. "Close your eyes, now, and go back to sleep. Everything's fine. I promise."

I want to believe her, but Celia has always tried to warn me when there's imminent danger. What did her cryptic words mean?

Then Janine, already half-asleep, murmurs, "I wonder why you were dreaming about horses...?"

And it takes all my willpower not to say, *According to a ghost who is usually right about these things, they might be coming to destroy us.*

Chapter 13

Whit

THE OLD MAN'S BODY is covered in purple bruises and deep, oozing gashes. It looks like he challenged a couple of grizzlies to a fight and lost.

But it wasn't bears that did this to him—it was the Family. They took his wallet, which was probably practically empty, and left a scrawled note: *Why beg when we can steal?*

Janine, in scrubs that are already bloodstained, points urgently at the victim. "There's major blunt-force trauma to the ribs. We need to secure the airway and prep for anesthesia," she says. "Get a double-lumen endotracheal tube. Keep up cricoid pressure!"

But there's no one else in the room to take her orders. Either the other medical personnel are attending different patients—or else they don't want anything to do with me. The lifesaving is going to be up to the two of us alone.

"Janine, I don't know what any of that means," I say through gritted teeth.

"He's got class-four blood loss and a possible flail chest!"

"So what you're telling me is that this guy is on death's doorstep and he's ringing the bell?"

She nods sharply. "Flail chest means he's got a piece of broken rib floating around in there. If it punctures a lung, he's going to be stabbed to death by his own bone."

At that moment, the old man's eyes flutter open. "Just let me go," he whispers. "I'm ready."

I shudder, remembering that this is the same thing that Sasha, a Resistance leader and one of our best friends, said as he lay on the ground with an arrow piercing his chest. I couldn't heal Sasha that day, and it nearly broke my heart. But I'm going to heal this old man if it kills me.

And if trying to heal Pearl was any indication, it just might.

But I shake my head firmly. "Sir, I've been to Shadowland and trust me, you don't want to make that trip."

It feels like a miracle when he offers me the smallest sliver of a smile. Then his eyes close.

"His heart's gone arrhythmic," Janine shouts.

She stays close by, monitoring his vitals. "His bones are brittle," she says. "They're not going to be easy to get back together."

"Nothing about this is going to be easy," I answer.

I concentrate intensely as my hands hover over his body. The air beneath them seems to shimmer as the magic flows from my fingers down into his wounds. My arms tremble with effort, but I need to stay calm and listen. I hold my breath, focusing, and then the old man's heartbeat pounds in my ears. The air through his lungs sounds like wind through dead branches.

Steady, I think. *Just keep breathing.*

My fingers feel electric, like they could burn just as easily as heal. My arms ache from the strain, but this time I'm *not* going to fail.

I close my eyes. My whole body's shaking violently. I can tell that I'm seconds from losing control... and then, maddeningly slowly, it begins to happen. I can sense the severed blood vessels reconnecting, the floating rib finding its place.

I hear Janine's relieved voice. "He's stabilizing."

I keep my focus on the old man. I hardly feel my own pain anymore.

Janine's right next to me now, her hand on my shoulder. "It's amazing," she whispers. "The contusions are fading."

The old man stirs. Moans. Then he blinks confusedly. "Where am I?" he asks.

I smile weakly at him. I've probably spent an entire week's magic on dragging him back from the brink of death. "You're in the hospital, but don't worry, we'll get you out soon."

"The pain," he says, touching his chest. "It's gone." His wonder-struck eyes search my face. "Who are you? Are you God?"

"Sometimes he seems to think so," Janine quips.

And just like that, the tension in the room breaks, and the three of us are laughing like maniacs. Relief floods my body. *He's okay. Everything's going to be okay.*

It's a fantastic moment for the ten seconds it lasts. But then hospital loudspeakers come to life, and they start blaring my name.

Chapter 14

Whit

THE HARSH VOICE over the crackling speakers orders me to report to the office of Dr. Amos Keller, the head of City Hospital, *immediately*. Like I'm some kind of truant kid, instead of the guy who just saved a man's life.

Dr. Keller's secretary won't meet my eye; he just points me toward the right door, a look of distaste on his face. I swear I hear him spraying disinfectant after I leave.

The doctor is waiting for me behind a giant black desk. He's long-armed and hairy, with a big, wrinkled forehead. I can see why the nurses call him the Chimp behind his back.

"Sit," he says sharply. It sounds like he's talking to a dog.

I sink down into a chair so small that my knees practically touch my chin. Dr. Keller glares at me for a long time, his arms folded across his broad chest. I shift uncomfortably as I wait for him to say something. The silence is excruciating.

"So," he finally says, "you think you can come in here with no training whatsoever and interfere with proper medical procedures?"

"Well, sir," I try to say calmly, "I think I've been helpful—"

"I couldn't care less what you think!" Keller interrupts, a vein pulsing in his forehead. "What I do care about is protocol: ensuring our patients receive modern therapeutic care and conventional, scientifically tested medicine. Not hocus-pocus, faith-healing, spell-chanting *crap*."

Now I'm a lot less calm. "My powers are not crap," I yell. "I just saved a man's life!"

But it's like he doesn't even hear me. "Do you know what a hallux valgus is?" he demands.

"No."

"How about gastrodynia?"

"No."

"Cephalgia, then."

When I shake my head, Keller lets out a snort of disgust. "If you can't identify such *simple* problems as a bunion, a stomachache, or a headache, how on earth do you call yourself a healer?"

"I don't need to know what it's called to fix it," I argue.

This infuriates him. "You fool, you probably don't even know where the spleen is."

"The *magic* knows how to heal," I tell him. "It's bigger and more powerful than I am."

His eyes grow cold. "Your ignorance is outmatched only by your hubris, Whitford Allgood."

"I'm practically killing myself down there to *save* other people. I'm trying to *help!*" I shout.

He stands up and pounds a hairy fist on his desk. "Do you really want to help people, you charlatan? Then stop your reckless, dangerous practices immediately!"

I stand up. He has no idea how many people I've saved! "But, Dr. Keller—"

"Don't speak to me again," he shrieks, flecks of white spittle flying from his lips. It's like he's completely lost control. "I can't stand the sight of you! If I hadn't taken the Healer's Oath, I'd stab this pencil through your trachea."

I begin to raise my fists. *I'd like to see you try*, I almost say.

But then suddenly Keller seems to calm down. He eases back down into his chair and adjusts his tie, like he didn't just threaten to murder me. "One of my best trauma nurses, Janine, defends you. She says you must be allowed to stay. And you will be . . . as long as you sign here."

He shoves a piece of paper across the massive desk. I reach for it, and my eyes dart down the page until I see what I'm dreading. *Authorization to remove unnatural and potentially sinister capabilities . . .*

I look at him in outrage. "You want me to *submit!*"

"You have one day to think about it," he says sternly. "Now leave my office. You're getting blood on the desk."

I put my hand up to my face, and it comes away red: my nose is bleeding.

The same dizziness I felt after trying to heal Pearl

washes over me, but I shake it off. I've got to get out of here. Wiping my face with my sleeve, I stumble into the hallway.

The secretary shrinks away from me, but the look of disgust on his face is still there. As far as these people are concerned, I'm a mortal enemy—and a walking biohazard.

Chapter 15

Whit

I DON'T THINK I slept at all last night, and by the looks of it, I'm not the only one. A line of bleary-eyed people snakes along the sidewalk outside the Government Lab. They're pale and nervous and talk in agitated voices as they shuffle forward, one by one, to meet their fate.

They're all magic makers, and they're here to be Excised.

Patriotic music plays from loudspeakers, and motivational banners hang from the lampposts: THE BEST POWER IS *HUMAN* POWER, and BE NOBLE! BE NORMAL!

Janine's holding my hand tightly. "'Just Say No to Magic'?" she reads. "What genius came up with these slogans?"

I don't answer, because I'm staring at the sign that reads THE ORDINARY IS EXTRAORDINARY in bright-blue letters. Though it's hard to admit, I realize that I kind of agree. My life was pretty great back when I was just a high school foolball quarterback. The biggest worries I had were my scores on my algebra tests and whether or not I'd get sacked on the playing field.

And if someone back then had said to me, *Okay, Whit, I'm going to give you some awesome, mind-boggling powers, but in exchange you're going to have to spend the rest of your life fighting evil wizards*, would I have agreed?

The truth is, I don't know.

Janine scoots closer to me on the bench, across the street from the crowd. I'm jittery with nerves and the five gallons of coffee I drank, and I tell myself that we're just here to look.

I need to see this. I need to know if there's a good reason a person would give their magic up.

A woman in an EXCISION IS EXCELLENT T-shirt walks up and down the line, handing out buttons with the same phrase. "I did it," I hear her telling a nervous-looking teenager, "and I've never felt better in my life. I finally feel *free*."

She's basically bouncing up and down with happiness. I try to remember when I last felt that upbeat, and I can't.

I have to ask myself: *Is magic really the burden she makes it sound like?* I've always thought of it as something that produces undeniable wonders. Sure, it has its drawbacks, like when bad magic wreaks total havoc, and good magic doesn't always work.

Just ask Pearl.

Oh, right, you can't.

I turn to Janine. "I see plenty of people going into the Lab. How come no one's coming out?"

"There's probably a recovery period, like with any other surgical procedure," Janine replies. "Or maybe there's just a back door."

"Yeah, I'm sure that's it," I say grimly.

Excision. I haven't thought about anything else for twenty-four hours. But I still don't know what I should do.

My sister would say it's a choice between who I am and who everyone else thinks I should be. But I don't think it's that simple. Like I said at the Council meeting, I'll consider anything that I think will help our City stand strong together. So my decision has a lot to do with honor and duty (a couple of things my beloved sister might *not* be that good at).

If all citizens shared the same, ordinary talents, wouldn't it be easier for us to unite? Wouldn't we stand strong and fearless together?

Janine, sensing my muddled mood, tries to distract me. "You know, when I was a kid," she says, "I had a magic cape. I was convinced it made me invisible. And everyone played along. *Hey, where's Nini?* they'd say, even when I was standing right in front of them."

I smile, imagining it. "Nini, huh? I bet you looked cute in it."

"For a while, maybe," she allows. "Then it got so old and holey that my mom finally hid it from me. I cried for *weeks.* And you know what she said? 'You don't need a cape to be invisible. The magic is in you.'" Janine laughs at the recollection. "Which is crazy, because I don't have any magical powers at all."

As screwy as I feel, I can't help but laugh, too. "So the moral of the story is...?"

Janine shakes her head. "I have no idea! That my mother is nuts?"

"Or that she figured out a way to get you to stop whining about your ratty old cape," I tease, and Janine giggles and jabs me in the ribs with her sharp little elbow.

The lighthearted moment passes quickly, though, as the line moves forward and the patriotic songs get louder. I can't help but think about how my mother never said a *thing* to me about magic powers when I was a kid—and she knew I had them!

The hard thing is often the right thing: that's what she used to say to me. The phrase is haunting my thoughts now.

"I don't know what to do, Janine," I say, watching an old woman and a little girl enter the Lab hand in hand. "What will life be like with no magic?"

"Well, I like it just fine," she says. "Actually, it's *better* than fine. A lot better."

And the way she looks at me now tells me that some part of her wishes I were normal, the way she is.

"Whit," she says, "there will always be something magical about you. Nothing and nobody is going to take that away."

66

I pull her close to me and hold her tight. If I'm no longer magic, I won't be a threat to our new government. I won't be called a demon. I won't be called on to wage epic battles against despotic sorcerers. My life with Janine will be quiet and sweet and ordinary—which is also *extraordinary*. And nothing will ever come between us.

I take a deep breath. Then I rise and join the line.

Chapter 16

Whit

TWO OVERSIZED AND vicious-looking orderlies wearing black scrubs watch me coldly as a nurse takes my blood pressure and listens to my thudding heart. When she's pronounced me "fit to undergo the procedure," Thug One grabs my right elbow; Thug Two takes my left.

"You don't need to drag me," I point out as they propel me down the hall. "I came here of my own free will."

In the silence that follows—well, Thug One sort of *grunts*—I begin to wonder: are there some people who don't come here by choice? Others who come willingly, but then change their minds? Are these goons here to make sure people go through with it?

I'd ask, but they're probably too dumb to understand the question, and anyway, I don't have time, because they're already shoving me through a set of swinging doors into an operating room.

The walls, floor, and ceiling are a cold and spotless

white. It feels like I've just stepped inside a king-sized refrigerator. There's a huge, gleaming machine in the center of the room—it's shaped kind of like a giant metal donut—and standing beside it is a kid I recognize from the last Council meeting. He was the short one in an argyle sweater, and he hung on Terrence's every word. But now he's in a white lab coat, and he's *smiling* at me.

It's how I imagine a boa constrictor would smile, right before it squeezed you to death.

"Good morning. Do you remember me, Mr. Allgood? I'm Dr. Starling," he says. Then he gives a little shrug. "Well, I'm not *really* a doctor, but then neither are you, am I right? Funny how our lack of proper credentials hasn't prevented us from working in health care."

"You can skip the pleasantries," I say. "I'm not in the mood."

He laughs and motions for me to come closer until I'm towering over him. He has pale skin and squinty eyes. Now he seems less like a boa constrictor and more like a human toadstool. He taps me once on the sternum. Hard. "Strip to the waist, *if you please*, and lie down on the gurney."

My instant dislike of Starling sparks a flare of regret about my decision. The Whit Allgood of a few years ago would have wanted to sock the guy and head right back out the door, and no security thugs could have stopped me.

But I'm a different person now. I remind myself that what I'm doing is important—and right. I'm doing it for the sake of the City. For the sake of peace. To get us all closer to the admittedly saner and more predictable world we *used* to live in, a world without magic.

Slowly, I lift my shirt above my head and lie back on the table. The black-scrubbed goons strap me down with leather bands, one across my chest and two at my wrists.

"Muscular, aren't you?" Starling says. "Strong. Probably to compensate for a certain weakness in the cerebral region." He giggles. "I'm only kidding. Isn't this fun? Now, don't move. I need to attach these electrodes."

He keeps up the chatter as he sticks cold suction cups on my hands, my chest, my head. There are even extra-small cups placed on my fingers. "Everyone asks if it's going to hurt. Since you seem disinclined to make such a query, I will tell you: not *usually*. But sometimes!"

That's hardly a problem. My *own* powers have been hurting me enough lately. And I've made my choice. I'm not turning back.

"Are you familiar with infrasound, Mr. Allgood?" Starling asks, attaching the last electrode and stepping back.

I don't look at him. "No."

"It's a very low-frequency sound, which can travel great distances and easily penetrate structures, vehicles, and people, of course. Depending on the number of cycles per second, it has very interesting biophysical effects. Such as the elimination of . . . shall we say, *unnatural talents*."

The gurney begins to slide back, pulling me inside the donut. It's dark and cramped inside—I wouldn't be able to lift my arms even if they weren't strapped down. I immediately feel claustrophobic. My breathing quickens. A low-frequency humming sound begins, then builds.

Outside the machine, Starling's still talking. He says something about possible side effects and complications, but I can't really hear him anymore.

My ears start to pop, and pressure begins to build in my head, as if there's a rising tide inside my skull. Then my heart begins palpitating, and I feel like I'm going to be sick.

The humming gets more intense. If you've ever wondered if you could *feel* sound instead of *hearing* it, the answer is, yes, you can.

And it *hurts*. A lot.

I try to clench my fists, but the tight straps at my wrists won't let me. The pressure in my head keeps growing. I will myself not to cry out as the pain moves deeper into my body.

It feels like I'm being stripped from the inside. As if there's a vacuum inside me—a kind of spinning, sucking vortex—and everything that's ever made me *me* is disappearing down into it.

I can't help it: I scream.

And then I lose consciousness.

When I wake up, however many minutes or hours later, I'm dry-heaving. Starling's standing over me, an oily, smug look on his face. He takes the belts off my wrists and chest.

"See, that wasn't so bad, was it?" he asks. He pats my arm, and I'm too weak to shake him off. "Now you're just like us!"

Then he drops his hand and steps away. His eyes glitter in cruel satisfaction. "Although, as we already discussed, perhaps not as clever." He sighs dramatically. "I wonder if your pretty girlfriend will still find you so special. *Do* let me know how that works out, will you? In the interest of science, of course."

I'd slug him if I could. But I can't lift my arms.

"Oh well, nothing we can do about that," Starling continues. "Now, *if you please*, I have more operations to perform." And he motions me toward the door.

I can't get out of here fast enough. I stand up—but then I fall to my knees. *I don't have the strength to walk.*

"Poor thing," Starling says sarcastically.

He gives a wave of his hand, and Thugs One and Two step forward again. Then they take me by the armpits and drag me out the door, with Starling's harsh cackle still ringing in my ears.

They leave me outside the rear entrance, pathetically crumpled on the pavement.

Chapter 17

Wisty

WHERE IS MY BROTHER?

I rode to Whit's apartment this morning: empty. I checked his favorite greasy-spoon breakfast joint: no Whit. And now I've scanned the face of every person in line outside the Government Lab: nada.

But the dull throb of dread in my guts tells me he's nearby, and that he's about to do something stupid.

Something we're *both* going to regret.

I'm a jumpy, jittery jangle of nerves. I pace up and down the street talking to myself like a crazy person. *Don't do it, Whit. Don't submit.*

At the corner, I see the Family's latest graffiti tag, spray-painted blood red on the side of a building. It's a series of intertwining *F*s, and next to that, a picture of a stick figure holding a gun to another stick figure's head. The drawing is crude, and for some reason that makes it even more chilling.

Below it is a simple, scrawled question: *Are you next?*

I shiver involuntarily. Walking on, I see more pictures: a hanging man, a headless woman, a person with a knife sticking out of his ribs.

Apparently the Family has developed a real artistic streak—although the subject matter totally sucks.

"Why doesn't that person have a head?" pipes a small voice.

I turn to see a boy in mismatched sneakers, looking worriedly at the savage pictures.

I smile reassuringly. "Someone just forgot to draw it, I think! Here, let's fix it." With a wave of my fingers (and a quick jolt of M), I doctor the drawings. First I turn the gun into a huge bouquet of roses. Then I add a head to the headless woman, giving her cross-eyes and a goofy, buck-toothed smile.

"All better?" I ask the kid.

He nods happily, and we give each other a high five before he goes skipping off down the street.

It makes me feel better—but only for about ten seconds. Then the anxiety's back again, nagging at me like an itch I can't scratch.

Whit, where are you?

I need an outlet for my energy or I'm going to blow a fuse. I figure some more magic will help, so, summoning my powers again, I turn a crow into a brilliant-green hummingbird. *Better, right?* I make a dying day lily open in bloom. *Cool.* I shoot a little jet of flame at a wasp and fry it to a blackened crisp. *Well, nobody's perfect.*

Then I snap my fingers, and a fire hydrant spews out water like a fountain. Out of nowhere, a dozen street kids appear and start splashing around in the cold stream, squealing with delight.

There's a little girl from the Lab line watching me. She's on her way to be Excised, and she probably doesn't even know what that means. I hope she's too young to remember the day she gave up her powers. Her beautiful, chaotic uniqueness.

I conjure a bright-red balloon and send it floating toward her. She reaches out for it. "Look, Mommy!"

The mother glares at me. "That's a renegade witch," she says angrily. "Don't touch that devil balloon."

The girl starts to cry, and immediately I feel terrible.

But not nearly as terrible as when I spot Whit walking up behind the girl and her mother. For a split second, I don't believe that the hunched figure could be my brother. He looks so...*diminished*. Like he's been completely hollowed out.

He's holding Janine's hand, and she's whispering something in his ear. He's walking so slowly, he could be a hundred years old.

Oh, Whit, what have you done?

A tidal wave of boiling anger and deep sorrow swallows up my heart. I don't know whether to run to my brother and take him into my arms or haul off and punch him in the face.

I'm leaning toward the latter, but instead I thrust my

arms in the air. And immediately all the fire hydrants on the street explode, sending streams of water shooting into the sky.

Then the bright cold droplets fall back down, like the million tears I'm too mad to cry.

Chapter 18

Wisty

RAGE CLOUDS MY VISION, but that doesn't stop me from leaping onto my bike and gunning it down the street, racing away from my broken shell of a brother.

I feel furious—and *abandoned*. We discovered our magic together. We used it together. We strengthened it together. And then Whit went and gave it up—like it was a childhood toy he'd outgrown. Without even talking to me first.

I lean forward, willing the motorcycle to go faster as the wind whistles past my ears. The world flashes by in a multicolored blur. Seventy miles an hour, now eighty and rising....

Even over the roar of the engine, it's as if I can still hear what he said to me after the last Council meeting. *You can't keep running, Wisty. One of these days you're going to have to slow down and grow up.*

I lean in as I take a roundabout at twice the posted

speed limit. Slow down? Fat chance. And if he thinks giving up my powers is what it's going to take to get me to grow up, then I guess I'm going to be immature forever. Because I'll never, *ever* do it.

What's Whit going to do now that he's grown up and normal? Learn how to cook? Take up knitting?

Furious as I am, I almost laugh as I picture him with a ball of yarn, a couple of needles, and the beginning of some ugly afghan. Maybe he could make a pair of fuzzy slippers for our mom, potholders for my dad, and matching sweaters for my cats.

The sharp blare of a horn jolts me back to the present.

Oh, holy M, I'm about to smash into the side of a van.

Time itself seems to slow down, but I can't. The only way out of this is *up*. Good thing I've got lightning-fast reflexes and a motorcycle engine so badass it could power a jet. I lean back, yank hard on the throttle, and with a big burst of M, shoot myself straight up into the air.

As I arc over the van, I glance down and see the terrified faces of three little kids. The big one screams like she's just looked death in the face.

Which, in a way, she has.

My tire clips the roof rack and tears a piece off. I land a second after it and screech to a stop.

I hastily reattach the piece with a quick hit of M—no harm, no foul, right? But then the man who was driving the van gets out and starts yelling and cursing at me. "What is *wrong* with you? You almost killed us!"

I'm about to yell right back when I see that tears are coursing down his face. His kids, too, are weeping and clutching at each other.

And then it hits me.

I really did almost *kill* them.

Guilt twists my stomach and takes my breath away. "I'm so sorry," I manage.

The man wipes his eyes and then spits on the ground. "Get out of here," he growls.

I turn to go, shocked at my own actions. I'm *dangerous*. Just like the Council said I was.

And though I tell myself that a lot of things in life are dangerous—killer whales, for example, and zombie wolves, and sharp kitchen knives (just ask Whit about the Carrot Incident)—I don't feel too good about earning a top slot on that list.

Chapter 19

Darrius

AT ROBERTS & SONS, a bustling supermarket that stretches along an entire City block, a middle-aged man sniffs at a cantaloupe, trying to determine if it's ripe. A woman in a too-tight dress compares the price of crackers. Twin boys doze in a double stroller.

Darrius, lingering casually in the store's doorway, savors the moment: the innocent calm of a room, right before all hell breaks loose. He *loves* times like this. But not as much as what comes next.

Pandemonium.

He gives the signal, and his black-clad minions burst into the store, streaming through doors and windows alike, armed with everything from sticks and rocks to axes and switchblades.

The screaming is instantaneous and deafening. Everyone's doing it, even—or maybe *especially*—the robbers. They howl like barbarians as they knock over displays, chase shoppers down the aisles, and plunder the shelves for food and drink.

The woman in the tight dress has fainted. Jake, a makeshift mask covering his eyes, holds a knife to the throat of the cantaloupe man. The twin boys scream themselves purple.

Amazing, really, how shoddy the security is, Darrius thinks. Two old, fat guards who were half-asleep at their posts are quickly dragged off to the meat locker. The Family's second-in-command, Sean, is already emptying out the safe.

Darrius disables the silent alarm system with a wave of his hand and then kills the lights, just for fun, savoring how the screaming gets even louder. *People are going to start bursting their eardrums,* he thinks. Not that he cares.

He makes sure that a Family member is stationed at each of the cash registers, emptying the contents of the drawers into sacks and pillowcases. He stops to admire the nimble efficiency of the kid named Sam, who darts around the store taking people's wallets and jewelry.

Everything's going perfectly according to plan, until a clerk comes leaping out of the shadows, a gun gripped in his hands. He's so fast that not even Darrius can stop him. He aims and shoots. There's a sharp popping sound, and Ellie, Darrius's third-in-command, falls to the floor.

Dead.

The clerk tries to keep shooting, but Darrius is upon him like a fiend. He flings the gun away and knocks the clerk to his knees.

The clerk bows his head, then looks up with desperate, imploring eyes. "Please—" he gasps. "Whoever you are..."

"My name is Darrius," the wizard shouts. "*Please?* Are you asking me to *spare* you? You have the nerve to ask that after you just put a bullet through the eye of a member of my Family?"

The clerk has begun to weep, and he's trembling so hard he's barely able to keep his balance.

"No, I don't think I will spare you," Darrius says, walking in a slow circle around the shaking clerk.

But he can't concentrate with all this noise. He makes a violent, slashing motion with his arm, and silence descends immediately. People can try to scream all they want, but considering their vocal cords have just been frozen, they're not going to have much luck.

Now Darrius can practically hear the idiot's bones rattling. He picks up a pencil from a cup near the cash register and holds it in front of the clerk's tear-streaked face. "See this?" he asks. "*This* is your femur."

And then he snaps the pencil in two.

The clerk shrieks in pain, doubling over his broken leg. (Naturally Darrius didn't freeze *his* vocal cords.)

Darrius breaks the pencil again. "Oops. There goes your other femur. That one was probably a compound fracture."

The clerk's screams are blood-curdling.

And Darrius enjoys them. He plays them like an instrument, making them rise and fall with each brief pause in the agony and each new broken bone.

The clerk is dead long before Darrius breaks every one of the 206 bones in his body. He incinerates the mess that's left, leaving nothing behind but a little gray hill of ash.

Then Darrius gives the shoppers back their voices, and the screams rise again in an earsplitting symphony of terror. He lifts his arms like a conductor, and when he brings them down again, he and his Family simply *vanish*.

Chapter 20

Wisty

AFTER NEARLY KILLING an innocent family, I decide to stick to second gear for a little while longer—you know, *defensive driving* and all that garbage. But when I turn down Garden Avenue, I hear the screaming and rev the engine.

Somewhere not too far away, dozens of people are completely *freaking out*. And as much as I'd like to believe it was a surprise concert by the Groaning Bones, the sound is distinctly distressed. In fact, it's bone-chilling.

It can mean only one thing: the Family has paid some people a very unwelcome visit.

Five seconds and a major turbo boost later, I'm outside Roberts & Sons eyeing the shattered glass and plugging my ears against the noise. A police cruiser comes skidding up, lights flashing, and Byron Swain leaps out, his black police jacket only half on and his normally coiffed hair sticking out in all directions.

"Wisty," he barks. "Inside with me."

I'm still feeling shaken up by my near-death-causing experience, but Byron has already grabbed my hand and is pulling me into the store. The lights are off, and people are cowering on the floor, screaming and crying.

Byron lifts his bullhorn. "Everyone, please calm down," he calls firmly. "The police are here. We have the area secured."

I glance around the dim room doubtfully. There could be any number of criminals tucked away underneath the produce displays, and I don't fancy a shiv to the Achilles tendon. "Are you sure about that?" I whisper.

Byron nods curtly. "You think they want to stick around to get cuffed? They're long gone, Wisty." He picks up the bullhorn again. "Once again, the area is secure. You're safe now."

The shoppers shakily begin to stand up. Some, though, still tremble on the floor in teary puddles.

Byron gestures toward the door. "There's a medical team outside for those who need it. My colleagues will take your statements by the blue van. Everyone to the exit, please."

Then Byron turns back to me, all business. "We need to locate the bodies," he says.

Even though I know the Family has no problem with killing, my stomach still lurches at the assumption of *dead bodies* lying around.

"Reports say there's one thief and one employee down. You take the front, I'll take the back."

Reluctantly, I walk over to the cash registers, their drawers hanging open like giant mouths. I see a few loose coins scattered on the floor and a knife with a broken tip. And then I see the body of a girl.

"Byron!" I yell, and he comes scurrying over.

Together we look at the fallen figure, masked and dressed in black, with an oozing, gaping hole in her head, right through the eye. I notice the tattoos on the girl's wrists—the entwined, calligraphic letter *F*s—and around her neck hang the dog tags I've lately seen on Family members. *Cousin Clara*, hers says.

On the floor, not too far away, lies the gun that probably killed her.

"So there's the weapon," Byron says. "But where's the person who shot her?"

I point to a small mound of ashes. "Right there," I say grimly.

"Wisty, that's *dirt*," he says dismissively.

"That pile of ash," I tell him, "is someone who tried to be a hero. I know magic when I see it, Swain. This is the work of a very powerful, very depraved wizard or witch." I kneel down and touch the tip of my finger to the ashes. A wave of sadness washes over me. "You were brave," I whisper. "But you had no idea who you were up against."

The fact is, none of us have any idea who—or what—we're up against. And now that my brother's a Normal, there's one less good wizard to fight it.

Chapter 21

Wisty

BYRON KNEELS BY THE THIEF, making sure that the slowly spreading pool of blood doesn't stain his chinos. He puts his fingers against her neck to check for a pulse.

"Like she could survive a shot like that," I say grimly.

"Gunshot to the eye and orbit, exit wound straight through the occipital lobe. Time of death, approximately eleven thirty a.m.," he says, and writes this down in his pad.

Then he reaches out and gently begins to untie the knots of her mask. I'm surprised by how respectful he is. Some would say she's nothing but a dead outlaw, but Byron treats her like a person. Like somebody's little girl.

Meanwhile, I start gathering up the ashes. *This* was someone's child, too.

"Wisty?" Byron's voice is strained.

"What?" It comes out sharper than I intended. But I'm so tired of the senseless violence.

"Come here. Is this..."

When I look down, I nearly cry out. My hand flies to my mouth.

"It's Clara Starr, isn't it?" Byron asks.

I can only nod. Clara was a member of the Resistance during The One's reign. I remember her reading bedtime stories to the orphaned kids in the abandoned department store we called home. I feel tears pricking at the corners of my eyes. "She was one of the good guys," I finally manage.

"*Was*," Byron repeats bitterly. "*Was* good. *Was* alive. And now? She's neither."

I touch one of the delicate *F*s around her wrist. "Why, Clara?" I whisper, as if she were capable of answering me. "What did the Family promise you?"

Byron rubs his eyes and sighs in sadness and exhaustion.

"Didn't know the job would be this hard, did you?" I ask him. "You thought it'd be all about flashing a cool badge and driving around in a fast car."

Before the Family's crime spree, Byron would have nailed me with a misconduct report for an accusation like that. But now he just shakes his head. When he looks at me, his eyes are full of pain. "I didn't think there'd be so much death," he says softly. "It's just so ... *unfair.*"

I take a sheet from a nearby aisle and drape it over Clara's body. Byron's right. This is a gruesome waste of life. And for what—the lure of a cult and the contents of a cash register? Suddenly furious, I kick a grocery cart. It falls over with a bang that makes Byron flinch. "This can't keep happening!" I cry.

Byron stares at me dully. "It can't, but it does. And no one can stop it."

Then he stands up and walks out the door.

I follow him out, my hands clenched in fists. "Don't talk like that, Swain," I yell. "You've played every side, seen every angle! You're a survivor, and *survivors don't give up!*"

But I don't even know if he hears me over the noise of the crowd outside the store. Reporters scurry around, badgering people for eyewitness accounts, and photographers cast about for a gruesome shot to put on the front page. It's like they want to terrify people just as much as the Family does.

"Enough is enough!" a woman yells, jabbing a finger at Byron. "The police—the government—you have to *do* something!"

"We're doing all that we can, ma'am," he responds flatly. And then he starts walking toward his squad car.

I watch him in disbelief. *This* is what he calls doing all he can? Spending five minutes at a crime scene and then hurrying away for a consultation with his fellow investigators?

"Byron," I shout. He doesn't turn around. "Agent Swain!" I try, but he ignores me.

And now I'm alone in a crowd of angry people. *Justifiably* angry people: everywhere they look, there's another spray-painted threat from the Family. *We are always watching*, says the scrawl on the side of an elementary school. *What's yours is ours*, reads the awning above a pharmacy.

And every day, more blood is shed.

If the police can't figure out how to fix it, someone else is going to have to. Someone like me.

I approach the woman who yelled at Byron. "You were inside, weren't you? I need you to tell me everything you saw."

She narrows her eyes at me. I'm not wearing a badge; I could be anyone. But then she decides to trust me—or maybe she just can't keep the horror to herself anymore. She reaches for my hand and starts squeezing the life out of it. "They came like a swarm of demons," she says. "All of them in black, and their leader...*Darrius*..." She begins to shiver, as if simply saying his name has chilled her to the bone. "His eyes were inhuman. He killed without touching."

"Can you tell me—" I begin.

But she barrels on. "He broke that poor clerk into pieces, and then he disappeared." Her eyes are wild with fear.

I keep my voice very soft and calm. "You mean Darrius ran away? Which way did he go?"

She shakes her head violently. "I mean he was there, smiling this terrible smile—and then, *poof*, he was gone." She drops my hand now, like it's something dirty.

I can't pretend this is the news I was hoping for. But at least I know his name now. "Did Darrius say anything to you?" I ask.

"No," she says. "All he had to do was look at me, and I knew everything."

"What do you mean, everything?"

"I saw what he wants," she says. She motions me closer. "He wants unimaginable power," she whispers. "Dominion over all things, living and dead."

Her words chill me. I wrap my arms tight around my body as the crowd surges, still protesting police incompetence and demanding justice.

Dominion over all things, living and dead.

You know how you can tell when it's going to rain? There's a new coolness to the air, a sudden change in barometric pressure. It's like that now, but it's not rain that I sense coming.

It's chaos.

And it's going to be up to me to try to stop it.

Chapter 22

Whit

IT'S OVER. DONE. *Finito.* I have the signed Certificate of Excision to prove it.

And here's the strange part: I feel...nothing.

Not nothing as in, *Oh, cool, that wasn't such a big deal after all.* No, I'm talking about nothing as in, *I cut myself shaving and I felt no pain. I looked at my bowl of cereal and felt no hunger.* And now, as Janine and I walk to the hospital under a bright morning sky, I can't even feel the sun's warmth.

I feel nothing.

Or maybe it's more accurate to say: I feel *nothingness.*

Janine, dressed in pink scrubs and her favorite combat boots, is trying her best to act like today's no different from yesterday. She smiles and talks, and I pretend to listen.

Right before we start our shifts, she stands on her tiptoes and kisses me deeply. "It's going to be a good day," she says, resting her hand against my cheek. "I promise."

I nod like I'm capable of believing her.

We hurry down the hall to the ER, where we find a boy lying in bed with a tear-streaked face, cradling his swollen, purple arm.

Janine takes a quick look at the X-rays and then nods. "It's a transverse fracture of the radius," she says to me. "In other words, a clean, simple break." She smiles at the boy reassuringly. "You're going to be just fine."

I breathe a sigh of relief. After days of major trauma cases, we finally have a mere *accident*—an injury I could have healed in my sleep.

Janine gives the boy a shot of anesthetic and prepares to set the bone. The rolls of casting plaster are soaking in warm water behind her, ready to be wrapped around the boy's small forearm.

"Just let me try," I whisper before I can stop myself. I didn't even realize I'd been thinking about it.

Janine shoots me a worried glance. "Whit—" she begins. But then she stops, unsure of what comes next.

I shrug like it's no big deal. Like I'm not dying to know if my M's really gone. "I just want to check and make sure the Excision worked!" I try to say airily.

Now that the boy's not in pain, we're not exactly in a desperate rush. Janine thinks about it for a second, then steps back. "Okay," she says quietly. "Go for it."

I move next to the boy's side and place my hand near the break. "How'd you do that, buddy?" I ask, smiling.

He sniffles. "Fell out of a tree."

"I did that a few times myself when I was your age," I tell him. "It happens to the best of us. Can you hold still for me now?"

He nods, and I bring my hand closer to the injury and begin to concentrate. What I feel first is anticipation. Maybe even *hope*. I home in on the break, knowing without an X-ray exactly where it is. And after a moment, I sense the telltale prickling, the tiny electric shocks of M that walk the line between pleasure and pain.

I can feel it—it's still there—

But try as I might, I can't make the feeling build. The power doesn't increase. And the bone doesn't knit itself back together.

My vision blurs and I have to reach out to steady myself against the table. *I can't heal.*

They say that amputees can still feel their missing limbs years after they're gone. I can still feel my missing magic, tingling and buzzing inside me, like something caught in a cage.

I bow my head low. *Finito*, I think.

Then I look up to see Janine watching me intently.

"Are you okay?" she asks.

"Well, the Excision definitely worked," I announce emphatically. I hold out my unmagic arms and flex my ordinary fingers. "No fuel in the tank, so to speak."

Janine nods slowly. Maybe even sadly, I can't tell. "Why don't you take a break, Whit," she says. It's not a question; it's an order.

I look at her, searching her face. Why does she look unhappy? Isn't this what she wanted? "Whatever you say." I stalk off.

Outside, in the hospital's decrepit little courtyard, the weight of my decision comes down on me. Hard.

But not quite as hard as it does a couple of hours later, when I'm fired from my job as an assistant trauma nurse. Because, as Dr. Keller makes perfectly clear, without magic *or* medical knowledge, I'm not much help in the ER.

I believe "as useless as a kickstand on a horse" was the phrase he used.

I am, however, still very strong, which is why he lets me stay on as a porter.

Yup, a *porter.*

So now they've got me taking out the trash—huge, reeking bags of it, which I drag from the garbage chute to the incinerator. One after the other, I feed them into the machine's fiery mouth.

It's sort of like looking into the pit of hell. Except it feels like I'm already deep down in it.

Chapter 23

Whit

"NOT SO SPECIAL NOW, ARE YOU?" sneers an orderly as he pushes a cart full of medical supplies down the hall. He swerves toward me, and one of the wheels rolls right over my foot.

I grit my teeth and don't answer. *I'm willing to do the work—whatever it takes to help.* That's what I keep telling myself.

I haven't seen Janine for hours. While she's in the ER saving lives, I'm working my way down a seemingly endless list of new and humiliating tasks. Emptying bedpans. Swapping out the boxes of disease-contaminated needles. Bathing the raging, hydrophobic psychos from the mental ward, including the guy who believes his own hands are a pair of vampire bats.

This isn't what I bargained for.

I'm scrubbing the bathroom floor on my hands and knees when the door flies open and Sula, the nurse who once called me an abomination, calls my name urgently. "There's a Code Brown in room two-thirteen," she cries.

I drop my rag and rush after her. I don't know what Code Brown means until I come skidding to a stop in the hospital room.

It's a bed absolutely full of shit.

The smell makes me gag, and I almost quit right then and there. But I say it again, out loud this time. It's become my mantra. "Whatever it takes to help." And then I suppress my disgust and begin cleaning up the mess.

To make matters worse, now lingering in the doorway and watching me with barely contained delight is Grant Volm, a sixteen-year-old wizard. He's usually hanging out with a gang of younger kids, probably because they're easier to impress with his silly light shows and magic card tricks.

I never liked him.

"Well, if it isn't Whitford Allgood," he laughs. "Ex–heroic wizard and current janitor. What's that phrase? Oh, yeah: 'The higher you rise, the harder you fall.'"

"Oh, hey, Grant," I say casually, tossing the foul sheet on the floor, right next to his shoe. "You here for your chronic hemorrhoids?"

His cheeks flush. He can't think of a comeback, so he mutters a spell and turns my uniform hot pink. "Ha! The old Whit would have thrown me out the window with a flick of his pinkie for that," he says. "But *you* couldn't do it if you had a catapult."

I take a step closer to him. "I could still break you in half," I growl. "Want me to try?"

Grant backs away. "As fun as that sounds, I've got to be going. There's a wizard meeting downtown. *So* sorry I won't see you there."

I'd give just about anything for one more second of magic: I'd *evaporate* him.

I'm still fuming when I trudge past the ER, pushing an enormous laundry cart. My heartbeat quickens as I hear the sound of Janine's voice.

"Cerebral contusions with subdural hematoma," she's yelling. "Patient unresponsive."

I muscle my way into the room. There are at least a dozen people in there, and I'm stuck at the back, straining to hear what's going on. A girl fell from a window—or maybe she was pushed, no one knows for sure. She's unconscious, and her entire left side is bruised and bleeding.

"Intracranial pressure is growing," someone shouts.

"She's got high blood pressure and respiratory depression," calls someone else.

Even I know that means the situation is critical. And I also know that *yesterday* I could have helped her. But today, I just watch as they try desperately to save her life. And then, horribly, I watch her draw her last breaths, convulse, and die.

Numbly, I turn to go and almost run into the old man whose flail chest I healed. He's hobbled up behind me and must have seen everything. Tears are streaming down his face. "Why didn't you save *her*?" he demands, clutching my arm with clawlike fingers. "Why an old man, and not that beautiful little girl?"

I don't answer, because I can't tell him the truth: that I have made a terrible, irrevocable mistake. In trying to do the right thing, I've betrayed everything that ever mattered to me.

Chapter 24

Wisty

THANKS, IN PART, to my memo about the Roberts & Sons robbery—which *just might* have suggested that the Council members "pull their heads out of their butts ASAP"— Terrence has called a joint meeting with the City's security forces.

And while I'm not late (for once), the Police Center auditorium is so packed by the time I arrive that I can barely wedge myself in the door. I'm jostled from every direction, and someone steps on my toes so hard I swear I can hear the bones crunch.

Up on the wide, floodlit stage sit the Council members, along with the police chief, the head of City security, and a few members of the capital's elite crime squad. (Although considering that Byron Swain's up there, too, maybe the word "elite" is a bit generous.)

Terrence raises his hands to call for silence, but the raucous crowd takes a long time to settle down. "Citizens,"

Terrence yells, "my fellow citizens!" Finally everyone hushes, and Terrence offers us a thin, ugly smile. "We meet today in response to a growing threat to our City's peace."

"About time," the man next to me grumbles.

"The secretive, larcenous, and bloodthirsty cult known as the Family is growing daily in strength and numbers," Terrence announces.

"You gonna tell me something I don't know?" the man asks loudly.

Terrence is oblivious, of course. "Their leader, the one they call Darrius, is an extremely dangerous wizard. He holds his members in complete thrall, and the myriad of crimes he subsequently induces them to commit are the very definition of heinous."

"Did he eat a thesaurus for breakfast or what?" I say, rolling my eyes, and the man next to me chuckles.

But then Terrence starts quoting figures—twelve robberies, sixteen assaults, and five murders in the past *week*—and things don't seem so funny anymore.

"We cannot stand by any longer while the Family terrorizes our City. We, the Council, have authorized new protective measures, which Marcus Andrew, our head of security, will now explain."

Terrence sits down, and Marcus, a pimpled giant of a nineteen-year-old, stands up, placing his huge hands on either side of the podium. "We will be doubling the size of the police force," he informs the crowd, which immediately hoots its approval. "These new recruits will be specially trained in an intensive one-week program focused on crowd control, arrest and restraint, and marksmanship."

My jaw drops. Did he just say *one week*?

"In addition, all police and security officers will be equipped with a magazine-fed, self-loading firearm—"

I can't keep my mouth shut now. "You're going to give these rookies *machine guns*?" I holler.

Marcus looks for the source of interruption and quickly spots me in the crowd. "I should have guessed it was you, *witch*," he says snidely.

"Exactly," I retort, "since I seem to be the only person willing to question the Council's *deeply questionable* intelligence."

But Marcus declines to take the bait; he turns his attention back to his audience. "As I was saying," he goes on, "we have a new weapon in our fight." He holds up a small, gleaming pistol. "This is one and a half pounds of lethality, capable of firing sixty rounds per minute. But unlike a traditional machine gun, these firearms are concealable and can be operated one-handed."

Marcus makes a dramatic show of distributing the new guns to the officers onstage, including Byron, who couldn't hit a barn door with a baseball bat. And to my horror, the room erupts in deafening applause.

"Have you gone insane?" I cry. "You people say that witches and wizards need to be Excised because magic is *dangerous* and *too hard to control*—and now you're handing out dangerous guns to people who don't know how to control them?"

Marcus sighs. "They will be trained, Miss Allgood, as I just explained."

I know I shouldn't flaunt my powers at a time like this, but I can't help it, I'm too mad. I rise above the crowd so that everyone can see me. And *yes*, I let myself glow a little bit. "You can't kill twenty people in two minutes with a club, or a knife, or even most magic. But you can—*and somebody will*—with those guns."

Marcus nods. "Precisely."

I want to bang my head against the wall. "But what if it's not Family thugs? What if it's the *wrong* people getting killed? Some rookie cop might shoot a hundred holes in someone before he even sees who it is!"

Marcus rolls his eyes and turns to Terrence. "She's tiresome, isn't she?"

Terrence glares at me. "She's a malcontent," he says. "Bordering on an insurrectionist."

I'm about to give them both a piece of my mind, but a new wave of thunderous applause sweeps the room. They're cheering for the guns, for the new police recruits, and maybe even for Terrence's insult. They're clapping and stomping their feet. Is this a government or a mob?

I rise up another six inches, and my fingers just *itch* to spark. "You're not going to kill Darrius with a gun! You need—"

"*Magic?*" Terrence interrupts, his voice dripping with venom. "Is that what you were going to say, you floating glowworm?"

"Yes, you—" I stop myself from saying *impotent slug.* "You need *good* people with *good* powers!"

Terrence looks like he'd like to jump off the stage and personally throttle me, but he knows I'd broil him first.

Marcus, who's calmer, smiles. "Mr. Speaker, maybe we should move on."

Terrence ignores him. Through clenched teeth, he speaks. "The Council has decreed that anyone working with the police force must be *Excised.*"

What?

Behind Terrence, several Council members exchange confused glances. Obviously, this is news to them, too.

My eyes blaze like they're on fire. "Arm the rookies and disarm the witch? You're a fool, Terrence," I shout. "And I *quit.* So you can take your Excision and shove it up your—"

Marcus raises a soothing hand. "I think we might be able to make a special case for a witch who has proved useful in the past," he says to Terrence.

"Useful!" I holler. "Is that what you call saving the asses of everyone in this City at least *twice?* Well, guess what—I'm done. Good luck with your new police force. I'm sure they'll be just *great.*"

And then I shove my way to the door. I'm burning with anger, and pretty soon I'm going to start singeing people.

"Oh, *Wisteeeria,*" Terrence calls.

I can't help it. I turn to face him. "What?"

"All the proper measures will be taken," he says coldly. "Against the Family, and against any *renegade citizens.*"

His pale-blue eyes bore into mine. And involuntarily, I shudder. Suddenly I don't know who scares me more: Darrius, or my own City leaders.

Chapter 25

Wisty

"WISTY! STOP!"

I whirl around, and there's Byron, waving his arms and scurrying toward me. (Sometimes I regret turning him into a weasel so many times; I think it permanently affected his gait.) "You can't just leave like that," he calls out accusingly.

"Oh, yeah? And who's going to stop me?"

"You should stop *yourself*," he scolds. "You're so damn hotheaded. You never listen to reason."

"*Reason?*" I scoff. "Is that what you call handing out guns to a bunch of scared newbies? If so, I believe we have different definitions of the word."

"I'm just saying, we've got to stick together."

"Well, *that's* funny," I say, "considering you basically abandoned me at a crime scene yesterday. What happened to you? Were you suffering from donut withdrawal?"

Byron gives me a wounded look. "Everyone has moments of doubt," he says defensively.

"But now you're all fired up again because you got a new gun. I never pegged you for such a typical male, Swain."

"Wisty, why are you always so angry?" he asks softly.

Honestly, the question makes me want to scream. "Maybe because every day, *more* people get robbed, and *more* people die, and the incompetent fatheads we chose to lead us are doing nothing about it!" I stomp my foot—the hurt one—and curse. "Scratch that: they're doing *worse* than nothing, because they gave people like *you* guns."

He looks at me for a moment, then shakes his head. "I can't believe how much I used to love you," he says.

"That has *nothing* to do with *anything*," I yell. The ends of my hair start to smolder; any second now, they'll ignite.

"It doesn't?" he asks. "Aren't you tired of feeling so alone?"

And sure enough, the red curls burst into licking flames. But I refuse to admit there's any truth to what he's saying. "I'm not tired of being alone. I'm tired of *you*," I say.

He frowns and opens his mouth—he's probably going to chastise me some more; he *loves* being up on his high horse—but then we hear the sirens. Another emergency.

My heartbeat quickens. I forget everything we've just said to each other; I dismiss all of Terrence's threats. "We've got to go!" I'm already on my motorcycle and gunning the engine. "Hop on the back!"

But Byron just stands there, in his new black leather cop jacket, his lips pressed in a firm, hard line. His right hand grips his new gun. "No, Wisty," he says. "You can't come this time."

Then he heads for his big, shiny squad car.

I can't help what happens next. I mean, *maybe* I could, if I felt like practicing a little impulse control. *Too bad I don't.* I throw my arms up into the air, summoning a rush of power, and an enormous gust of wind lifts Byron's car— and flips it over when he's less than ten feet away from it.

"Yeah, maybe I should submit," I yell. "But I'm not going to. *Ever.*"

But Byron doesn't even look surprised by his upside-down car. "I know, Wisty," he says. "I know you better than anyone. Even your brother. Now please, just go home. If I see you at the scene, I'll have you thrown in jail." And then he turns and walks away.

Chapter 26

Wisty

WHEN I GET to my apartment, I'm still steaming—literally. I kick aside the pile of boots and jackets by the door and clomp my way into the living room. Of course it's a mess in there, too: stacks of magazines, heaps of throw pillows, and so much cat hair it looks like I have a fur couch.

Aren't you tired of being so alone?

Byron's question rings in my ears. *No,* I think.

But also yes.

I decide that maybe a little housekeeping will cheer me up, and I've almost gathered up all the floor detritus when my doorbell rings. I freeze, my hands full of dirty clothes. It rings again, then again. Considering pretty much no one ever comes over, I approach the door cautiously, dropping my laundry on the floor in the foyer.

Even before I turn the knob, I smell the unmistakable aroma.

Pizza.

My mouth starts to water. I fling open the door, ready to welcome my mom and dad, or even Whit the Normal— whoever's out there with my favorite pie, a mushroom and onion with extra cheese. (One of the problems with living solo is that you have to feed yourself; I'm even worse at that than I am at cleaning.)

But outside on the stoop is a group of four teenagers, none of whom I've seen before. They're dressed head to toe in black. And they're obviously not here to deliver me a pizza, because they're already eating it.

"Oh my god," a girl with red braids is saying between bites, "this is, like, the best pie ever."

A guy of about seventeen, with dark curly hair, looks up at me and smiles. "Oh, hey, Wisty," he says. "Can we come in?"

"Who are you?" I demand. But judging by the black clothes, the shiny dog tags, and the *F* tattoo on this guy's hand, I already know the answer to my question. My pulse begins to pound. These people are probably killers.

But the weird thing is, I'm not getting a murder-y vibe right now. They seem relaxed. Neighborly. Friendly, even.

Although no one's offered me a slice of pizza, and I'm starving.

"I'm Brother Mike," says the tall guy. "That redhead there is Sister Annie Rose, and the short one's Cousin Willie."

Willie smiles at me with crooked teeth: I don't smile back. I notice Mike doesn't introduce the other guy, the one who's so big he looks like he could influence the tides.

"Mind if we come in?" Mike asks again.

It's weird how normal they seem. How...*nice.* Not to mention casual and happy, attitudes that don't describe anyone else in my life right now. As crazy as it sounds, I'm kind of drawn to these people. And I'd commit *several* crimes in order to have a slice of that pizza.

But I'm not going to let them in my house.

"I'm sort of in the middle of a spring clean," I say, shrugging. "Now's not the best time."

Mike sighs. "Well, that's too bad. We came a long way, and it's kinda chilly out here. So you're not being very hospitable." A slight edge has crept into his voice. But then he smiles. "Hey, whatever. We don't demand good manners. But here's the thing. Darrius wants to talk to you."

I hope that the massive shiver that shoots up my spine isn't visible to anyone else. "So?" I say, as coolly as I can.

"So, basically, Darrius gets what he wants. And he *wants* you to come *visit.*" He hands me a piece of paper with an address scrawled on it.

I'm liking Mike less and less. "Oh, yeah? Well, I'm not a member of your little freak Family. I don't have to play by your rules," I say.

Annie Rose's eyes widen. I think I hear her say *Uh-oh.*

The giant dude steps forward. His forearms are as big as Holiday hams. "You might not respond effectively to requests or persuasion," he rumbles. "But how about unrestrained brute force?"

I keep my eyes on Mike. "Your friend's got a pretty big vocabulary for a rhinoceros," I say.

The big dude takes another menacing step forward.

"Otis," Annie Rose whispers, "calm down."

But Otis is smacking his fist into his palm, hard and unhurried, like he wishes it were my face. It's *so* cliché.

As for me, I can feel the tingle. The promise of firepower. I don't really want to torch my porch, but I'll do it. Come to think of it, it's a nice night for a barbecue.

"Step back, Cousin Otis," Mike orders.

"Good for you," I say. "You just saved his worthless life."

Mike shakes his head. "It's disappointing, Wisty. You're not nearly as smart as they say you are. Your behavior is... dangerous."

"If you think I'm afraid, you don't know anything," I say.

He smiles, cruelly now. "You *should* be afraid. Because there's a lot to be afraid of. A pretty, young girl like yourself, living all alone in the big scary City?" He looks meaningfully at my tall, narrow windows. "Ever so breakable," he whispers. His eyes glint.

"Get off my porch," I say.

Mike gives me one final burning look. "As you wish," he says.

And then he and his friends turn and slip away into the darkness, leaving me alone.

Very, *very* alone.

I'm still holding the scrawled address in my hand. Yesterday, I would've given this to the police and helped them take down Darrius and the Family. But today?

The edges of the paper blacken and curl as I watch. A moment later, it's nothing but cinders.

Chapter 27

Whit

I'M SLUMPED AT the kitchen table. My whole body aches, and I'm so tired it's hard to tell whether I'm asleep or awake.

"Voilà!" Janine slides a steaming plate of spaghetti and meatballs in front of me. It smells spicy, garlicky, and delicious. *Oh*, I think. *I guess it must be dinnertime.* But that's pretty much as far as the thought takes me. My head's basically a swirl of tired, worn-out confusion.

"It's food, Whit," Janine says after a while. "You pick up a fork and you put it in your mouth." She mimes chewing.

"Yeah, I know," I say. Meanwhile I'm thinking, *Wow, I'm so far gone that I need directions on how to* eat?

Finally I take a bite. "It's great, Janine. It's my favorite," I tell her.

She gives me a funny look. "I know that, silly. That's why I made it."

"Oh—right."

We eat for a little while in silence. But I can tell that Janine's troubled. Part of me is sympathetic, while another part is like, *Hey, join the club.*

"Was the hospital really awful today?" she asks eventually.

I nod. "You don't know what *bad* smells like until you've done psych ward laundry," I say. I twirl a few noodles around the tines of my fork. "But that isn't even the problem."

"Then what's the matter? You don't seem like yourself."

I surprise us both by banging my palm against the table. "Exactly," I shout. "*I am not who I was.* The Whit we both knew *doesn't exist anymore.*"

Janine reaches over and puts her hand on my arm. "But you're still you," she says soothingly.

"On the outside, maybe," I retort.

She shakes her head. "No, it's more than that, Whit. You still love spaghetti and meatballs, you still laugh at the same dumb jokes, you still can't ever seem to match your socks, and you're still a sucker for puppies, cop shows, and asinine buddy movies. I mean, right?"

I can almost hear her unspoken thought: *You still love me... right?*

I do—I mean, I'm pretty sure I do. Honestly, I don't know *what* I feel, because I'm hollow inside.

And the bitter irony, of course, is that Janine encouraged me to become this way.

I hold her gaze as I speak. "Can you understand what

it's like to undo yourself, Janine? Un-become yourself? Can you imagine what it's like to be *utterly different* from the way you were the day before?"

"I'm trying, Whit. I—"

But I don't let her finish. "Can you fathom the pain of knowing that from now on, you will always be this *lesser you*? This *pale imitation*?"

Janine looks at me with wide, worried eyes. "Whit, you can't say those things."

"Why not?" I ask bitterly. "It's the truth."

She takes my hand between hers, pressing it reassuringly. I watch her fingers curl sweetly around mine, and all I can think is, *That hand of mine used to* heal, *and now it takes out filthy, reeking garbage.*

Abruptly I stand, pulling myself out of her grip. "I need to get some air."

And before she can say anything, I'm pushing my way out the door, into the cool darkness of the street. I hurry down the sidewalk as if I have any idea where I'm going.

I figure I'll just walk until I can't walk any more, and then who knows? I pick up a stone from the street and fling it as hard as I can.

You can't run away from yourself, my mother used to say. To which I would reply, *Just watch me.*

I'm all the way down near the wharf when I realize I've been hearing the same muted but insistent sound for blocks. It's a low, steady hiss—like wind, except that it's not the wind.

The sound has been following me.

Suddenly I'm aware that I'm being watched. It's not just the matter of the new security cameras that the Council has begun to install. No, it's something else. I can sense... *magic.*

There's a charge to the air, a crackling whisper of suppressed power. But obviously it's not coming from me.

I stop under a streetlamp, my hands balled in fists. "Wisty? Is that you?"

Silence.

I raise my voice. "Fine! I don't care who it is! Just *leave me alone.*"

No one answers me. The wind picks up and blows an empty trash bag along the gutter. Then it comes to rest, right at my feet, like a sign from the universe.

You, Whitford Allgood, are a deflated, depleted sack of nothingness.

Chapter 28

Wisty

AN HOUR AFTER Mike and his gang leave, I'm cruising to the south side of town on my motorcycle. I'm going the speed limit, but my brain is *racing*.

Am I insane? I'm insane! goes the inner dialogue.

Should I really go see Darrius?

No! He incinerates people!

Well, you could, too, if you tried.

Yeah, but I won't. That's a big difference.

Okay, fine. Chicken.

I'm not a chicken! Maybe I just don't really want to meet this guy.

What do you have to lose?

Oh, I don't know, my life?

Well, it's not like it's going that great for you these days, is it?

I shake my head in disbelief. I'm fighting with myself

while simultaneously steering said self to the abandoned factory that I now know is the Family's headquarters.

If I get out of this alive, I should probably go see a shrink.

I know I can't defeat Darrius alone; he's far too powerful. But this way I'll at least see what I'm up against. "Know your enemy and know yourself and you can fight a hundred battles without disaster"—somebody said that once, and it makes sense to me.

As I near my destination, the streets grow even more desolate. There's trash scattered all over the sidewalks, and a snaking, fetid canal loops around behind the building like a moat. I swear it's ten degrees colder over on this side of town.

I take a deep breath at the factory door. Yes, I am definitely insane.

But there's nothing to be done about that now, and I didn't come all this way to chicken out at the last minute. I throw my head up and my shoulders back, steeling myself. And then I yank open the door and step inside.

Before me is a vast squatters' camp. Kids are everywhere—working, lounging around, play-fighting. For a second I'm overcome by a rush of memory. This feels so much like our Resistance hideout. Except that *we* were fighting for good, of course. These kids: not so much.

I haven't taken two strides into the room before I'm stopped by a firm hand to the sternum. I look over to see who's got the *nerve* to touch me, and my mouth falls open so far, my chin practically hits the ground.

It's the golden-eyed hunk who tried to talk to me after the Council meeting. He's gazing at me so intensely I can actually feel it on my skin. "Wisteria," he purrs. "So glad you changed your mind and decided to accept my invitation."

I shake my head in confusion. He's not—he *couldn't* be—

"I'm Darrius."

Oh, damn: he *is*.

His eyes are ringed with dark lashes, and his eyebrows have a striking arch—the kind that changes an expression from good-humored to cruel in an instant.

"We meet at last," he says, smiling. His voice is so quiet that I have to lean in close to hear.

The air around him almost crackles with electricity. He radiates power the way a fire radiates heat. And I can't help it: I'm drawn to it.

I always have been. It's my biggest weakness, and I honestly don't know how to control it, no matter how much trouble it's gotten me into in the past.

But I refuse to let him knock me off my game. I lower my voice, too. "I just came here for the pizza."

Darrius throws back his head and laughs. "I'm afraid we're all out. But Brother Wilson can make you something. Are you hungry?" He gestures to a dark-haired kid standing near a cookstove, next to a long table still covered in the messy remains of dinner.

I shake my head. "No, thanks." I don't trust the little cult member; who knows what he'd slip into the mac and cheese.

"Boogers, probably," says Darrius.

I start—did he really just *read my mind*?

Darrius laughs again. "I didn't read your mind, if that's what you're wondering. Your doubt was written all over your face." And then he whispers, "It's not unfounded. Trust me."

"Oh," I say lamely. When I glance around the room, I notice that most of the Family members are now watching us. "I don't know why I'm here," I say.

This, in a way, is very true, considering that the sane part of me is screaming, *Run!*

Darrius is still smiling. "You came to see what we're all about."

I snort derisively. "I *know* what you're all about. Murder, robbery—"

Darrius interrupts me. "Oh, that," he says. "That's just a bit of fun to make the time pass."

I can't believe his nonchalance. "You're sick," I spit.

Darrius ignores this. He motions me over to the side of the room, to a cluster of old furniture with dusty, faded cushions. "Sit here, Wisty, on the love seat," he says. "Don't you think that's a funny name for a piece of furniture? 'Love seat': I wonder who thought of that."

"I *definitely* didn't come here to talk couch nomenclature," I say, perching on the edge of a bench.

121

He looks at me with delight. "And to think that Brother Mike said you weren't that smart!"

My eyes dart over to Mike, who's polishing a knife across the room. "*That's* the pot calling the kettle black," I mutter.

Darrius sits down close to me, and my breath comes quicker. Something about him agitates me in a way that's both exciting and frightening. "Anyway, Wisteria," he says, "you object to our... *hobbies*. Here's my response: the world is a vexed and chaotic place. The souls of men—and women, and girls and boys—are dark. I merely empower the members of my Family to enact their hearts' desire." His eyes gaze into mine. "You see, it's all about *self-actualization*."

I hope the scorn I'm feeling is as plain as the nose on my face. "Spare me the psychological BS, why don't you," I say. "Tell me who you are and why you're doing this."

He bites his lip and smiles while looking me up and down. My core temperature rises, three degrees at least, and a bead of sweat forms on my upper lip.

"You can't beat us, Wisty," Darrius says softly. "So why not join us?"

"Never."

"Why so quick to refuse?" he asks, looking wounded. "My feelings are hurt." He leans closer to me, his body language an unnerving mix of flirtation and *menace*.

"I'm not interested in assault and murder," I say. "By the way, do your thugs need to hang around like this? They're creeping me out."

Darrius looks over at the three behemoths lurking nearby, swords dangling from their leather belts. "Gabriel, Michael, Thomas: you may retire," he says sharply. Then he turns back to me. "There. I'm unprotected now. But what about you? I can't very well ask you to put down your weapon, can I?"

"I have a feeling you've got a few weapons of your own," I say.

Darrius chuckles. "I might know a bit of hocus-pocus," he allows. He reaches for my hand, but I pull it out of his reach. "Join us," he urges. "Just for a day."

"No, thanks," I say.

His expressive brows arch in disappointment. "You are not to be persuaded. I see. Well, it was an honor meeting you."

I stand up. "I wish I could say the same."

"We won't hold your decision against you, Wisteria," Darrius says, rising. He holds out his hand, and this time I take it.

When our fingers meet, I feel an electric shock that takes my breath away. A thousand colors flash before my eyes. I see comets, dizzying snowy peaks, a blazing supernova—

I rip my hand from his grip.

Then all I can see are Darrius's golden eyes, gleaming with magnetic and terrifying power.

Chapter 29

Wisty

I'M SO RELIEVED to be home—to have escaped Darrius's spell unharmed—that I barely notice that not all my dead bolts are locked.

Or that my cats don't appear to greet me in the hall.

Or that all the lights are off.

So when the pillowcase gets yanked over my head and strong arms grab me viciously from behind, my first thought is, *Wisty, you oblivious, effing idiot.*

I twist in the person's grip, yelling and kicking wildly. I've almost got an arm free when a punch to my gut doubles me over and leaves me gasping and retching.

Good thing I didn't eat, or my dinner would be all over the inside of the pillowcase.

The arms yank me up again, and I take another punch to the guts.

I dry-heave for a minute, and when I'm done, I stagger upright. I'm seriously *pissed.*

I squeeze my eyes shut and clench my fists, and the M jolts through me almost immediately. My palms blaze with heat, and whoever's held me from behind yelps and lets go.

"You'll want to ice that," I say, snatching the pillowcase away from my face and flinging it to the ground.

It's dark in my apartment, but I can see the dim shapes of the intruders. There are three of them.

I stand in the middle of the room, knees bent to keep my center of gravity low. My palms still blaze, sending tongues of light into the corners.

"Who's next?" I hiss, and almost before the words are out of my mouth, a shadowy figure launches toward me.

He or she—or *it*—tackles me, sending me spinning back toward the floor. I land on the rug with a thud that knocks the wind out of me.

The person now sitting on my chest growls like an animal. I see dog tags glinting in the light. *What's your name, Brother Bloodshed?*

Hands circle my wrist with cold, inhuman strength. I summon the fire inside me, and it arcs out of my hands, round and burning like tiny meteorites. These fireballs explode right at my assailant's shoulders, but instead of consuming the figure in flame, they flicker and sputter—then fizzle out, as if they've made contact with ice.

So he has powers, too.

But it's just a mercenary, a hired gun—that's what I tell myself. No match for a witch with a desperate desire for self-preservation. My fear and rage ignite a flaming

125

sphere just inches from my chest. My opponent is knocked backward, cursing, and when the other two people—one guy, one girl—charge me, I scramble to my feet and slam my back against the wall so no one can come at me from behind.

I pick up a lamp and hold it like a club. "Who's next?" I scream.

When the girl makes a move, I swing the lamp wildly. There's a sickening crack as I hear it connect against the side of her head. Blood shines on her cheek.

But I've stepped away from the wall, and that lets the big guy get behind me again. He throws me to the ground and puts his knee between my shoulder blades. He lifts me up for a second, then flings me back to the ground, and I swear I hear my collarbone snap.

The good thing about adrenaline? I don't even feel the break.

I manage to slither away, my breath coming so hard and fast it seems almost deafening in my ears. I'm behind the bookcase now, and I take the few seconds I've got hidden here to regroup.

This is it, I think. *Fight, or die.*

And so, with a blood-curdling scream, I leap up from behind the bookcase. Flames shoot out of every cell of my body. I'm a human inferno. I set everything, *everything* alight.

And evil powers aside, my assailants are flammable. They cower for a moment in the brilliance, and then they flee.

A moment later, the sprinkler system in my apartment comes on, quenching the flames and drenching the furniture. I collapse on the floor, letting the cool droplets hit my burning face.

We won't hold your decision against you, Darrius had said.

Yeah, right. I'm sure that's not the first—or last—of his lies.

Chapter 30

Wisty

I'M TOO AGITATED, too *bruised*, to sleep. (And even if I *could* rest, the sprinklers turned my bed into a wading pool.) So I wrap a scarf in a figure eight around my shoulders—a makeshift collarbone splint—and then I go outside.

The streets are quiet and empty. I guess Terrence's stepped-up police force hasn't made capital citizens feel safe enough to take nighttime strolls. Hell, I'd be scared, too, if I hadn't already been jumped by Family members. But I assume they're done with me for the night.

I stride quickly through my neighborhood. I'm hoping the cool night air has healing powers, because I have a headache so intense I see rainbows whenever I look at a streetlight.

I take stock of my current situation: it's not pretty. The most powerful wizard in the City is out to murder me. Terrence wants to Excise me. Marcus thinks I'm an instigator, and as far as Byron is concerned, I'm a knee-jerk rebel with the emotional maturity of a two-year-old.

It's not a question of who's my enemy anymore. It's more a question of who isn't.

I miss my brother.

The thought takes me by surprise. And then an image of Whit flashes before my eyes. He's racing down the foolball field, pursued by the *entire* opposing team—but he outruns them all to score. Immediately after that comes another, darker image: Whit bent and broken after he gave up his powers. And I feel like I've just been punched again.

I wonder what my brother's doing right now. Watching foolball on TV? In bed and snoring already? Drinking tea and making an afghan?

Regretting his choice?

I wish I could talk to him, even though it's almost midnight. I wish he could heal my aching collarbone. I wish... well, I wish a lot of things.

I'm feeling sort of sorry for myself, honestly, but the farther I stalk down the street, the more the self-pity turns to anger. I know life's not fair and blah blah blah, but don't I seem to get more than my share of hard knocks? I didn't *ask* to look death in the face tonight. I don't *want* to always be fighting. And I'm sick of people looking at me like I'm either their savior or public enemy #1, depending on the day. (It's usually the latter.)

When do I get to be simply Wisty, City teenager, eating a pizza with some friends?

Never, it seems.

Or—on the other hand, maybe *tomorrow*, if I gave up my powers, too. I'd have a nice normal life then. Or so they tell me.

But here's what I have to say to all who think I should submit: I raise my two middle fingers, and flip off the entire sleeping world.

Suddenly, all the streetlights down the avenue shatter. Shards of glass fall to the ground like jagged snowflakes, and I'm in utter darkness. My heartbeat pounds in my throat. "Who's there?" I yell.

I reach for a stick—a weapon—but it catches fire in my blazing hand.

And that's when I realize that it wasn't Darrius, or any of his henchmen, knocking out the lights. It was me.

Making magic by mistake.

Oops.

Chapter 31

Wisty

IN THE MORNING, I wake cold and ravenous. I guess that's how it works when you spend the night on a park bench. (Note to self: don't do *that* again anytime soon. No matter how trashed your apartment is, it's still way better than sleeping outside with a bunch of raccoons.)

I flex my stiff fingers. Nothing catches on fire, which I take as a good sign. Last night's bout of uncontrolled magic can remain my little secret.

As long as it doesn't happen again.

Half an hour later, I'm banging on a brass door knocker and yelling, "Hello, hello?" until my throat hurts. I'm about to give up when the door finally opens, and Byron sticks a sleepy head out.

He blinks at me in confusion. "Wisty?"

I shove my way past him into the house. "No, the *tooth fairy*," I say.

"What are you doing here?" he asks. "What happened to your face?"

I take a deep breath; obviously I need *help*, and I don't have anyone else to turn to. But instead I say, "I'm really hungry. Can you make some eggs?"

Then *she* shuffles into the hall, still in her pajamas: Byron's new girlfriend. She's small-boned, like me, and her hair is red. If I squint, it's practically like looking into a mirror.

Except she lacks my countless cuts and bruises, of course.

"Hi," she says, taking a few hesitant steps toward me. "I'm Elise."

"Wisty," I say sharply. "Your evil twin."

Byron, to his credit, gives a little snortlike laugh, but Elise just nods, smiling.

"Eggs?" I say again.

Byron rolls his eyes at me. "Fine. But you know, it's generally considered polite to *call*."

"Yeah, and not show up at six a.m., whatever. But I slept outside last night, you know."

He puts water on for coffee and starts cracking eggs into a bowl. "Why?"

"Because I was attacked by Darrius's thugs. They practically murdered me in my own apartment. I didn't want to stay there."

Elise gasps, but the expression on Byron's face doesn't change. "That sucks," he says tranquilly.

"No kidding! They're animals! So what we need to do is storm their headquarters, Byron. I know where they are now, I—"

Byron cuts me off with a wave of his spatula. "Wisty, there is no *we*."

I tear off a hunk of baguette and shove it into my mouth. "Excuse me? What does *that* mean?"

"It means that you chose your side," he says. "And it's not the same as mine."

I consider flinging the rest of the baguette loaf at his head. "Well, it sure as hell isn't the same as the Family's," I retort. "Byron, we've been friends *forever*. Aren't you going to help me?"

Byron gazes at me steadily. "I've helped you a lot, Wisty," he says. "And somehow it always ends up costing me."

"I'm not asking you to do it alone, dummy," I cry. "It can be a police raid."

"Sure," he says, nodding, "a police raid. Led by the witch who everyone on the force wants to burn at the stake."

I gape at him. "Seriously? You're going to bring my popularity into it?"

"Or lack thereof," he mutters.

That's it. The bread goes flying, and it clocks him on the ear. I turn to Elise. "Sorry I had to do that to your boyfriend. But he needed it."

Her eyes get wide—they're a very lovely green, I notice. "I throw socks at him sometimes," she whispers.

I flash her a quick smile. Maybe she's not as meek as she seems.

Byron's stirring the eggs in the pan now, and they smell so good I feel like I might faint. "The thing is, Wisty," he says, "if Darrius is as powerful as we think he is, and if his people have powers, too—isn't it a suicide mission?"

"Well, what's our other option? Standing around and just letting him keep robbing and killing us?"

"We have to come up with a plan," he says. "We have to think before we act." He shoots me a look that says, *We know how much you suck at that.*

"Nope, not my style," I acknowledge.

"Well, maybe it's time you changed, Wisty," he says.

I look at him in his slippers and his kitchen apron, with his cute little bungalow and his sweet, redheaded girl-friend. "Maybe it's time I changed you and Elise into ferrets," I yell.

Elise's eyes widen again. She should really learn a different facial expression.

"Wisty," Byron begins, but I'm already stomping out the door, scrambled eggs be damned.

Back out on the street, I turn around and see Byron and Elise standing together at the window, watching me with furrowed brows. Judging me. Even worse, feeling *sorry* for me.

Screw it, I think. And with a wave of my hands, Byron

and Elise become the cutest little ferret couple you could ever hope to see.

I wonder how ferrets feel about scrambled eggs. Because by the time that spell wears off, it's going to be time for Byron to rustle up some dinner.

Chapter 32

Whit

"HURRY UP, ALLGOOD," shouts today's sadistic supervisor, Joe. "I thought you were supposed to be so *strong*."

A grunt escapes me as I heave the enormous trash bags into the incinerator even faster. It's the hardest workout I've ever had—not to mention the most humiliating.

"You've got two more floors to go," he says. "Then report to the psych ward for bathroom duty."

I nod grimly. I've decided not to talk, because if I open my mouth, every single curse word I've ever heard is going to come spewing out.

In the past two days, I've been yelled at by doctors, harassed by nurses, and berated by janitors. Patients glare reproachfully at me. And that old man, the one I healed? He's like my damn shadow. He follows me around, demanding to know where my powers are.

I'd like the answer to that question myself. Did they get

sucked into that machine? If so, could I go and get them back? Or were they simply vaporized?

"Allgood!" Joe shouts. "You dropped something."

The contents of an entire trash bag are strewn on the floor: bloody bandages, adult diapers, paper towels covered with scum. Bile rises up in my throat. And Joe, who obviously sliced open the bag and dumped its contents on the ground, just stands there, waiting.

I glance down at my heavy-duty rubber gloves. *If you beat him with a pipe*, says a small, dark voice, *you wouldn't leave any fingerprints on the weapon.*

Too bad that's just a fantasy. I bend down and start cleaning while Joe watches me with his arms crossed, smiling in cruel satisfaction.

In the afternoon I'm supposed to be on guard duty—the one tolerable part of my new job. I patrol the ER and the surrounding hallways, on the lookout for Family creeps and anyone else aiming to pick a pocket or raid a drug supply closet.

It means I'm near Janine. I can catch glimpses of her now and then, or hear her voice coming from the ward or the break room.

What's weird is that I can't decide if this is a good thing.

"Oh, poooorter," Joe sings. "Laundry time."

I pick up the last scraps of trash and toss them into the bin, then trudge upstairs to gather the dirty sheets from a hundred rooms. I'm not even halfway done when

Dr. Keller appears, his bleached teeth gleaming in a fake smile.

"Aren't you industrious," he says. "And here I thought you were good for nothing."

I feign deafness. *La la la, no bald jackasses around here!*

"I'm glad to see you know your place now," he says. With his foot, he nudges the laundry cart, and it begins to roll away.

I hurry to catch it—but then *Janine* gets to it first. She's striding down the hall with another nurse, and I can tell by the look on her face that she was just laughing.

"Look, it's your protégé," Keller calls to her. "Doing the work he's best at." Then he turns to me. "Something smells. I *do* hope it's not you."

Janine, who hears him, flushes. She opens her mouth to say something—but then she shuts it again. Her friend giggles, and then whispers something into Janine's ear before following Keller away down the hall.

When we're alone, I turn to Janine. "Thanks for having my back," I say sarcastically. They're the first words I've said all day.

She reaches for my hand. "Oh, Whit, I'm sorry! But look, Keller's mean to everyone. His entire staff hates him."

"Yeah, well, they hate me, too, in case you haven't noticed," I say.

She shakes her head firmly. "No, they don't."

Are you blind? I almost ask. "Janine, I've never been treated like this. Under The One, I was an outlaw—an enemy. But I was worthy of *respect*. Now I'm nothing. No, scratch that—I'm *less* than nothing."

"It's going to get better, Whit," she insists. "Tomorrow I'll go talk to the other nurses."

That's not good enough. "I'm tired of this 'you're still the same person, everything's going to be okay' crap," I yell.

Janine looks taken aback. "What do you want from me, Whit? Do you want me to tell you that you screwed up? Why bother, when you already believe it?"

"So you think it was a mistake?" I demand.

She looks at me for a moment before she speaks. "No. I think it was the right thing to do. But maybe you weren't ready for it."

I scoff. "Maybe I wasn't ready to be kicked around by every damn person in this hospital."

Janine looks pained. "I can't stand up to Keller, Whit. I'll lose my job."

"Right," I huff. "While I'm losing my *sanity*. You don't understand how hard it is."

Janine steps toward me. "I told you, I'm trying," she says, eyes pleading. "I love you."

And now comes the time when I'm supposed to say *I love you, too.*

But instead I say, "I'm sorry."

And then, "I can't do this anymore."

Chapter 33

Whit

JANINE'S RUNNING AFTER ME down the hall, calling my name, but I don't stop. I sidestep a gurney, careen around a corner, and leap over a mop bucket. A doctor has to dive out of my way as I nearly crash through the emergency exit to the outside world.

Free. And I am never going back to that place.

"Whit," Janine's calling. "Wait!"

The grief in her voice stabs me in the heart. And I hesitate, because this is practically the first real feeling I've had since I was Excised.

"Come back," she cries. *"Please!"*

But I can't turn around. I can't see her tear-streaked face, or I'll weaken, and right now, I just have to keep going.

And so I pick up the pace.

I haven't run like this since I was on the foolball field. At first my legs are stiff, but then I find my stride, and pretty soon I feel like I'm flying.

Well, here's *one* thing I'm still good for. Maybe there's a future for me as an express delivery boy.

As if.

Janine's voice fades in the distance. Pretty soon all I can hear is the rasping of my breath and the pounding of my feet. And still I keep going, past the museum, the market, the library, my old high school—past everything that was once a part of me. I run until I'm lost.

If I were Wisty, I'd shoot off fireworks of distress. I'd topple trash cans and set off car alarms and light the trees on fire. I wouldn't care about being a total public nuisance, because the destruction would make me feel better.

But I'm not Wisty, and I'm not magic. These days, the only thing I am is all the things I'm not: *not* a jock, *not* a healer, *not* a wizard, *not* a hero.

And not a boyfriend, now, either.

Chapter 34

Whit

WHEN MY MOM opens the front door, she stares at me for a split second before her face breaks into a welcoming smile. As she waves me inside, I find myself wondering: *Do I somehow* look *different, too?*

"My dear Whit," she says, standing on her tiptoes and planting a kiss on my cheek. "I'm so glad you're here. I've been worried sick about you and your sister."

"You have?" I ask. Because it's not like she's *called.*

"Oh, yes! Everyone's talking. Have you heard the Council's new and horrible position on magic?" Her brow furrows, and she plucks agitatedly at the sleeve of her blouse.

My breath catches in my throat. "Uh—yeah," I manage.

"We're going to organize a protest," she goes on. "You can help us. Your father's been in contact with Mrs. Highsmith and several other magic folk—"

In no way am I ready to have this conversation. I turn

around, heading straight for the cupboard where they always keep the cookies and flinging it open. I know: *rude*. I shove four gingersnaps in my mouth at once.

My mom frowns. "Please *chew*, darling. I can't have you choking to death in the kitchen."

With my mouth full, I can only nod.

"All this talk of submission and Excision," she continues, wiping the crumbs away distractedly. "It's just awful. They're actually getting people to give up their powers. Can you believe it?" She gazes at me, incredulous.

The lump in my throat makes it hard to swallow the cookies.

Again, I just nod.

Yeah, I can believe it.

Then my dad comes up from the basement, wiping his hands on his flannel shirt. Lately he's been trying his hand at carpentry, a hobby Mom refers to as "making sawdust."

"Son," he booms, "excellent timing! You can test out one of my *handcrafted* chairs."

Mom shakes her head, and a quick smile lightens her worried expression. "Ben, dear, don't ask Whit to risk life and limb by sitting on your rickety furniture. He's already endangering himself by trying to eat all the cookies at once."

Dad grins back at her. "I know you think I should use my powers, Eliza. But then it wouldn't be half as fun!" He takes a handful of gingersnaps, too. "You don't use magic in the kitchen, do you?"

"That's my little secret," she says, winking.

Then they both start laughing. My mom, temporarily forgetting about her Excision worries, starts telling me about some Dad-related furniture disaster, and my dad cheerfully protests throughout. It's like we're just another *happy, magic family.*

I can't stand it. I feel like a liar, even being in the same room with them.

"I, uh, need to tell you something. . . ." I begin. But what am I supposed to say next? That what I did is killing me? That I hate who I am now? *Hey, Mom and Dad, you know how I've, like, fought a bunch of evil wizards and stuff? Well, guess what: the person most dangerous to me was my own self! Isn't that soooo ironic?*

I'm stuffing some more cookies in my face while I try to figure out how to start, when I'm saved by the sudden appearance of *Wisty,* who comes bursting through the kitchen door with a black eye, a cut on her forehead, and her hair sticking out every which way.

She's the last person I expected to see here, and she looks like hell. My first thought is, *Oh, god, is she okay?* And my second: *Now admitting what I've done is going to be that much harder.*

My mom shrieks and runs to her. "Wisty! What happened?"

"I had some, uh, rude visitors," she says in her typical offhand manner. "It's nothing." She lets them both hug her for a minute, then she pulls away and tries to smooth down her hair.

"Aren't you going to say hi to your brother?" my mom asks, still eyeing Wisty's wounds.

Wisty glares at me. It's the first time I've looked her in the face since I went to the Government Lab. Her eyes are cold and hard, and the cookies—yeah, I took more—turn to sawdust in my mouth.

"No," she says flatly.

Mom clucks her tongue. "You got hit on the head. That's making you grouchy."

"I said it's nothing, Mom," Wisty says. "Quit worrying about it."

"It's *not* nothing," I say. "What's wrong with your shoulder?"

Forget fire: I swear she could turn me to *ice* with that look.

"*Nothing*," she says again.

She can be as rude to me as she wants, though. I'm her big brother, and I'm going to help her whether she likes it or not. "Come here," I say. She protests, but I make her sit down—I've wrangled unruly patients before.

Albeit, not ones related to me. Not ones who seem like they'd sooner scratch my eyes out than say hi.

I gently palpate the collarbone, and she winces. "Ow!"

"Sorry. The good news is it's not broken. But it's badly bruised. You need a better splint."

And Wisty's no dummy; she knows she needs help. So she holds her breath and waits, glowering, while I re-splint her shoulder. Then I clean and bandage her cuts while our parents observe nervously.

"Glad to see they didn't take *all* your healing powers," she sneers when I'm done.

The room falls immediately still.

Then: "Whit?" my mom says questioningly. "What is Wisty talking about?"

I feel like I'm going to be sick, but I steady myself against the couch. No more putting it off.

It's time to confess.

Chapter 35

Whit

WISTY, AS USUAL, beats me to the punch. "I know what you did and you never should have done it!" she barks.

I take a startled step back. "Whoa, hang on, sis. Maybe we could have a reasonable, adult conversation about this."

But once Wisty gets going, there's no stopping her. "It's too late for that! You should have talked to us, you stupid idiot! Instead you went and *submitted*, and you'll never be the same again."

My mom's cheeks pale. "You *didn't*," she whispers.

"He *did*!" Wisty shrieks.

My dad stiffens, and then he turns and gazes hard into the fireplace, like if he looks at it long enough, some genie'll pop out of the ashes and tell him the secret of life.

Or maybe tell him why his only son let himself be Excised.

I do want them to understand. "It wasn't an impulse,"

I try to explain. "I thought about it for a long time. And I believed it was the right thing to do."

Believed—not *believe*. But they don't pick up on my use of the past tense.

"Did I call you a stupid idiot already? I can't remember, so I'll do it again. You're a stupid, sneaky, idiotic idiot!" Wisty yells—just like she's four years old again and I've taken her favorite toy.

"The Council said we needed to stand together, as *equals*," I say, keeping my voice steady. "That made sense to me."

I'm hinting at the truth because I can't bear to admit it to them—that I've regretted every second of my life since the Excision.

"But your powers..." my mother begins.

"They're gone," I say flatly.

Wisty shakes her head. "It's just so imbecilic and sad."

"I did it for the City," I yell.

"And look what good it's done," Wisty cries, tears springing to her eyes. "Nothing! It's done *nothing*! All it's done is make you *weak*."

And I don't know what to say to that—because she's right.

"I just don't get it," my mom says. She's staring down at her hands because she can't bear to look at me anymore.

"It's because it makes no sense at all," Wisty says, her eyes narrow and mean. But hey, at least she'll look at me.

Meanwhile my dad has decided that the fireplace isn't

going to offer him any miraculous wisdom, so he turns to face me. For a second I hope he's going to be the voice of sanity, help Mom and Wisty see reason. But then he whispers, "How could you?"

Being so near to them, and yet feeling so far away—it's unbearable.

"You gave up your *birthright*," he says, disbelieving.

"I told you," I insist. "I was trying to do the right thing."

My dad straightens his shoulders. He's standing up as tall as he can, but he's still five inches shorter than me. "And now *we* are trying to do the right thing when we say this: you've made your choice, and now you have to live with it. We can't help you, Whitford. I'm sorry, but this is no longer your home."

My mom gasps, and even Wisty looks surprised. But they don't protest. I turn to both of them, asking without words: *Are you really banishing me?*

It seems the answer to that question is *yes*.

So I bow my head and turn to go.

As I leave behind my childhood home, I shake my head in disbelief. I thought I'd hit rock bottom, but it turns out I'm still falling.

Chapter 36

Whit

I'M RUNNING SO FAST it's hard to think—which is the *point*. But somehow, bitter thoughts haunt me anyway. In the course of a single day, I've sprinted away from everyone who truly matters to me. And as far as I can tell, only Janine was sorry to see me go.

If I thought I felt empty before, well, that was nothing. I had a job, a girlfriend, a family. And now what? I have the clothes on my back, the money in my pocket, and the quick-moving legs now carrying me back into the City. Maybe I'll keep running until I come to the end of the world—or drop dead. Whichever comes first; I don't care.

I tear down street after street, my breath coming rough and fast. I pass men and women coming home from work, waving to their neighbors before climbing the steps to their warm houses. I smell dinners being cooked. Every now and again I catch a strain of music, or the sound of the evening news.

Almost in spite of myself, I slow down—as if just being here is the closest I'll get to having a family ever again. The neighborhood seems peaceful, despite the graffiti scrawled on stoops and the surveillance cameras scanning everything. Maybe because it was never bombed under The One's reign of terror, it feels like a sanctuary.

For everyone else, anyway.

"The sky is one whole, the water another; and between those two infinities, the soul of man is in loneliness." Somebody said that once, but I don't remember who.

Still running, but more sluggishly now, I glance up at the evening sky. It's filling up with glittering points of light.

And that's when the loneliness really hits me. *Even the dumb stars have friends and family*, I think. *Even trees grow in clusters, and even rats run in packs. People build entire cities because they don't want to be alone.*

Maybe this is why they call it runner's high. If you go far enough without stopping to rest, you start thinking weird things. And then maybe you even start *seeing* weird things, too.

Things you can't believe.

Really.

Like, I *can't believe* what I'm seeing right now.

Spilling out of every alley, and clattering up the center of the street, are *horses*.

Chapter 37

Whit

THEY'RE RUNNING LIKE they're being chased—or maybe even being whipped. But they don't have any *riders*. Steam curls from their nostrils, and their flanks shine with sweat and foam. Their muscular necks strain forward as their black eyes bulge.

I blink and give my head a hard shake. For a second, I'm still convinced it's some kind of crazy hallucination, an endorphin-fueled nightmare. But then a woman starts to scream, and I know I'm not making this up.

The sound of their hooves builds to a thunderous roar, and all along the street, car alarms start to go off. A storefront window shatters, hit by a rock flung up by a horseshoe.

The last time I saw this many horses, they were carrying the evil Mountain King's soldiers to battle. But these beasts aren't the shaggy-coated ponies of that alpine land—they're sleek, sinewy, and enormous. So where on earth did they come from? And where are they going so damn fast?

"*What's happening?*" the woman shrieks.

But no one has an answer for her.

A stray dog who'd been nosing around in the trash makes the mistake of stepping out into the sidewalk. It yelps in terror as it tries desperately to get away from the onslaught of horses. But it's not fast enough, and we watch in horror as it's trampled under a stampede of pounding hooves.

The woman's still screaming, but I can't hear her anymore. A black horse races past, just inches away from me. As the force of the wind knocks me backward, I see its rolling eye, wild with fear.

I'm pressed against the side of a building, dumbstruck. And then I remember the dream I had—the last time my dead first love came to visit me.

You're in terrible danger, Celia had said. *I see an army of horses.*

Suddenly, although I don't know how to explain what I'm seeing yet, I know what to call it.

It's an *attack.*

BOOK TWO

LOVE OR DESTRUCTION

Chapter 38

Whit

THEY'RE RACING TOWARD the City center, and I follow them. I'm not as fast as a sprinting horse, but I can pretty much keep up with the stragglers.

Above me, people lean out their windows to watch. Some are cheering like it's the Running of the Bulls, while others look on in shock and horror. I'm the only person crazy enough to be down on the street, dodging flying hooves and steaming piles of horse poop.

Because, for one thing, I need to know what's going on. And for another: *What have I got to lose?*

The City's siren begins to sound, its wail cutting through the night like an inhuman scream. I'm trying to remember: did *The Book of Truths* say anything about a plague of horses? A cavalry without riders? How is it that these *animals* are mounting an attack? And what are they going to do? Overrun the City? Demand higher-quality hay and an end to the glue factory?

Maybe this is somehow the Family's doing. Maybe they decided that the robberies and murders weren't causing enough chaos, so they brainwashed an army of equines. Maybe a battalion of wolves comes next, or a squad of bears....

But pretty soon I'm out of theories, and simply running is all I can manage. I'm falling behind the main band of horses, but I'm neck and neck with a sorrel mare that seems kind of directionless, as if she hadn't gotten the memo about where to gallop. She's so close I can almost touch her muscled shoulder.

Could I?

Legs pumping, lungs screaming, I reach out—and I manage to grab a fistful of her mane. I sprint beside her for a moment, my feet hammering on the pavement while my fingers tighten around the long, tangled hairs. Then, using the last ounce of adrenaline I've got, I launch myself into the air—and up onto her back. I land hard, and her coat's so slick with sweat I nearly slip off the other side. I grab tighter to her mane and squeeze my legs around her heaving sides.

She bucks in response to the sudden weight, but she can't shake me off. We pound through the streets, and the whole world rushes by in a blur. I might be on the back of an enemy mount, but it's a ride like I've never experienced before.

Another ten minutes of a hard sprint and we've reached the City center. In the vast municipal courtyard—the one ringed by all our important government buildings—a huge barricade of police cars and army tanks has formed.

So *clearly* I'm not the only one worried about this riderless herd.

There are hundreds upon hundreds of soldiers, plus police officers in full-body riot gear. The Council's new recruits stand side by side with grizzled veterans in a snaking line of defense.

All of them have their guns drawn.

The horses, instead of continuing their mad rush, pull up short at the near edge of the square—as if halted by a hard tug on invisible reins. A stallion neighs, and a few beasts paw the cobblestones with their hooves. But for a moment, a strange quiet descends as animals and people face off beneath the floodlights.

I slide off my borrowed mount and duck into a nearby doorway. Whatever happens next, I've got no need to get shot by a poorly trained rookie cop with a nervous trigger finger.

My shelter allows me to catch my breath. It also gives me the perfect ground-level perspective when, a minute later, all hell breaks loose.

First, the horses rear up on their hind legs—and then they *charge*. Manes flying, they thunder across the square toward the barricades. The police on the other side hesitate: do they kill a riderless horse?

But then, in a blinding flash of amber light and a deafening rush of wind, the horses' *riders* appear. *Out of thin air.*

They simply *materialize*—right onto their horses' backs, spurs immediately biting into the straining flanks.

They shriek as one, in a language I've never heard before. A tongue of guttural barks and snarls, as if they're no more human than their mounts. But they're men: huge, bearded men, armed to the teeth with everything from cudgels to rifles. And they're thundering down upon the City's defenses, which suddenly look *pitiful*.

The first line of City soldiers stands its ground. "Fire!" shouts a voice, and bright flashes spark in the muzzles of their guns. An army tank shoots a rocket toward the enemy's left flank, and it explodes in a bright ball of fire. I see horses stumble, men knocked from their mounts.

And for a moment, I think we have a chance.

But hundreds more riders surge forward, and as they charge, they lift their cudgels over their heads. Each weapon begins to glow with a terrible amber light.

Confused, the City forces hesitate—and then the collective glow shoots outward in lines of fire, torpedoing toward men now frozen in horror.

In another second, they're simply gone.

Annihilated. Evaporated. Obliterated. Not even ashes left behind.

The second line of City forces had their guns lifted—but then they drop them and just run.

The riders spur their horses forward, guns blazing,

cudgels glowing. The army tanks mount a brave stand, but soon they, too, are overrun.

In a matter of minutes, our battle with the magical, unknown foe is over.

Needless to say, we lost.

Chapter 39

Wisty

I WAS SURE my TV screen had broken during my fight with the Family—after all, the *rest* of my apartment sure got busted to smithereens—but at five o'clock in the morning, it suddenly flickers to life. First comes a shrill beeping noise, then a crackle of static, and then a familiar voice begins to speak.

I sit up, groggy and stiff from a night spent on the couch. It takes a minute for the picture to come into focus. When it does, I gasp.

It's *Darrius*.

My blood chills as his golden eyes, gazing steadily out from the screen, seem to bore deep into mine. When he smiles, he shows a row of perfect white teeth.

"Greetings, citizens," Darrius says. "I address you this morning as your new leader."

Wait—*what?*

For a second, my half-asleep brain thinks he's only on *my* screen. You know, so the sadistic bastard could torture me mentally as well as physically. But he's talking to *the entire City.*

Which, I realize, is actually worse.

Darrius's expression is positively serene as he goes on. "Last night, at approximately ten p.m., Terrence Rino, acting on behalf of the Council, surrendered all rights of City governance to me."

Instantly it's like I've been socked in the gut. All the air goes out of my lungs, and for a second, the room actually goes dim. I blink and rub my eyes, but when I stop, Darrius is still there.

My stomach twists into a knot of fear and dread. I can hardly believe it. Last night, while I was sleeping, Darrius somehow took over the City.

I'm almost overcome with shock—and with *guilt.* I could have stopped him, if only I'd acted earlier. If only I'd had help.

"Damn you, Byron," I shout. "Why didn't you side with me when there was still time?"

Meanwhile, on-screen, Darrius is still addressing his new constituency. "Here beside me, citizens," he says, "you will recognize a familiar face: a former Speaker wrongfully deposed and exiled."

The TV camera shifts to the side, and this time I nearly choke. It's none other than that traitor General Matthias

Bloom, whom I personally *besieged with monkeys* before *banishing to the infernal desert*. Bloom's face shines greasily, and his toupee is worse than ever.

"There is no need for alarm," Darrius goes on. "The order your City was lacking is being restored."

"By whom?" I yell at the screen. "*You?* The *Family?* The very people who were destroying it in the first place?"

I run to the window, expecting to see black-clad, dog tag–sporting thugs policing the streets with billy clubs in their hands. Instead, though, I see no one at all. And that, too, is scary.

Darrius's calm voice continues on the screen behind me. "This new Rule of Law will result in an atmosphere of peace and an environment of order," he says. "We need no longer live in fear."

But then, as I watch out the window, a truly frightening pair of bearded, heavily armed men trot up the street on horseback, silver badges flashing. A woman who'd stepped outside to get her morning paper takes one look at them and scrambles back inside, slamming the door behind her.

Is that what Darrius calls order? Scaring people into self-imprisonment? Also, who in the holy hell are those giant hairy dudes on horses? They're *definitely* not from around here.

I turn back to the TV screen. Now Bloom has taken the microphone. His eyes glint—he always *loved* a captive audience.

"As Leader Darrius has said, now is not a time for

fear," he assures his viewers. "We will do all that we can to maintain harmony during this period of transition, and we ask that you do the same."

"Why don't you choke on your own tongue?" I scream at the screen. I know what Bloom means by "harmony." He means *subjugation*.

But my rage can't banish my growing sense of fear—for my City, and for myself.

Because let's not forget that *both* of those men, in addition to exhibiting extremely scary sociopathic tendencies, have tried *very hard* to kill me.

Chapter 40

Wisty

OVERNIGHT, THE CITY CHANGED from a place of peace to a place of fear. From my childhood bedroom (yeah, I ran home to my parents—can you blame me?), I watch the armed Horsemen march up and down the street. They're all at least six and a half feet tall, with chiseled features, cold blue eyes, and sunbaked skin; they look like they'd flay you alive if you so much as glanced at them funny.

My mom and dad are in shock, too. Every ringing hoofbeat is a reminder: the life we were living yesterday is *not* the one we're living now.

Because now looks a lot more like hell.

Sometimes I close my eyes and try to pretend, just for a second, that the world isn't falling apart around me. It almost never works.

My mom knocks lightly on the door before opening it and sticking her head in. "He's on again," she says.

"Again?" Darrius's primary weapon—besides those horrifying Horsemen—seems to be the video screen. Every hour he's back on it, *orating*. Cajoling. Threatening. Manipulating.

Whatever he thinks will bring people over to his side. (As if the guns and the troops and the magic weren't enough?)

Now he's up against a plain blue background, gazing out as if he can see each and every one of us in our homes, and he looks...well, beautiful.

Hateful, but beautiful. Unfortunately, power suits him.

"—grateful for your understanding the importance of these *minor restrictions in movement*," he's saying.

I turn to my mom. "What's he talking about?"

She's twisting a dish towel in her hands like she's trying to strangle it. "No one can go anywhere without papers justifying their destination," she says. "People might be able to go to their jobs, for instance, but they can't visit a friend."

"You're kidding," I cry—though of course I know she's not.

She shakes her head. "We'll be given assigned times for going to the market, or the hardware store...."

"But *why*?" I ask, incredulous.

And it's almost as if Darrius can hear me. "When disobedience of the law is widespread," he intones, "such as it was under the previous government, it is necessary to *reevaluate* what we might once have considered *necessary freedoms*."

Then Bloom takes the microphone and flatly announces that anyone walking after dark without permission could be shot on sight.

"Holy M," I breathe.

My dad, watching from the doorway, remarks, "You like their good-cop, bad-cop routine? Darrius explains; Bloom decrees."

"It's obvious that Darrius is calling the shots, though," I say. *Bastard*, I think. And I can't help but notice how Bloom wears a uniform and glowers at the camera, while Darrius smiles in a black cashmere V-neck—as if it's important for our new overlord to rock the business casual.

"These are dark times," my mom whispers.

"You think?" I say.

She frowns. "Honestly, Wisty, is the sarcasm necessary?"

"Sorry. Habit."

"It's okay." She takes a deep breath. "We have to keep each other safe from Darrius, Bloom, and the Horsemen— whoever they are, and wherever they came from. But we also have to organize a resistance." She pauses. "It's so good that you're here."

"It is?" I ask. "I know I've got a reputation for being a bit *fighty*. But what am I supposed to do against the most powerful wizard I've possibly ever encountered? Tell me, Mom, because I've been trying to figure that out."

"You join forces," my mom says.

"With who?" I ask. "You, Dad, and Mrs. Highsmith? That's not much of an army."

Tears suddenly spring to my mom's eyes. "I wish Whit were here," she whispers.

My dad, still in the doorway, buries his face in his hands. His voice, when he speaks, is muffled. "I never should have sent him away."

No, I think, *you shouldn't have.*

But then Whit shouldn't have let himself be Excised, either. So whose fault is it, really?

Chapter 41

Whit

FROM WHERE I'M CROUCHED, I see mostly hooves. Sometimes I catch glimpses of the Horsemen's boots, trimmed with snakeskin and feathers. And occasionally a squirrel skitters through my line of sight.

That's pretty much it.

Not that I expected anything else. I knew right when I crawled in that, while a giant concrete drainpipe isn't the worst place to call home, it's damn close enough.

The funny—or *unfunny*—thing is that it feels right to me. I've got nowhere to go, so why pretend that I do? I'm embracing my fate.

Let's say it again now: *the fate I stupidly chose.*

I've scavenged a handful of musty blankets, full of holes and mouse droppings. Layers of cardboard make up my mattress. They're not what I'd call soft, but they act as insulation, keeping the cold of the concrete from seeping into my bones.

Pride won't let me sneak back to my apartment for a pillow, or maybe another warm coat. Because if I take something, Janine will notice it's missing, and then she'll think of me.

I don't want that.

Besides my pitiful bedding, I've got some matches, some candles, and a *geranium*. Seriously. Someone threw it away because it was basically 98 percent dead. But I repotted it in an old coffee can, and it's looking pretty good now. There's a bud—just a tiny pink speck—that's going to turn into a nice flower one of these days.

See? Just when you thought there was no hope.

Actually, I'm being sarcastic. There *is* no hope.

At the other end of the pipe, the one that faces away from the street, is a pit where I build a fire sometimes. I heat chili in the coals and eat it, spoonless, right out of the can. Ditto chicken soup and canned spaghetti and meatballs.

As a structure, my pipe is as solid as it gets: while I'm tucked inside it, the world can go to hell around me.

And it seems like it is.

There's shouting on the street, and I peer out to see a pair of Horsemen stopping a man and demanding, in their strange, guttural accent, to see his papers.

"I have to go to my mother's," the man pleads. "She's old. Her boiler's not working."

The bearded man on the gray horse sneers. "No papers," he grunts. "Criminal."

"No," the man says, "I just—"

Quick as lightning, the Horseman riding the bay clubs him on the side of the head. The man crumples to the ground, and they stand over him, taunting: "Get up, get up! *Run home to Mama.*"

After a few moments, the man struggles to his feet and tries to hobble away. But the Horsemen follow him. First they walk their horses behind him, and then, as he picks up speed, they urge them to a lope.

I can see his terrified face as he tries to go faster, and if I could magically give him the speed and strength of my legs, I would.

As they near him again, they begin to grin. The first one throws a rock, hitting the man in the back and knocking him down. The second spurs his horse over the man's prone body—and I watch, in horror, as the animal tramples him.

To death.

And I do nothing. Because there is nothing I can do.

I bury my head in my blankets and curse myself, for the millionth time, for giving up my powers. I bite my lip to keep from screaming. I stay like that until I hear the footsteps. Close by.

Getting closer.

Now right outside.

I grab a can of beans as a weapon. But then *Wisty's head* appears in the opening of the pipe, upside down. Her long, windblown hair brushes in the dirt.

"Well, well, well," she says.

Then she drops all the way down and quickly scuttles into the pipe.

"Can't wait for you to invite me in," she says. "There are Horsemen just around the corner." Instead of hugging me, or even meeting my eye, Wisty looks around the drainpipe. "Nice digs," she says dryly. She reaches for a blanket and sits down cross-legged. "Candles, wool blankets, a plant— if there was a decorating magazine for homeless dudes, you'd be in it. This is totally hobo chic."

I decide to take her joking as a good sign. Maybe she doesn't hate me as much as I think she does. "How'd you find me?"

"*Magic*," she declares.

I can't take it; I look down at my powerless hands. "Comes in handy, doesn't it?" I say softly.

"Oh, Whit, I could just kill you," she cries, hitting the side of the drainpipe in frustration. "But you've already half killed yourself."

Tell me about it, I think. But I don't say anything.

"You can't stay here," she says.

Finally our eyes meet. "Really? Where am I supposed to go, Wisty? Tell me what I'm supposed to do."

She bites her lip like she's trying to hold something back. Something she knows will crush me even further than I've already crushed myself.

"What?" I ask.

She shakes her head. Whatever she was thinking, she's

not going to tell me. "You have to come with me," she says. "You have to see what we're up against."

"Even if I can't help?" I whisper.

She doesn't answer. She just holds out her hand. "Come," she says.

And so I do. Because Wisty, my *baby sister*, calls the shots now—and she knows it.

Chapter 42

Whit

WISTY CARRIES FORGED PAPERS, but just in case, we keep to the back alleys.

"Where are we going?" I ask, but she's too busy watching out for Horsemen to answer. Too busy telling me how much everything's changed since I "slithered into that moldy drainpipe."

She pokes her head out of the shadows, scoping out the street before scurrying on to the next narrow corridor. As we go, she ticks off what's been outlawed. "Video games, dancing, congregating in numbers greater than three, growing or consuming squash or squash products...and going anywhere without permission, *obviously*."

"Whoa, hang on. Darrius outlawed *squash*?"

Wisty spits derisively into the street. "That was Bloom. Apparently during part of his exile, he survived on pumpkin rinds. Now he can't stand the sight of the stuff—which is pretty ungrateful, if you ask me. It's like a shipwrecked dude outlawing lifeboats once he gets back home, you know?"

She shakes her head, almost smiling now, and I realize just how much I've missed her.

I wish I could tell her that.

We pass under a bridge tagged with *Long Live Darrius* in giant letters, then turn up the alley behind the Municipal Library. Its doors are chained shut, and its windows are covered with plywood.

I get a sinking feeling in my stomach. "Did Darrius shut it down—just like The One did?"

"Not *exactly*," Wisty says. "But he didn't issue passes for it, so no one can legally go there. And he reclassified all librarians as nonessential workers. You know what *that* means."

I shake my head. "Uh, no."

"Seriously? Have you been living under a log?" She stops herself. "Oh, right, basically you have. If you're deemed a nonessential worker, you get assigned a new work duty. You don't pick your job, and you don't get paid." Wisty shudders, and her voice goes hard. "In other words, you become a *slave*."

I'm trying to wrap my head around this as we make our way past the roller rink, the mall, and the stadium—all closed. The new community center had barely opened its doors before Darrius decided to shut them again.

A *slave*. I thought I had nothing left to lose, but I do: my freedom. The freedom of my friends and family.

"Well, here we are," Wisty says, giving me a false, bright smile.

Behind her is the art museum. Its doors are chained together, too. There's even police tape strung between the pillars, as if art itself is a crime.

She knocks lightly a few times on one of the boarded-up windows, like she's announcing our presence. But to whom? Then she pries up a corner of the thin wood and motions me inside. "After you," she says.

I squeeze past her and worm my way through the broken pane of a window. A piece of glass catches the collar of my shirt, and some skin, too. As I drop down into the main hall of the museum, I feel a thin trickle of blood running down my neck.

Wisty lands much more gracefully behind me.

It's dim and echoey inside, and it takes my eyes a minute to adjust. When they do, I gasp. Every painting on the wall, every sculpture, has been horribly defaced. Spray paint mars the marble statue to my left; the canvas nearest me has been ripped to shreds.

I'm shocked into silence. The One may have stolen our art—but Darrius has *destroyed* it.

Wisty doesn't give the ruin a second glance. "This way," she says.

I follow her down metal steps to the museum's basement. In the huge, cinder-block room that smells like mold and turpentine, I get my second major shock of the day.

The room is full of *kids*. Dozens of them—maybe even a hundred—big, little, and in between. Kids I *know*. My heart does a somersault in my chest.

It's the *Resistance*.

They've come together again.

Chapter 43

Whit

WISTY GIVES ME the first real smile I've seen in days. "The gang's all here," she says.

Without even thinking, I scan the room for Janine. She was a Resistance leader, after all. She braved death on the icy slopes of the Mountain King's peaks. She fought by my side against two evil despots.

But I don't see her anywhere.

Enormous Emmet, one of the original Resistance members, comes striding over and claps me on the shoulder. "Good to see you, man," he says. "Too bad it's not under better circumstances."

Ross hurries over next. The last time I saw him, he was DJ'ing the City-wide party to celebrate The One's defeat. He was best friends with Sasha, who died in my arms in the ice-bound forests of the Mountain Kingdom. "Whit," he says solemnly, and I know he's remembering our lost friend. "Glad you're here."

Then Wisty introduces me to new Resistance members. There's Serena, a beautiful black-haired girl with the green eyes of a cat; Greg, a blond surfer type with his arm in a sling; and Lily, a little fireplug of a redhead who looks me up and down, wrinkles her nose, and says, "You need a shower."

No doubt she's right. "Where's…" I start to ask. But suddenly it's hard for me to even say Janine's name.

Emmet frowns. "JD, our former weapons expert?" he asks. "He plays for Bloom's team now."

Ross nods grimly. "Darrius has turned a number of our members against us."

I know I should care about this JD person's defection, but I don't. "Actually I was wondering about—" I begin.

But everyone's talking at once now, trying to catch me up on everything I've missed.

"Darrius found our first hideout," Emmet tells me. "This is headquarters number two."

"He took fifty of us in that raid," Serena adds, and beside her, Sam starts telling me about narrowly escaping a gang of Horsemen while Lily describes Bloom's terrifying night patrols. The voices swirl in a blur around my head, and for a second I wish for the solitude of my drainpipe.

Then, out of nowhere, a gong sounds. Emmet nearly jumps out of his skin, and Wisty and I unconsciously grab each other. We turn around to see Ross, standing on a wooden crate above the crowd and grinning. "Effective way to call a meeting, don't you think?"

"Effective way to get your teeth knocked in," Emmet mumbles.

"Now that we're all here," Ross continues, "we have a few things to talk about."

But we're not *all here,* I think. Was Janine one of the fifty people taken? And if so, to where?

"The root of the alliance between our new leaders remains clouded in mystery," Ross begins. "How did Darrius and Matthias Bloom find each other?"

"A dating site for psychotic dictators?" Sam jokes.

"An Assholes Anonymous meeting," Serena calls.

Ross allows a flicker of a smile to cross his face. "Bloom was exiled to the desert by our very own Wisteria Allgood." He claps, and a few people in the audience hoot in support. "We think that's where Darrius is from, too, as well as the barbarians they call the Horsemen." He pauses. "And today, our scouts tell us that more Horsemen are coming."

"But Darrius is in power already," Lily says. "What does he need more of those ugly sand cowboys for?"

Ross's brow creases with worry. "We believe they want to take over our City."

"Uh, haven't they already?" Wisty points out.

Ross shakes his head. "Right now there are only a few hundred of them here, acting as Darrius's enforcers on patrols and as guards at the Old Palace. But there are *thousands* more in the desert, biding their time. Life out there's hard, you guys—and they're *tired* of it. They want what we have." He stops and looks at each of us in turn. "And any day now, they're going to *come for it*."

"And what happens to us?" Serena asks softly.

"Slavery—or death," Wisty says. Her voice is sharp and bitter. "I doubt they care which."

Ross nods briskly. "What we must remember is that we have many enemies. We need to gather all our powers in the fight against them."

The room erupts into chaos again—people shouting out questions and giving voice to their fears—and amid the noise I collar Emmet. "Where's Janine? Have you seen her?" I ask.

He shrugs his giant shoulders. "I don't know. She's not with us."

My heart sinks. If she's not with the Resistance, does that mean she's against it? I'm desperate for answers—about Janine, about the Horsemen, about everything. And there's only one place that just might have some of them.

"What about *The Book of Truths*?" I call. "Is there any advice or reassurance for us there?"

Ross looks pale all of a sudden. He hesitates.

"Go on," I urge. "Tell us."

Reluctantly, he opens a tattered copy and flips to the right page. "'From ashes and exile, vital leaders rise,'" he quotes. Then he grimaces.

Beside me, Wisty jumps up. "*Exile?* That sounds like Bloom! And turning people to ashes—that's what Darrius does! *The Book of Truths can't* mean they're right for us."

Her hands twitch in agitation, and I wonder if she's going to spark.

I don't claim to always understand *The Book of Truths*, but I have to admit, this wasn't the reassurance I was looking for. "Maybe there's another explanation," I suggest.

"I hope so," Wisty says darkly. "Because if there isn't, we're doomed."

Then Emmet slings his arm around Wisty's shoulders and gives her a little shake. "Come on, Wist," he says. "Think of all the battles you've fought! When have you ever been afraid of insurmountable odds?"

Her eyes slide over to me. "Before," she says quietly, "I had *help*."

I turn away. She doesn't need to keep reminding me of what I've given up.

"You'll have a lot of help this time, too," Emmet says. "I mean, come on—look at us! We're going to kick some wizard ass!" He grins bravely, and everyone in the room starts to cheer.

My heart surges with pride. This gang of teenagers is going to figure out a way to take out the most powerful wizard the City has ever faced.

But they won't have my magic to help them, and I'm not looking forward to the moment when they realize it.

Chapter 44

Wisty

I PEER BOTH WAYS down the darkened streets, poised to run at the slightest hint of hoofbeats. But everything's quiet, so I motion my friends out from the shadows of the alley.

Emmet creeps along as quietly as he can, but he steps on Serena's heel. "Ouch," she yelps, then claps her hands over her mouth. "Sorry," she whispers.

We're breaking two laws right now, simply by walking around: it's after dark, and we have no papers.

Yes, we could be shot on sight. As my brother keeps reminding me.

But we're on a midnight mission: we want people in the City to know there's still hope, even if it doesn't feel like it. Even if Darrius is making us slaves, and *The Book of Truths* seems to tell us that we've gotten what we deserve. We need to prove to the City that the Resistance still lives.

We arrive at a small plaza, where I break law number

three by making a pyramid of miniature pumpkins. Silly as it looks, it's a coded message to a population living in terror and dread. *We are here, and we will not give up.*

"Perfect," I say, making a final adjustment to the arrangement of Bloom's vegetable enemy #1.

"Punishable by ten years in the slammer," Emmet crows, moving one of the pumpkins an inch to the left. "There. Now, *that's* perfect."

Serena punches Emmet in the arm. "Assault!" she says. "Twenty years' hard labor."

Then Emmet runs ahead, stops, yanks down his pants, and moons us. "Indecent exposure!" he giggles. "Thirty!"

"Guys, come on. This is dangerous," Whit pleads.

My brother's right, of course. But what *isn't* dangerous these days? We all know Bloom would sooner shoot a man than smile at him. So maybe it seems crazy to be joking around like this, but sometimes you have to blow off steam. Sometimes you have to give your so-called leaders the finger.

When we pass one of the City police stations—now occupied by Horsemen, Family members, and other traitors to our government—I shoot a jet of blue flame from my palm. I've got another message, but this one's just for Darrius. *This is our City, not yours*, I burn into the side of the building. *Are you listening, Darrius?*

"Okay, sis, that's enough for now," Whit says.

But I'm only getting started. I turn to face him, hands on my hips. "You think? Because *I'm* not sure it is." I point at a pile of newspapers and cardboard boxes waiting to be recycled. A tendril of smoke curls up, and then—*whoosh!*—the pile goes up in orange flames.

"*Arson*," I sneer at Whit. "How many years for that?"

The fire climbs up a trellis on the police station, and an alarm begins clanging.

Emmet starts to look nervous. "Uh...I don't know if that was such a good idea," he says.

But there's still fire inside me, and it's itching to get out. "Well, maybe you guys don't want to stick around for *this*," I say. And I fling my arms into the air, and the streetlamps begin to blaze like klieg lights, and then sparks start arcing out of them. Any moment they'll explode in a shower of scarlet embers.

I want to shout and dance in the light—I want to feel the burn on my skin. I will *not* let Darrius put out my fire.

I'm spinning madly, shooting off sparks, when suddenly there's an arm around my neck, and it's pulling me into the darkness. I fight it, kicking and scratching, and then another hand clamps down hard on my mouth so I can't bite.

I'm blind with fear and rage, but the arms are too strong. They're pulling me deeper into the darkness, dragging me away from my dancing flames....

And then they let me go.

I whirl around, fists raised—and I'm face-to-face with Whit.

"*Hush*," he whispers. "The Horsemen are coming."

Behind him, Serena and Emmet stare at me in fear and wonder. And I understand why. Because when you're breaking laws established by murderers, you *really ought to be quiet about it*. Unless you want to eat a bullet for your midnight snack.

Chapter 45

Whit

DARRIUS'S FACE FLICKERS onto the TV screen at five a.m. *Again*. If this dictator business doesn't work out, he's got a bright future as an alarm clock. (Not that he managed to wake Wisty up; I can hear her snoring in the next room.)

He serenely wishes us a good morning, but then he quickly hands the microphone to General Bloom, and without preamble, Bloom launches into the latest set of rules. "Public parks have been closed, pending further notice. Benson Polytechnic School is now closed, as is the Drake Academy of Art and Science. Citizens residing in the City's eighth quadrant will be receiving their relocation assignments within the week."

More closures, more forced relocations: it makes me want to kick the screen in. They promise we'll earn our freedoms back, once we learn how to comport ourselves. They say in the meantime, we should be grateful we're still alive.

"Contrary to what you have been led to believe," Bloom likes to say, "existence is not a right. It is a *privilege*."

I unplug the TV—I've had enough of them for now. And then I get dressed, even though the sun's not up yet. I grab a breakfast bar from the cabinet and scrawl a quick note for my mom. I slip outside before anyone's up to ask me where I'm going.

After Wisty's obnoxious display last night, I made up my mind to take a different approach.

Which is why I'm going to join the slave brigade at Work Site #1.

It's not as crazy as it sounds, I swear.

Work Site #1 is a giant pit in the middle of the City. A full square block in size, it was supposed to be the foundation of a new cultural center. Once Darrius came to power, though, everything changed. Instead of building support columns for the future building, people were forced to dig the huge hole still deeper. And if you believe what you hear, the labor of excavating rock and mud is literally *killing* people.

I've decided my job's going to be helping them survive. I *can* do that, even without my healing magic. I'm also going to find out why they're digging. And maybe, just maybe, I'll figure out a way to stop it.

We have to fight with the weapons we've got, after all: that's what I keep telling myself as I join the hordes of unwilling workers. My weapon, for now, will be subterfuge.

One of the Horsemen grabs my arm and quickly clamps

a strange metal band around my wrist. Before I have time to look at it more closely, he motions me and hundreds of other bleary-eyed people down rickety ladders into the vast, muddy hole.

It feels like I'm climbing down into the pit of hell. But instead of fire, there's rock and mud and cold, wet sludge. The only sounds are the clang of the shovels and pick-axes and the groans of the filthy, miserable workers. The air smells like sweat and piss and worse. I've seen a lot of suffering in my life, but this just might take the misery cake.

"You do not rest. You do not talk. You *work*," the Horse-man shouts from above, "until the bell sounds. The only excuse for not working is *being dead*." He pats the gun slung across his shoulder and smiles cruelly.

"But being dead *must* be better than this," whispers someone nearby.

I can already tell he's got a point.

As I walk farther along, I notice that all around me, carved into the walls of the pit, are the beginnings of tun-nels. Muddy figures labor in the rocky, gaping maws—but there's nothing to see but darkness. Where will the com-pleted tunnels lead? Are we building a subway system down here? A network of new water lines? Are these tun-nels supposed to be *mine shafts*? And what's up with my weird new bracelet?

I try to ask a fellow slave as I pass by, but he shakes his head in warning—we aren't supposed to talk. When I try again, he swings his pickaxe so close to my feet that I have to jump back.

I join a group of about a dozen workers by the mouth of one of the tunnels. None of them say anything to me, either—why risk a lashing? But I nod at each of them in turn, trying to say, *I see you. You're not simply a faceless slave.*

I move next to a red-bearded man wielding a pickaxe. I decide to risk speech again. "I'm Whit," I say as I slam the shovel into the earth.

At first I think he hasn't heard me. But then he says simply, "Stan."

"Do you know—" I begin.

"Shut up," he says, not unkindly.

And so for a while I do. And I work.

The sun beats down on us as we dig, and I don't think I've ever been this hot in my life. Sweat stings my eyes and pours in rivers down my back. Within an hour of shoveling, huge blisters form on my hands. When they pop, the shovel handle grows slick with blood and pus. The dust from the shattered rock billows up, getting into my eyes and nose and covering my hair in a fine gray powder.

And still I dig.

And dig.

Each minute takes an hour, and each hour is a lifetime.

My lungs feel like they're filled up with dirt, and I'm so hungry I think I could fill my stomach up with it, too.

"When do we eat?" I whisper to Stan.

He snorts. "Eat what?"

I guess that answers my question.

We're allowed a five-minute break in the afternoon, when the sun blazes so brightly it feels like the whole world's on fire. By now I'm too dehydrated to sweat.

For a few moments, I catch my breath, supporting myself against the wall of the pit. Above me, a group of Horsemen gathers around at the lip of the pit, inspecting a map and arguing in their foreign tongue, interspersed with smatterings of words I can understand. I hazard a few steps closer, hoping to hear something more. I think I catch the words "open" and "deep" and "gate."

Open deep gate? What does that mean?

I'm thinking about asking Stan when a woman near me stumbles, cries out, and then falls to the ground, facedown in the dirt. I move as quickly as I can to her side—which, considering my state of exhaustion, is not what I'd call speedy. When I turn her over, her mouth lolls open; she's barely conscious.

Stan hurries over, too. "Don't let them see," he whispers urgently. "They'll take her."

I'm guessing he *doesn't* mean to the hospital.

Together we drag her toward the mouth of a tunnel and prop her up against the cold rocks. There's a deep gash on her forehead, which I clean with a cloth from the kit I brought. My hands are shaking with exhaustion, but I manage to steady them enough to place bandages on the wound. The woman's eyes flutter open, then fall closed again. Stan begins shoveling right in front of her, blocking her from the Horsemen's view.

Behind us, the nearby workers are still digging. But they're watching us, too, and I swear I can see a spark of hope in their eyes. I can imagine what they're thinking: *What if we worked together—if we didn't just leave the weak and injured to their fate? Might there be a way to survive this?*

I know the guards can't see me right now, so I'm not afraid to speak. "We're going to watch out for one another," I tell them. "If you're hurt, come to me. If I can't help you, I'll help *hide* you. Okay? We're going to get through this. *We stand together.*"

They nod, slowly, and my spirits lift. This small, quiet moment could be the first step toward an uprising.

For a little while longer, I dig with renewed energy. But then I hear the screaming.

All of us look over to the bent figure of a woman. Behind her stands a Horseman, his whip raised. He brings it down hard across her back, and I see the skin open up and the blood run down. He does this three more times, while the woman's shrieks seem to shatter the air. When it's over, she collapses in the dirt, silent. And then the Horseman holds out a pitcher of water, and he pours it over her back.

And the screaming begins again.

"Salt water," Stan says, turning away in disgust. "That's how they do it around here."

I feel sick to my stomach. This is so much worse than I ever could have imagined. I know that the minute the

Horseman leaves, I'm going to go help that woman—but for now, I'm just useless.

"We stand together," I remind the people around me. "Together, we are strong."

But I don't sound as convincing this time.

A tall, wild-eyed woman reaches out and grabs my arm. "There's nothing to be done, new boy. You know what we're digging here, don't you?" She jabs a finger at my chest. "*Graves*," she says. She kicks at a rock and curses. "For *ourselves*."

Chapter 46

Wisty

IF THERE WERE a prize for stupid decisions, then surely my brother would win it: that's what I'm thinking as I gaze down into the enormous pit of Work Site #1. He's somewhere inside that hellhole, and I've got to get him out.

Dig, dig, dig: Darrius and Bloom must be trying to work these people to death—that's the only explanation I can come up with. But I'm not going to let anyone else kill my brother, because that's *my* prerogative. (Metaphorically, I mean. In reality, I'll only kick his ass a little bit for being so insufferably good-hearted and principled and *idiotic*. I mean, what sort of person *voluntarily* enters a muddy pit teeming with slaves? I'm seriously doubting his capacity to make sane decisions now.)

I walk slowly along the upper lip of the pit, from one end to the other, looking for a pair of familiar muscled shoulders and a shock of too-long blond hair. But there are hundreds, if not thousands, of people down there. They're covered in dirt from head to toe, too, which makes it hard to tell them apart.

Me, I'm disguised as an old woman—just a bit of magic, plus some clothes from my old dress-up trunk—so I assume I'm safe from being collared by Horsemen and handed a shovel.

Except, as it turns out, I'm *not*. I've just caught what I think is a glimpse of Whit when I'm grabbed roughly by the arm, spun around, and then held face-to-face by a huge and hideously ugly Horseman.

"Why aren't you working?" he yells.

His breath's so bad I momentarily choke. "Sir," I manage, "I'm a grandmother—surely you don't—"

But he's already dragging me toward the ladders at the entrance to the pit. I claw madly at his arms, but I might as well be a kitten for all he notices. "Let me go," I shriek. "You ugly, stinking barbarian!"

A handful of other Horsemen come over to watch and laugh at this spitting, cursing old woman. I can feel the burn inside my skin, like I'm going to combust. But I don't want to blow my cover right now—and even ringed by flames, I don't know if I'm a match for half a dozen of these thugs.

Still yelling and scratching, I'm taken down into the muddy earthen maw, and there they clap some band around my wrist and then let me go. Someone pushes a shovel into my hands—a shovel so heavy that, if I were as old as I look, I wouldn't even be able to lift it.

I can't help it: I spit on the ground at a Horseman's feet.
He cuffs me across the cheek so hard I see stars. "Dig, old
woman," he barks. Then he shoves me toward the other
slaves.

As I hobble my way across the pit to where I think I
saw Whit, I wonder if I might *also* win a prize for stupid
decisions.

It's so much worse than I could have imagined down
here: a seething, stinking mass of brutalized humanity,
wordlessly ripping the earth to shreds. For a minute, I
consider shape-shifting into a bird and getting the hell out
of here. But then I tell myself that I came here for a reason.
A reason named Whit.

"Hello, *Whitford*," I say when I finally locate my brother.
I say it brightly—to hide the nervousness that's quickly
turning to dread.

He turns around and gives me a blank look. He's filthy
and sweating, and there's a big cut on his shoulder.

"Don't you recognize your own sister?" I ask.

His eyes go wide, and then he grabs my arm and drags
me halfway into the mouth of a tunnel. "Don't let them see
you talk," he whispers fiercely. "Wisty, is that really you?
What are you *doing* here?"

"I came here to ask you the same question," I say. "Well,
not exactly—I actually came here to break you out. But
that didn't quite work."

"Obviously," he says. Then he startles me by slamming
his fist into the rock. "Wisty, this place is a *death trap*," he

nearly shouts. "Do you know how many people I've seen carted away? The answer is: you don't *want* to know. And they're not coming back!"

I shake his hand off. "Hey, *I* can escape this dump. All I have to do is duck into a corner and *poof*! I'm a cat! Even the Horsemen can't make a *cat* dig."

Whit shakes his head. "Your powers won't work in the pit, Wisty," he says.

"What do you mean?" I demand.

He gestures to the bracelet the Horsemen gave me. "That blocks magic," he says.

I look at it—it's so small and innocent looking. It's almost pretty. Whit's obviously wrong about it. "How come I still look old, then?" I counter.

"Why don't you see what else you can do," Whit says flatly.

"Fine." I point my finger at a small pile of rubble, and I can feel the M begin to spark and flow. But then, instead of releasing, it keeps swirling around inside me, like my body's a cage it's locked inside. I focus with everything I've got, and a tiny blue flame shoots from my fingertip. The ends of my hair begin to smoke, and a few curls spark. But that's it.

It's definitely not enough magic to bust us out of here.

"Uh-oh," I whisper.

"Yeah, and that's not all," Whit says. "If you leave the site early, or fail to report to work on time, it shocks you. Just little shocks at first, like tiny bee stings. But they get worse. Stay away too long, sister, and you'll get cooked—from the inside out."

I can feel myself grow pale. "What?"

Whit nods. "It happened to Stan's brother. Ask him if you want details. But personally, I wouldn't recommend it." And then he turns his back on me and starts digging.

He can't be right—can he? If he is, I'm in deeper trouble than I thought.

A finger is gently tapping my arm. "You better start working, ma'am," a woman tells me. "The guards are on patrol now, and they'll beat even *you*."

Unsure of what else to do, I pick up my shovel. Within minutes, my shoulders are screaming in pain. My forearms feel like sticks of fire. And for *hours* it goes on like this.

When it seems like I can't even stand up for another second, a red-bearded man comes over and takes my shovel away. "You rest," he whispers. "I'll cover for you."

"Who're you?" I ask.

He shakes his head, as if it doesn't matter. "We stand together," he says. He nods toward Whit. "He leads us. Soon we will rise up."

Well, I'll be damned, I think, looking at Whit with new eyes. Maybe my brother's not quite as idiotic as I thought.

Maybe.

Chapter 47

Whit

WE WERE FINALLY released after fourteen hours of labor, but now there's a Horseman patrol marching up and down our street—back and forth, back and forth, like some kind of lethal parade.

Wisty curses because the bracelet's still preventing her from shape-shifting. *Now she knows what it feels like to be me*, I think.

We wait in the shadows for a long time, until there's a momentary break in the patrol, and then we scurry around to the back door of our parents' house.

It's locked.

"Seriously?" Wisty hisses.

I'm about to shoulder my way through it when it swings open, and my mom stands there, backlit, with a look of shock on her face. At first I think she's going to turn me away. But then she gives a little cry and flings her arms around my filthy neck.

"Oh, Whit," she cries, "I'm so glad you're home."

Wisty gives my mom a quick hello and heads straight for the refrigerator. I could eat every scrap of food in the house, too, up to and including whatever's in the compost bin, but first I stop and lock eyes with my dad.

I'm surprised to see that his are moist.

"Son," he says quietly. He reaches for my callused hand and shakes it. "It's good to see you."

I search his face for any sign of doubt. "You sure about that?" I ask.

He nods emphatically. "I made a mistake," he says. "I can only say I'm sorry. So very sorry."

I pull him toward me in a hug. "It's okay," I tell him.

And I mostly mean it. Because yeah, they tossed me out on my you-know-what. But we've got much bigger things to worry about now.

Like how to take a thousand starving, terrified, despairing slaves and turn them into an army.

After Wisty and I get cleaned up, we sit at the kitchen table, picking at the brown bread and dried meat that we were rationed. With my stomach growling in dismay, I close my eyes and picture a huge hunk of lasagna on my plate, with salad, and garlic bread, and olives, and…well, you get the idea. But instead of the heavenly scent of marinara and melted cheese, the odor of incense comes wafting into my nose.

A moment later, in breezes Bea, our favorite aunt, wearing a crazy pink caftan and rocking more jewelry than a cross-dressing pirate.

She deposits a delicious-looking yellow cake in the center of the table, and then swoops down and plants a kiss on the tops of both our heads. "So glad to see you both," she says. "It's been far too long! Whit, you need a haircut. Wisteria, you look lovely. I'm glad to see you've gotten your combination skin under control."

Old-lady-Wisty scowls and smiles at the same time, as Aunt Bea settles into the seat between us and folds her braceleted arms.

"So," she says brightly, "what's new?"

"Oh, not much," Wisty says, eyeing the cake but obviously not wanting to be rude. "Just a little slave labor, a bit of starvation, and some murderous tyranny.... You know, the usual." She picks up a crust of bread and starts gnawing.

Aunt Bea chuckles, but then her face turns serious. "Things can't go on like this," she says.

"No kidding," I mutter, and my stomach rumbles loudly in agreement. "Every part of my body is in pain."

Aunt Bea takes the mug of tea my mom has just handed her and says, "Your parents and I have been told to report to Work Site number three tomorrow."

I suck in my breath sharply. Why hadn't they mentioned it?

My mom smiles sadly. "We didn't want to worry you," she says.

"It's going to be fine," my dad says. "I've done plenty of manual labor in my day."

Not like this you haven't, I think.

"Have you figured out what the digging is for?" Aunt Bea asks.

I shake my head. "Not unless you can tell me what 'open deep gate' means."

Bea looks thoughtful for a moment, but then she shakes her head. "No, that doesn't ring a bell. But you've been organizing, yes?"

"I've made allies," I say. "Everyone's exhausted and terrified, so it's not easy. But I think I've got some people who'll help me out when the time comes. I just need a few more on my side." I reconsider this. "Well, a lot more."

Bea reaches for our hands. "*Both* of you will be crucial in this fight," she says.

"But what do we have to offer?" I ask. "I mean, Wisty's bracelet dampens her powers, and me—well, I was Excised."

"*The Book of Truths* tells us," she says. "It hints at the concept of how power can be divided and multiplied simultaneously."

Wisty wrinkles her forehead. "I know I skipped a lot of math classes, but that makes no sense."

"What *does* it mean?" I ask.

"It's not entirely clear," Bea admits. "But I believe it has something to do with you two."

"*The Book of Truths* has been about as comforting lately as one of those fortunes you get in a cookie," Wisty says. "'News of a long-awaited event will arrive. Your lucky numbers are five, three, and nineteen.'"

Bea smiles. "*The Book of Truths* is a poem and a riddle. Its words say as much about the reader as they do about the future."

Wisty snorts. "I don't need it to tell me about *me*. I need it to tell me about how to kick some Darrius ass."

"Watch your mouth, darling," Aunt Bea says. "What I do know is this. There is a way this regime can be defeated."

"Specificity would be helpful right about now," I say.

Aunt Bea laughs. "My dear, if I knew how it was going to work, believe me, I'd tell you. Right now you just have to trust."

"Trust what, though?" Wisty asks.

"And trust who?" I say.

"We all have many questions," Aunt Bea says. "We must *trust* that the answers will come."

We all look at one another for a minute—worried, tired, scared—and then she says brightly, "Who wants cake?"

And we demolish that thing in two minutes flat.

Chapter 48

Darrius

WAITING ON THE marble steps of the City Capitol, he bounces on the balls of his feet, flickering in and out of sight in agitation.

Where is the redheaded witch?

He's spent altogether too much time thinking about Wisteria Allgood.

With her family, he is unconcerned. Her brother has been neutralized, and the parents' powers are laughable—if Darrius's magic was a sword, theirs was a toothpick. But Wisty holds a power so great that even *she* can't comprehend it.

How close Darrius has come to her so many times. And she's always danced away, never appreciating either the power of her gift or the luck of her survival.

It *galls* him.

He really should have killed her when he had the chance.

He spots Diana, Sybil's replacement, striding across the square toward him. She's tall and dark haired, with eyes such a startling and mesmerizing blue that she almost always wears sunglasses to hide them. She claims not to like the attention, but her low-cut dresses suggest otherwise.

Darrius waits until she's climbing the Capitol stairs, waits until she's on the step just below him. "Stop," he says. "What is the report?"

A flicker of confusion crosses her face. Normally he kisses her in greeting.

"The report," he says again.

She sighs. "The witch is still at large," she says.

"Her apartment?"

"Trashed," Diana says. "Empty."

"What about her brother's place? Her parents' house?"

"No signs of her there, either. But I have regular patrols watching those places, Darrius."

Darrius says nothing. A patrol is a fine idea, of course. But the Horsemen are a half-witted, inattentive lot, better suited to murders than stakeouts. If Wisty walked by them with a hat pulled low over her eyes, Darrius doubts they'd recognize her.

Must he do *everything* himself?

He has no interest in walking the streets of this wretched City of slaves. He wants Wisty brought to him, as the saying goes, on a silver platter.

"We'll find her," Diana assures him.

Darrius leans down and plucks the sunglasses from her face. Her eyes are so very blue.

"But why haven't you found her *yet*? That's the question I'm interested in." He runs a finger along the plane of her cheek. Her skin is cool and smooth.

She reaches up and takes his hand. Kisses his fingertips.

"I can't understand why you're so obsessed with her," she says. "I really don't see what the big deal is."

"You wouldn't," he says.

Diana stiffens. "What's that supposed to mean?"

"You disappoint me," Darrius says softly.

"How? By not knowing the whereabouts of some freckled witch?" Diana sniffs derisively. "She can't be that important."

She reaches up for his belt buckle, and then she pulls him down to her step.

Darrius sees that she's already abandoned her duty—that she thinks failure is acceptable. She stands on her tiptoes and kisses him on the mouth. Delicately at first, and then harder.

Darrius feels a surge of anger that turns to desire. And then the feeling shifts again, to what could almost be called sadness. Diana does not understand the gravity of the situation, and there is no room in this world for those who do not understand.

He stands with his arms hanging at his sides. He kisses, but he doesn't embrace her.

"What is it, Darrius?" she asks, pulling back. "Are you

really so mad? I'll find the little minx if it means so much to you. Tomorrow."

Darrius shakes his head. It's too late for that. He bends down to kiss her for the last time. Bittersweet.

And then he raises his hands, and he touches Diana's slender waist with only the tips of his fingers. Instantly he feels the rush of his magic flow into her body. It happens so quickly: one moment she is a living girl, and the next she is nothing but ash.

He's alone on the white marble steps again. Alone with a pile of cinders. "I'm disappointed in you, Diana," he says. And then he walks away.

To find Wisty.

Darrius is brooding, still flickering in and out in annoyance, until a pleasant idea comes to him. Rather than looking for Wisty himself, he'll send his new deputy. That homely but clever young fellow.

Byron Swain.

Chapter 49

Wisty

EVERYONE SAYS *I'M* the reckless one, but if you ask me, Whit's little exercise in team spirit is going to get us killed.

Despite not yet knowing what we're digging for—or toward, or away from, or *whatever*—he has just informed everyone nearby that we need to quit doing it.

Just look *like you're digging*, Whit tells us. *But don't actually dig. Don't give them what they want.*

And the people around us nod like this is a good idea!

Now, I'm all for skipping out on manual labor—that's part of the reason I'm still in old-lady disguise, because even those barbaric Horsemen aren't going to murder an old lady for being slow. But they'd have no problem whatsoever giving a granny ten lashes, which is the punishment for "insufficient effort."

How do you fake digging? It's a lot different from faking paying attention in physics. I should know, because I was *excellent* at that.

Whit demonstrates what he's talking about. He heaves his shovel into the dirt, and the muscles in his arms and back strain visibly with the effort. Then he wrenches the shovel back out—but instead of lifting up a pile of earth, he withdraws a mostly empty blade. Then he dumps a smattering of pebbles onto the jumble of rocks behind him.

"The Horsemen aren't close enough to monitor the piles," he tells us. "They just watch to make sure we're moving."

Again, I seem to be the only one feeling skeptical here.

Whit narrows his eyes at me. "You in?" he asks. "Or are you working for them?" He nods up toward the guards on the lip of the pit, to the Horsemen with their cudgels and guns.

"Oh, I'm with you," I say. "Blood relation, loyalty, blah blah blah. But where's the uprising, Whit? When do we get to start *that*?"

"When we come up with a *plan*, Wisty," he says through gritted teeth. "Unlike some people, I like to think things through."

"Unlike some people, I get a little impatient for action," I retort. I smash my wretched bracelet against a rock, which hurts it not one bit. I would kill for a dose of magic right now.

I try to summon it again. Surely my powers are stronger than an enchanted piece of silver! I clench my blistered hands into fists and will myself to burn.

And that's when I see *him*.

Darrius.

Adrenaline floods my limbs and my heart skitters wildly. But something's wrong with my fight-or-flight response, because I just *freeze*. I might as well be a granny-shaped rock.

I keep my face pointed to the ground, even though I look nothing like myself.

Just dig, I think. *Just dig for real this time.*

Darrius speaks for a while to one of the foremen, and then descends the steps into the pit. Perhaps it's Take Your Despot to Work Day. All of us are filthy, wearing ripped and bloodstained clothes, but Darrius sports steel-gray slacks and a carefully ironed collared shirt. He steps scrupulously over piles of rubble. Over prone bodies, too—the fallen slaves that the Horsemen haven't yet carted away to jail or worse.

I start shoveling faster, and pretty soon I'm flinging rocks like they're grains of sand. I'm going to make a mountain behind me in record time.

Whit hisses, "Slow down."

At first I think he's just being uptight about how I'm actually *working* instead of pretending to, but then I realize that he doesn't want me to draw attention to myself. Considering the level of exhaustion and demoralization around here, anyone moving faster than a trudge is going to stand out.

I shovel more slowly, but I can tell Darrius is getting

closer. I don't even have to see him or hear him now, because I can *feel* him.

I don't know if anyone else notices it—the way the air around him carries an electrostatic crackle. But I can feel my body responding to it. My M drawn to it, magnetically, against my will.

If he comes much closer to me, I'm going to catch on fire, bracelet or not. And all the disguises in the world aren't going to cover *that* up.

I can't let it happen. So, closing my eyes in concentration, I imagine showers, rain, a deep, cool bath. The depths of the ocean, the polar ice caps—anything but heat. Still, my shirt prickles with electricity, and the little hairs on my arms stand straight up.

It's not working. I open my eyes again. Next to me, Whit's hammering away like a model slave. His knuckles are white, except for the part where they're bloody from the work.

Watching him, I suddenly remember a time when we were little, when our parents took us to the ocean. I played in the water, and Whit spent the entire day building a sand castle. It seems like a million years ago. But thinking of it now—of the waves, salty and cold, and the wet sand being coaxed into towers and moats—calms me. My pulse slows. My skin stops stinging with heat. I'm no longer on the verge of spontaneous combustion.

And yet I can sense Darrius approaching our corner of

the pit. I put my hand to my face: has the spell worn off? Is my skin freckled and unlined?

I nearly sigh with relief when I feel the thin, papery flesh of my cheek. I still look ancient.

But still—as if drawn by some invisible, supernatural signal—Darrius comes ever closer.

Chapter 50

Wisty

THE FOOTSTEPS HALT directly behind me. I stiffen. I swear my heart stops—and then, a second later, it comes to life again, beating so loud and wild I'm sure he can hear it.

Darrius is mere *inches* away. Did he pause here at random? Or did my magic pull him toward me? I can't turn around to look; I just have to keep shoveling, the terrible drumbeat of my heart pounding in my ears.

Then I feel the warm, insistent pressure of a *hand* upon my shoulder. The fingers dig into my collarbone, and then they turn me, ever so slowly, around.

I'm face-to-face with beautiful, golden-eyed Darrius, the latest in the line of men who've wanted me dead. His brow furrows, and he looks at me carefully. I can't move, I can't breathe. I can't even look away from his eyes, no matter how much I want to.

For a second, for a minute, or maybe for a thousand

years, I don't know—we stand that way, gazing at each other. I can feel my M inside me, roiling, smoldering, *aching* to come out. I can feel his, too, but it's different.

It is icy cold.

Then Darrius's mouth shapes itself into a kind of smile. "Tell me, what are *you* doing here?" he asks. His voice is almost amused.

"Just working," I manage to croak.

He clucks his tongue. "A shame that someone such as you would labor like this." He gestures to the muck all around us. "A bit *strenuous*, isn't it?"

I tear my eyes away and look at the ground, shrugging. I still don't know if he's talking to me as Wisty, or me as an old woman. Considering it's a matter of life and death, I wish I knew the answer.

"Actually, you're doing important work," he declares. "So important, you have no idea."

I decide to risk a response. "I thought we were just here to dig until we died. Sir."

Darrius throws back his head and laughs. "Oh, no. It's much more complicated than that." He glances over to a girl who's crying as she shovels; she can't be more than twelve. "Citizens of all ages, coming together as one, united in pursuit of a fantastic goal."

And that's when I realize I'm safe: Darrius thinks I'm really an old woman. I almost shout with relief, but I catch myself.

I'm emboldened now. "Please, young man," I warble.

"What *is* our goal? I...I heard something about a 'deep gate.'..."

A flicker of something—surprise? uncertainty?—crosses Darrius's face, and his hand shoots out and grabs my throat. I gasp and stumble forward, my heart racing. "Where did you hear that?" he demands.

But I can't talk, because his hand's around my windpipe.

He looks around at all of us, and I can tell he's itching to turn someone—anyone—to ash. I can't breathe, and my sight grows dim. Just when I'm about to lose consciousness, his expression returns to its familiar cold calm, and he releases me. "That is not for you to know, old woman," he snaps. Then, offering me a flinty smile, he turns to go. "Until the time comes," he whispers savagely.

When he's gone, I have to sit down and catch my breath. It was a narrow escape—but it was an *escape*. And that's what matters. "Did you see that?" I crow to my brother. "Darrius had no idea who I was! Guess he's not as all-powerful as he thinks."

Whit whips around, his eyes blazing. "You got *lucky*, sis," he says. "So don't go around congratulating yourself too much, okay?"

I'm so sick of his nagging I could scream. But inside me is a new flame of hope. I felt my magic leaping when Darrius was near me, bracelet be damned. And if I've got magic, I will not be afraid.

Chapter 51

Wisty

MY AUNT MUST have gotten off slave duty early somehow, because she's waiting for us when we stumble into the house. As I yank my boots from my blistered feet, I allow my face to return to its normal, unlined pallor. *So long, wrinkles, see you tomorrow!*

There's a pot of thin soup on the stove, but Aunt Bea's out in the living room, half-buried among stacks of ancient books and yellowed, crackling papers.

"Come in, come in," she calls, as if she's the one who lives here. "Whit, dear, the soup's not going anywhere, so put that spoon down. There are more urgent matters to attend to."

My parents limp in the door a moment after we do and immediately collapse into their favorite chairs: a leather recliner for my dad and a velvet wingback for my mom. She looks utterly drained; my dad stretches his legs out, cracks his knees, and grimaces. "We spent the day dredging the riverbank," he tells us.

"Do you know what for?" Whit asks.

"Of course not, dumbbell," I say, swatting his leg. "Darrius doesn't tell people his plans, remember?"

Mom shoots me a dark look. "No, we don't know, but there's no reason to talk to your brother like that, Wisteria."

I hate it when she calls me Wisteria.

"*Right*," Whit says to me, "and there's no reason to risk your life, not to mention everyone else's, because you can't keep your big mouth shut in front of Darrius."

I bristle. "Excuse me for trying to find out what's going on, instead of just slinging rocks like an idiot. Maybe if you had some brains to match your brawn, you'd actually come up with a plan."

"Maybe if you ever stopped for one second to use that brain you're so proud of, you could *help* me, instead of always making things worse."

"You're just mad because you got the lash. That wasn't *my* fault. I guess those Horsemen keep a closer eye on the rock piles than you thought they did."

Whit starts to respond, but then Aunt Bea claps her hand over his mouth. His eyes go wide, but he quiets down.

"*Anyway*," Bea says brightly, "mysterious slave labors aside, things are looking up. I told you there was a way, and I believe that I have found it."

I look at Aunt Bea—with her thick granny glasses, her frizzy, uncombed hair, and her kooky clothing draped over her tiny, birdlike frame—and I think, *Is this batty old biddy really our best hope for survival?*

She holds up a tattered volume bound in wine-colored leather. "This is a little-read addendum to *The Book of Truths*," she says. "And in it, I discovered something miraculous."

Her eyes spark with life, with hope.

And almost against my will, I find myself leaning forward, desperate to hear her words. Maybe she really does hold the key to our salvation.

She looks hard at me and my brother and shakes a finger at us. "No more fighting," she says. "Do you understand me? This will not work unless there is no anger. There must be only love."

"*What* won't work?" I ask.

"The *procedure*," she says simply. "It's very simple. I think. It will either work..." She trails off.

"Or?" I ask.

"Or it will destroy you," she says brightly. "Now listen very carefully."

Chapter 52

Wisty

GAZING DOWN AT the book she holds in her clawlike hand, Aunt Bea trembles with excitement. My parents and brother, too, are on the edges of their seats.

But suddenly I've got the feeling that I'm not going to like what comes next.

Aunt Bea clears her throat, and then she begins to read in a low, singsong voice. *"Not one but two / The fire splits through / Heal the rift / Cleave the gift."* She looks up at us, beaming, and then says it again. *"Not one but two / The fire splits through / Heal the rift / Cleave the gift.* See how simple it is?"

I'm about to say that I don't understand, until it suddenly clicks. "Wait a second. You want *me* to give *Whit* some of my powers, when he was the stupid idiot who gave them away? Is that what you mean? Because *no way.* You've got to be crazy."

Aunt Bea tsk-tsks at me. "Remember: only love," she says again.

"Wow, I'm sick of hearing that already," I say. I look over at my parents. "Do *you* think this is a good idea? If you decide to cut off your arm, Mom, would you expect Dad to happily give you one of his?" I demand.

My mom tries to reach for my hand, but I scoot away. "I don't think that's the right comparison, dear," she says. "For one thing—"

But I don't want to hear her explanation. I can't believe they're asking this of me. Give half my powers to Whit in a procedure—as yet *undefined* and *unexplained*—that may or may not *kill me*?

Or kill *us*. Whatever.

I glance over at Whit. He's practically slobbering with hope and excitement. Of course he wants his powers back, whatever it takes. But who's to say he won't decide to submit again and throw *my* magic away?

"Wisty," my aunt says, "I'm not feeling any love."

"Yeah, well, neither am I," I shout. "This is insane." I point to the bracelet on my wrist. "What about this? Have you noticed it *prevents magic*?"

Bea looks startled. "I forgot about that."

Beside me, Whit sighs in defeat. "Well, it was a nice thought," he says softly.

"Don't be so easily discouraged, Whitford," my aunt admonishes. She grabs each of us by the wrist, covering up the bracelets with her palms.

I notice that she doesn't have a bracelet of her own. "How did you—" I begin.

"Hush," she says. She closes her eyes and begins to hum, a note so low I can barely hear it.

I feel the sparks—the tiny electrocutions—that Whit warned me about. I grit my teeth as they grow in intensity. Just when I think I'm going to cry out, there's a loud crack, and the pain is gone.

On the floor are two broken metal bracelets.

"How the hell—"

"It doesn't matter," my aunt says. "Now listen up. You must focus. I know this seems improbable, but it's our only hope. Your power is great, Wisty—as yours was, Whit. By sharing this power—by dividing it—I believe it will then multiply."

"*The Book of Truths* said so," Whit agrees.

"I didn't hear that part of the prophecy," I point out.

Aunt Bea smiles at me. "One is never sure of anything, my dear. But I believe in *The Book of Truths* and the possibilities it suggests. How power willingly shared can grow even stronger. How power given is power gained."

I look to my parents, who are watching me with love and dread.

"Please," my mom whispers.

In resignation, I bow my head. "If this is what it really says—if this is what we need to do in order to fight Darrius—I'll do it."

"Remember to love," my aunt whispers. "It's the most important part." Then she addresses both of us. "Now face each other, please, and clasp hands."

Still reluctant, I take Whit's hands in mine.

"*Not one but two / The fire splits through / Heal the rift / Cleave the gift*," Bea begins chanting.

Apparently it's up to us to figure out how the rest of this works. Whit and I meet each other's gaze. I guess it's time to heal the rift.

"I'm sorry," he whispers, "for being the reason you have to do this."

I give him a half smile. "Well, I guess I'm sorry for being so mad at you all the time."

"I'm sorry you got sucked into the slave labor," he says.

I shrug. "I'm sorry I didn't bring more Resistance members with me to bust you out. Because that was really stupid." I bite my lip and frown. "I'm not going to say I'm sorry for being impulsive, okay? Because that's just who I am. But I'm sorry if I've been sort of a pain in the ass."

"Sort of?" Whit laughs. Then he turns serious. "You're fierce, sis. You're the firegirl."

I nod. "You're strong," I tell him. "You fix things—and people."

Then we just look at each other for a minute, sort of sadly, but hopefully, too.

Love, I remind myself, *love*. It's either that, or destruction.

Chapter 53

Whit

I FEEL HOPE in every single cell of my body. And fear. But most of all I feel gratitude. "Thank you," I whisper to my sister.

She smiles and squeezes my fingers.

When we finally close our eyes, we concentrate hard: on the sound of Aunt Bea's whisper, on the poem that's transforming itself into a spell. We focus on *believing*.

It's not long before I feel Wisty's hands heating up. At first our palms get sweaty, but then her skin grows so hot that the sweat dries. Soon I want to pull away—it *burns*. But I know without being told that we're not supposed to break contact.

I can feel Wisty's concentration. This *has* to work—and I'm trying not to feel terrified that it won't.

Our parents have joined in the chant now, their voices low and steady.

As our focus deepens, the air in the room seems to hum

and vibrate. If I opened my eyes, I imagine I could almost see the molecules sparking.

I grit my teeth as the heat grows still more intense. It's not just in Wisty's hands now. It's in the air between us—a bridge of invisible fire, running from her racing heart straight into mine.

But then something changes. Wisty seems to pull back, and the heat starts to die down.

"I can't," Wisty whispers. She's shaking, but I can't open my eyes.

I don't know what she means, and I'm afraid to ask. She can't make it work? Or she can't make herself give up part of her power?

Yes, you can, I think. *Yes, you can.*

Her fingers tremble against mine. "Please—" she gasps.

The heat stops burning me, and I know she must be giving up.

"*Not one but two / The fire splits through*," I urge. "*Heal the rift / Cleave the gift.*"

Yes, I have selfish reasons for wanting my powers back. But I also want to bring Darrius *down*. And for that, my sister needs to help me.

She's crying now. I know what she's feeling: an aching, sucking pull, like her soul's being yanked from her body. I felt that way myself, in the Government Lab.

I can't believe it, but in a way, I'm Excising my own sister.

Wisty gasps, then cries out. "Oh, Whit, it *hurts*—"

And that's when I pull my hands away. *That's* when I decide it isn't worth it. Darrius can rule forever—I can't do this to my own sister.

"Wait," Aunt Bea cries. "Don't stop now!"

The urgency in her voice reminds me of what she told us before we began: *This will work, or else it will destroy us.*

Pain sears my eyes and head, and right now, it definitely feels like we're closer to destruction.

Weeping, my mom reaches for our hands and binds them together again, covering them with her own. My dad, too, comes from his chair and joins us.

Can they share their power, too? Or will we all go up in a giant ball of flame?

My parents and Bea are almost shouting now, repeating the poem over and over until the words are sounds without meaning.

Wisty shudders, sobs, flings her head back in agony. But she won't let go of me. Her hands have become vises.

And then suddenly, her heat surges again. The temperature in the room rises, and I can feel flames licking at my chest. I know it should be burning me, but this time it's not. My heart feels like it's going to explode from all the energy flooding into it.

The room begins to glow, and the light comes streaming through my closed lids. When I open my eyes, I see the whole house lit by golden, leaping tongues of fire— burning nothing, just dancing in the air above Wisty's head.

She opens her eyes, too. They're bloodshot, red-rimmed.

"They're above you," she whispers. "The flames."

I don't dare look, but I think I know what they mean, and I want to scream with happiness. Wisty gave me her gift. *I'm magic again.*

Finally letting go of Wisty's hands, I stand up. I'm taller than I've been in weeks. I'm strong and certain and unafraid. I've been given back the only part of me that ever really mattered.

I reach down for Wisty, and I pull her up to me. I clasp her to my chest.

"You did it," I whisper. "Thank you."

She smiles through her tears. "You owe me, bro," she says weakly. *"Big-time."*

Chapter 54

Whit

I BARELY SLEEP at all that night, and in the morning, I'm out of bed even before Darrius and Bloom make their daily pre-dawn address. I hurry through the still-dark streets, on the lookout for any of Darrius's thugs. Soon, the City will be waking up, and its citizens will be heading out to the chain gangs. But not me: I'm going to a different work site. To a place—and a person—I never should have left.

I'm out of breath when I finally arrive at the hospital. For a few minutes, I just stand outside, observing. I watch silhouettes passing by in front of the windows; I see the automatic doors swishing open and then closed. It's almost funny: I used to spend the majority of my waking hours there, and now I'm afraid to go inside.

It's not about running into Dr. Keller, though, or any of the other doctors or nurses who feared and cursed me. It's about seeing Janine.

I need to do it.

I *want* to do it.

But that doesn't mean it's easy. I'm nervous. Jittery. Excitement and dread slosh around my guts in some weird emotional soup. *Pull it together, Whit*, I think. But it's half-hearted encouragement, and it doesn't help much.

I go around the back of the building, past the trash compactors I got to know so well. Trying to be as unnoticeable as possible—which is hard for a six-footer like me—I sneak up the stairs to the emergency room area.

Janine's territory.

The hallway is bright, and it smells like disinfectant. I breathe in deeply. Who would have thought I'd miss the smell of bleach? Or the familiar sound of heart monitors? Or the way the fluorescent lights on the ceiling flicker and hum?

I hear Janine's sweet, familiar voice before I see her.

"—he swears it's a hernia," she's saying, "but it's just a pulled muscle. So don't let him tell you any different. And for god's sake, don't *look* at it."

"Gotta love the hypochondriacs," says another voice wryly.

They laugh, and then the other nurse says something I can't quite hear.

"Sure," Janine calls. "See you later on the rounds."

And then she's coming toward me, walking alone, looking down at a chart instead of where she's going.

My eyes drink in her shiny dark hair, her slender, graceful frame, the pale long fingers of her delicate hands.

I will her to lift her face so I can see that, too: her green eyes, her quick smile, the single dimple on her left cheek.

Watching her, I'm just about bowled over by the pure idiocy of my actions. I can't believe I left the way I did, and I wish I could take it all back.

I remind myself of the stupid decision I made that day outside the Government Lab, and how fate and love and magic helped me reverse it.

I was *lucky*.

Can I be lucky again? Can I undo the second-most-stupid decision I've ever made? I know I can't rely on magic with Janine. But I still need the power of love and fate on my side.

As she slowly approaches—still reading the chart, inching her way along the hall—I hold my breath. I love her more than ever. More than I ever thought possible.

Closer and closer she comes. I catch a whiff of her lilac perfume, and I'm almost overcome by memories of holding her, kissing her, lying beside her. The images seem so real I could reach out and touch them.

I don't want to scare her, so I whisper. "Janine—"

But she jumps anyway. She looks up. And when she sees me, she goes white. Her mouth opens, but not a sound comes out. She stares at me for what feels like an eternity, her lips still tantalizingly parted.

"Janine," I say again. "It's me." As if I could be anyone else.

But then she just shakes her head at me—slowly, sadly. And she turns on her heel, and she walks away.

The pain in my heart comes on fast and hard. I gasp for breath.

Sure, I'm magic again. But I've just discovered a bleeding wound that my hands can't heal.

Chapter 55

Whit

I CAN'T SIMPLY STAND in the hallway, waiting to be discovered. I start walking in the other direction, not even paying attention to where I'm going. And that's how I find myself in a forgotten corner of the hospital, outside a small room where a boy lies curled in a bed.

There's no one else around. Not a doctor, not a nurse, not even a parent.

When I enter the boy's room, his eyes barely open before closing again. His chart hangs on a hook at the end of the bed, so I quickly scan it. I read about his acute leukemia, and even I, with my utter lack of medical training, can see that his blood counts are terrible.

But as I once told Dr. Keller, I don't need to know what's wrong in order to fix it.

Excitement surges in me. I'm *back*, and I'm going to do whatever it takes to help.

"Hey there," I say gently. "Do you mind if I sit with you?"

The boy's dark eyes flutter open again. Slowly, he shakes his head no.

So I sit on the hard chair near his pillow—the chair that should have held his mom or his dad. Probably they *did* used to sit with him, but then Darrius turned them into slaves.

"How're you feeling?" I ask.

He winces. "You don't want to know."

I reach for his hands. "Can I try to help?"

The boy considers this for a moment before nodding. "Can't hurt me worse than I already do."

So I stand and place my hands on his chest, and I concentrate on his blood, on the cancerous cells that are destroying it. My M flares, then sputters, like an engine that's been cold too long.

The boy squirms beneath me. It's possible I shocked him.

"Sorry," I whisper. "Just give me a minute."

I realize that I don't know if this is going to work. Like Aunt Bea says, I just have to *trust*. And so I close my eyes, and with every cell in my body I focus on the healing magic of my hands.

Soon I can feel the power building, and it hurts. It's a different kind of pain than I felt down in the pit—it's somehow better and worse at the same time. I recognize it. I welcome it.

"Mister?" the boy says softly.

I ignore him. I squeeze my eyes shut. And then I feel it, streaming out of me and into him: the magic. The light. The cure.

When I step away, he's staring at me with eyes as black as coal. He takes a deep breath, then lets it out in a sigh. "What did you do?" he whispers.

I have to hold on to the bed to keep from falling down. I'm sapped. "I think I fixed you," I manage.

Then I gather my strength and hurry to the next room. To the next person who needs me.

And that's how it goes for the rest of the morning. I find people. I put my hands on them. And I heal them. It's like I don't even have a choice.

The doctors and nurses crowd around, pointing at me and yelling for me to leave, but I ignore them. I stumble from room to room because yes, I'm weaker than I once was. Healing people kind of feels like it's killing me.

But I'm doing good. And so tell me: what's a better way to go?

Chapter 56

Whit

I'M FUSING AN old woman's broken hipbone when I hear the sirens. At first I think it's a squad of ambulances, and I shudder to think of the casualties I'm about to be faced with.

But then that familiar, loathed voice crackles over the loudspeaker.

"Whitford Allgood," says Dr. Keller. "Proceed to the nearest nurses' station *immediately*." He stops and clears his throat. "Be forewarned: should you remain at large, the police have been summoned. And they will find you."

At large? That's what he calls going from room to room and risking my own life to save people? I wish I had an ounce of energy to spare so I could find him and punch his lights out.

In the distance, I hear the shouting of Darrius's lackeys. But I try to remain calm and focused on the healing. *Whatever it takes to help.*

I don't want to think of what might come next. How if the police find me, I'm as good as dead. If I'm not shot on sight, I'll face the firing squad soon enough. Bloom will see to that—and he'll enjoy the hell out of it.

No way, I think. *I'm not going to give him that satisfaction.*

I press my hands harder on the old woman's hip. I realize that I have to go, even though I'm not quite done with the healing. I put a hand on the woman's bony knee, I look her in the eye—and I *lie*. "I think you're going to be okay now," I tell her. "Just—just have a doctor look at it, okay?"

She nods mutely, but her eyes shine with grateful tears.

And I feel like a monster.

That does it. I can't leave. I push up my sleeves and summon my powers again. But they come more slowly now, in weak, almost reluctant pulses. I start to wonder: *Am I somehow using my magic up?*

The M begins to flow the very moment I hear shouts from the floor below us. I grit my teeth as the healing ache begins. There's a rushing sound in my ears, and my eyesight starts to get dim, as the magic takes its energy from every cell in my body.

I only need a few more minutes—

But then the woman grabs my wrist with her clawlike hand. "*Go,*" she commands. "Go *now.*"

When I hesitate, she slaps my hand away from her hip. "I know who you are," she says urgently. "You have to save yourself." She takes a deep breath. "And then, maybe, you can save all of us."

I wait another second, but then I make myself pull away. "Thank you," I whisper.

"Thank *you*," she answers.

And then I'm racing down the hall toward the emergency exit. I hope it hasn't occurred to Keller to lock down the hospital—otherwise I'm looking at a showdown with armed officers, and I *know* I'm not up to that yet.

Just as I near the door, red emergency lights start flashing and the alarm begins to blare. I curse, turn back around, and head for the window—the only other way out. If only I could shape-shift! But I don't have the juice for that, either.

I grab a broom leaning against the wall and, holding it like a baseball bat, I slam it against the glass. The pane cracks, and with one more hit, it shatters.

"You're going to have to pay for that," says a voice.

I turn and see Janine standing in a doorway. Her hands are on her hips, but she's looking at me with . . . well, with what almost seems like affection.

My heart does a leap in my chest. I want to run to her and scoop her up in my arms and kiss her until she promises to forgive me. But I don't have time for that, because certain death is on its way up the stairs. I throw one leg over the sill. "You can put it on my tab," I say, smiling.

"Be safe," she whispers.

I glance down to the ground. It's probably a twenty-five-foot drop. "If I hurt myself," I say, "maybe you can heal me."

She nods slowly, and then she smiles.

And so, with the image of her smile in my mind—and a new glimmer of hope in my heart—I launch myself out of the window and into the air.

Chapter 57

Wisty

BY NOW I KNOW the Horsemen's patrol routes. But even if I didn't—even if I ran smack-dab into a pack of those bearded barbarians—they couldn't catch me, because a horse is no match for a 1250cc motorcycle.

I race through the streets in a low, black blur, shooting off sparks. Some of them land on the new posters of Bloom's face (oops!), and so I slow down a little to watch them burn.

When I pass the City police lot, its parking spaces full of cruisers and prisoner transport buses, the opportunity to wreak a little havoc is just too tempting. Downshifting to third, I send a wave of magic rolling toward the vehicles. The first row of cars flip over like toys, their wheels spinning in the air. I've still got the power! Giggling like a maniac, I flip the next row. Windshields shatter and alarms go off. All around the parking lot, horns start blaring, and I can't stop laughing. The upside-down cars remind me of bugs stuck on their backs—but there's no one but me who can turn them back over.

When the first City police come stumbling out of their offices, I gun the engine. I toss them the bird, and then *whoosh*—I'm gone in a flash.

I'm *free*, and it's exhilarating.

Yeah, I know Darrius is looking for me. I know that soon, I'll have to fight. But for now, I just want to remember what it's like to feel unfettered and alive.

And weaker, says a small voice inside.

But I ignore it.

A few blocks from the City center, east of the giant pit where I spent those miserable days, I stop in front of a big old brick building. It used to be a meeting place for City leaders of government and industry, but now it's been transformed into an armory.

I park my bike and walk the perimeter. Stacks of guns and ammo are visible through the windows. These are the very guns that Terrence Rino gave his policemen—and that Darrius so easily confiscated and stockpiled.

As if Darrius needs more weapons.

I wish the area were deserted: I'd shoot a jet of fire through the glass and the whole place would blow sky high. But I know the surrounding buildings are full of people, cowering like rats, hoping against hope not to be captured and taken to the pit. I can't risk blasting them to smithereens.

But if you asked me how I'd rather die—in a sudden

burst of fire or by the slow torture of the pit—you can bet which one I'd pick.

While I contemplate my options, I decide to *decorate* the building a little. After all, the blank brick walls are practically screaming for it. With the flame from my finger, I burn in enormous, looping black letters *The Resistance Lives* and *Die, Darrius, Die.*

It makes me feel even better.

"Up to your old tricks again, I see," says a voice behind me.

I whirl around, fists raised—but it's only Byron Swain. His hair is slicked back with its usual excess of product, but he's not wearing that cop jacket of his, which surprises me. He loved that thing so much he probably slept in it. Instead he's dressed in what looks almost like a military uniform. "What are you doing here?" I demand.

"Oh, just out for a stroll," he says. But his voice sounds strained, and I can tell he's lying. He glances up to the side of the building. "'The Resistance Lives,' huh? Interesting." His eyes dart around nervously.

I squint at him. He's acting weird. "What's up with you?" I demand. "You still holding a grudge about the ferret business?"

Byron laughs—a hollow sound. "No," he says. "You know *me,* I forgive and forget." Then he mutters something to himself, something that I can't hear. Except for maybe the word "Darrius."

I move closer to him, fists still clenched. *"What's that?"*

"Nothing," Byron says, stepping back. Then he frowns. "Tell me," he says, "have you seen any of those Resistance-type folks around here?"

"Why?" I ask. "You finally going to join it?"

Byron pales. "N-no," he stutters. He begins fidgeting. He rubs his hands over his arms the way you do when you're cold. Except it's about seventy degrees out.

The hairs on the back of my neck rise up. Something's definitely off. "What's going on with you, Weasel Boy?"

"It's all your fault," he says softly.

"*What's* all my fault?"

"They took her," he wails. "I have to get her back."

"Took who?"

"Elise," he says. His face crumples. "I'm sorry, Wisty." Then he reaches into his pocket, pulls out a whistle, and blows it. The shrill sound pierces the air.

My heart begins to pound, but I try to play it cool. "Who took her, Byron? Why are you sorry? And what's that whistle for? You get a new dog or something?"

Byron doesn't answer me. He just watches me for a minute.

"What?" I demand. "Why are you looking at me?"

For still another moment, he doesn't speak. Then he says, "I'm memorizing you. Just in case."

"Just in case *what*?" I demand.

But then the answer comes out of the alleyways in a mad, roaring rush. It's ten mounted Horsemen, cudgels raised. Coming at *me*.

Because Byron, with that stupid, innocent-looking whistle, has just summoned them.

"Just in case I don't see you ever again," he calls.

The air is a blur of leather and raised fists, and the Horsemen howl in their cruel-sounding language. I'm frozen in shock; my brain seems to be short-circuiting. In another millisecond, they'll be on top of me.

"I'm *sorry*," Byron cries.

Holy M.

It's over.

Chapter 58

Wisty

I SQUEEZE MY EYES SHUT against the coming blows. But then my faltering brain jolts back to life, and I realize the magic I have to do.

Assuming I still can.

To my surprise, the transformation is almost instantaneous: my body shrivels, my fingers curl, and my skin vanishes under a coat of inky-black fur. I'm a *cat*—and the Horsemen don't know what to make of it.

I race between the legs of the nearest one, my claws skittering on the pavement. Shrieks of anger erupt behind me as the Horsemen urge their mounts to take up the chase.

My body's so small and light, I feel like I'm flying over the cobblestones. My senses sharpen: I can hear mice scampering behind trash cans, I can smell milk going sour on a windowsill, and I can almost taste the air as it goes rushing into my lungs.

As I run, I curse Byron Swain to the ends of the earth. I vow to turn him back into a ferret, and then, still in cat form, I'll eat him alive.

That is, if I can make it out of this messy situation.

The horses are gaining on me. When I round the corner into an alley, a hoof grazes one of my back paws—a millimeter more, and it would have crushed it. I yowl in fear and rage.

And then I remember: cats *climb.*

With all the power in my back legs, I launch myself up a nearby tree. My claws catch the rough bark and my front legs hug the trunk. Up I go, as fast as I can, my panting breath in my ears sounding as loud as the cries of the Horsemen.

One has dismounted and is hacking the base of the tree with an axe.

Idiot, I think as I near the top.

Up here the branches are thin, and they bend under my weight. The sharp-edged leaves tickle my stomach. But it's only a few feet to the roof of a building, and I know I can make it.

Another of the Horsemen is already climbing the fire escape as I launch myself into the air. For one thrilling, terrifying second, I'm sailing thirty feet above the ground— and then I land safely on the tar-paper roof.

A hundred pigeons rise into the air, panicked, wings flapping.

Not gonna eat you, I think, but there's no way to tell

them that. I race to the other side of the building, and from there it's just a quick leap to the next rooftop.

There, I pause for a moment to catch my breath, hidden in the shadow of an air-conditioning vent. I can still hear the Horsemen looking for me; I just can't tell exactly where they are.

I hazard a glance over the side of the roof. Six of them are down there, waiting for me. They shout and point.

An arrow whizzes past my head, then another. Next they launch grappling hooks, and pretty soon they're halfway up the side of the building.

All this for a cat! I think. But still—it's time to get down.

On the far side of the building is a half-collapsed fire escape. It could never support a human's weight, but a feline's is no problem. I scamper down the rusting steps. I almost lose my footing once, but my claws save me. I wish I could keep them after I turn back into myself.

As soon as my paws hit the ground, I shoot down a narrow alley.

And I think I'm safe, until I hear hoofbeats behind me. I duck down another, narrower alley. I can feel my powers waning. I'm going to collapse, or I'm going to flame out. I don't know—but it's not going to be good.

Then I see a sewer grate up ahead. With nowhere else to hide, I slip in between the bars.

And then, panting, gasping for breath in the fetid air, I watch as the Horsemen ride closer and closer.

And then they pass me by.

Chapter 59

Wisty

WHEN THE COAST IS CLEAR, I slink back into the sunlight. I consider licking my fur—cats *do* clean themselves, after all—until I realize that I'd rather have sewage and trash on my body than in my mouth.

I lope toward a sheltered courtyard where I can make my transformation. In it, bright flowers spill from window boxes, and a ring of marble benches call out to be sat upon. In truth, all I want to do is curl up in a patch of sunlight and sleep. But I can't, because I don't know how safe I am. I need to return to myself, find my bike, and get the hell out of here.

So I shut my eyes and will myself back to my body: to the long, pale, hairless limbs I'm used to. I feel myself stretching out, lengthening; I feel the weight of gravity pulling on me harder as I grow.

When it's over, I open my eyes and gasp.

I'm not alone in the courtyard.

There's a Horseman in here, too. He's abandoned his mount, and he takes a giant step toward me.

He smiles, showing me a mouthful of yellow teeth. "Proud of ourselves, are we?" he asks. His voice sounds more like a growl than it does speech.

I look around the courtyard for a weapon. A stick, a rock—*anything*—because I don't know if I've got any magic left in me. But there's nothing but dirt and flowers. I take a step backward. "Yeah, for a little while there I was doing okay," I say.

He sniffs, grimaces. "You stink," he says.

I shrug as nonchalantly as I can, as if we're just having a friendly conversation. "Must've been that last sewer," I say. Thinking, *Dude, have you smelled yourself lately? Those leather pants make you reek like a rotting cow.*

"Silly cat," the Horseman says. "Do you know what we do with kitties where we're from?" But he doesn't wait for me to respond. *"We eat them."*

"Really," I say calmly. "Where are you from, anyway?" He's definitely chattier than the other Horsemen I've encountered. He seems to actually have a good grasp of our language.

He takes another step closer to me and casually pulls a dagger from his pocket. The blade glints evilly in the sun. "I come from the desert, catgirl—don't you know that?"

I take another step back; he takes another one forward. "Well, I might have guessed it," I allow.

"Life's hard out there. Hot. Ugly. People like you can't

even imagine." He smiles again. "I'm one of the nice ones," he says.

I need to stall him for another minute, until I've built up a little juice. "Oh, yeah?" I ask. "How so?"

He wipes the blade on his shirtsleeve. "I keep my weapons sharp. Death comes quicker that way."

I reach my foot back again, but it hits the wall of the courtyard. There's nowhere for me to go. "Wow, you *are* nice," I say. "Let's be friends."

He grunts, which I *think* is supposed to be a laugh. Hey, it's not every day you can make a killer crack up.

"Do you have powers?" I ask him. I'm flexing my fingers behind my back. I think I can feel the telltale spark.

"Maybe," he says slyly. "Want to see?"

I smile at him for the first time. "Let's check out mine first," I say, and I fling my hands forward, palms facing toward him.

Blue light shoots from my skin. He raises his arm to block it, but he's not fast enough. The light surrounds him, bombarding him with electric shocks. Little ones at first, but they quickly grow in violence and intensity.

He stumbles, reaching for his sword. But he can't grasp it. He begins to scream and writhe. His dagger clatters to the pavement as he convulses in agony. And then, a moment later, he falls down beside it, dead.

Electrocuted. Cooked from the inside out.

And I have to smile again. I've got Darrius's bracelet to thank for *that* particular idea.

But as I turn away from his prone body, my vision blurs and darkens, and I have to steady myself against the wall. I'm breathing hard and my legs feel like jelly. Magic has never wiped me out so completely before. *It's okay, Wisty*, I tell myself. *You'll be fine in a minute or two.*

Yet I have to lean there, propped against the bricks, for what seems like hours, until the weakness finally passes. Until I can see again.

When I straighten up, blinking in the bright sunlight, I ache all over. And I'm scared.

I guess discovering a new vulnerability will do that to a girl.

Chapter 60

Whit

"HE DIDN'T EVEN KNOW what hit him," Wisty gloats, tearing the dried meat on her plate into little shreds. "Poor dumb Horseman. I almost felt sorry for him."

My mom shakes her head in resignation. She probably *does* feel sorry for the Horseman—she's never approved of killing, not even the bad guys.

"It's a necessary evil," I remind her now. "It was him or Wisty. Be thankful your daughter's a badass."

Mom puts down her fork and gazes at me sadly, not even noticing that I've cursed at the dinner table. "I know," she says. "But when is it going to end? When do we get to stop living in fear?"

My dad laughs grimly. "That's the million-dollar question, isn't it?" he says. Then he stops and gets this wistful, faraway look in his eyes. I wonder if he's remembering a world before The One Who Is The One—or if he's imagining a world after Darrius.

I mean, assuming there's going to be such a thing.

I'm about to jab him in the shoulder when he snaps out of it. He looks at both of us in turn. "So, you two, what's the plan?" he asks.

"I like how you just assume we've got one," I say.

"Well, we do," Wisty says to me. "Don't we?"

"Sort of," I say. We spent the afternoon hashing one out—which *really* isn't that much time.

Wisty kicks me under the table. "It's very simple," she says. "Right, Whit?"

"More like very desperate," I mutter.

"What, dear?" asks my mom.

"Nothing, Mom," I say. I don't want to upset her even more by admitting the outlines of our plan. Our *pitiful plan*.

But my dad's looking a lot more optimistic all of a sudden. "So tell us more," he says.

Wisty shakes her head. "Really," she says, "the fewer people who know about it, the better."

Probably *she* doesn't want to upset them with our plan's pitifulness, either.

"As your father—" my dad begins.

But Wisty raises a hand and cuts him off. "Dad, may I remind you that we've saved this City *twice*? Don't you think you ought to trust us by now?"

I wonder if it's only me who can hear the waver in her voice. That sneaking sliver of doubt she probably wouldn't acknowledge even to herself.

My dad shifts uncomfortably in his chair. "Of course I trust you," he says. "But I'm also afraid for you."

My mom nods, looking like she's on the verge of tears.

And hell, I'm afraid, too.

But then Wisty gets this funny smile on her face. "I've got something to show you all," she says. "It's going to make you feel a lot better."

And I think, *You do? It is?*

She reaches into the bag that's hanging on the back of her chair and pulls out...well, what looks like a giant *bone*. She holds it triumphantly aloft for a second, and then sets it with a loud thunk on the table. My mom visibly recoils.

"What is that *thing*?" she asks.

"It is," Wisty answers, pausing dramatically, "a petrified camel's leg. Technically, its tibia, I believe."

"But *why is it on my table*?" my mom wants to know.

"Is it from a Horseman?" I ask.

Wisty nods. "Yep. Pried from the dead hand of—"

"Enough," Mom says, making a move to cover her ears.

My dad hesitatingly pokes it with his index finger. "Is it magic?"

Wisty shakes her head. "Nope."

"Is it a weapon?" my dad asks.

"Yeah, does it shoot arrows or something?" I ask.

Wisty smiles. "No and no." She turns to me, looking almost giddy. "Whit, you're going to appreciate this." She taps it lightly with her finger while she explains. "It proves what I hoped was true about the Horsemen. They *don't actually have powers.* All they've got is bad attitude and brute force."

I hold up my hand. "Wait a second. First of all, I don't know why you're only telling me this now." I shake my head in confusion. "And second of all, I saw them *materialize* that first night, right onto their horses' saddles. And you're telling me they're not magic?"

Wisty smiles. "That was a trick, dear brother. Special effects. A few moments of invisibility, courtesy of Darrius. Whereas I have subjected this bone to the most rigorous of scientific testing—"

I snort. "Dude, you totally failed science."

Wisty glares at me. "I'm not a *dude,* jockstrap."

"Ahem," says our mom.

"Okay, fine." Wisty sighs. "So I showed it to Aunt Bea. And she did some mumbo-jumbo chanting over it, and after half an hour she pronounced it completely and utterly *un*magical. Then she cross-checked it with *The Book of Truths,* which said something about 'ossified superstitions' and 'an enemy's illusions.'" She pauses. "'Ossified,' referring to *bone,* Whit—so you see, I remember a *few* things from science class."

"This is very interesting," my dad murmurs, scratching his stubbled chin.

Wisty just smiles smugly. "The point is, this isn't a weapon, you guys—it's a good-luck charm. A superstition." She holds up the bone triumphantly again. "The

Horsemen are just desert rats. Mercenaries. Idiots. Which means: *we can take them*."

Then she loses her grip on the bone and it clatters to the table. My mom jumps halfway out of her chair in surprise, then reaches out and swats it off the table and onto the floor.

As I look at it spinning harmlessly down there, I realize that Wisty's right. Aside from that first night, I've never seen a Horseman do anything remotely magical.

And I feel a tiny spark of hope. "I gotta hand it to you, sis," I say. "Maybe we *can* take them. Because we're a much higher form of idiot."

Chapter 61

Whit

DEEP IN THE PIT at Work Site #1, Stan doesn't recognize me at first, though I saw him only days ago. His eyes are bleary, and his shirt's nothing but ribbons of filthy, stained cotton. Lash wounds scar the skin on his arms and shoulders.

"We stand together, huh?" he eventually growls. Then he spits on the ground at my feet. "Where were you when they killed Molly?"

I suck in my breath sharply. Molly was the one with the wild eyes; I guess she was right about digging her own grave. "I was coming up with a plan," I say.

"While we were doing your digging," Stan nearly shouts.

I shove my spade into the earth, noticing how the tunnel is deeper now. It slopes downward, getting narrower as it goes. And I still don't know what it's for.

"Hey, I came back to this hellhole, didn't I?" I retort. "Put my tracker back on and here I am," I say. (I don't mention that it doesn't work anymore—that it's held together with tape.)

Stan's eyes widen, and his expression gets a lot less pissed all of a sudden. "How'd you get it off?" he whispers.

I put my hand on his scabbed shoulder. "*Everyone's* going to get theirs off. Today's the day we rise up against the Horsemen."

That's when Stan starts to laugh. "Us? Fight them?" he gasps. "That's the funniest thing I've heard in days."

"They don't have powers," I tell him.

He stops laughing. "Huh?" he says, confused.

"They aren't magic. They're just men. And there are more of us than there are of them. We can take them."

Stan looks up—at the Horseman sentries stationed every twenty feet around the lip of the pit, and at the others who ride their mounts in endless circles around the perimeter. As he stares, his eyes narrow. I can see the realization dawning on him: he's seen them maim and mutilate and murder, but he's never seen the Horsemen use magic.

His posture straightens almost imperceptibly.

"We can take them," I repeat urgently.

Then Stan's shoulders slump back down and he turns to me, his eyes sunken and desperate. "Look at us, though," he says. "We're more dead than alive."

Glancing around me, I have to admit he might be right. The workers can barely stand, let alone dig or fight. They are broken in body and spirit, victims of bondage and famine.

"The guards don't even let us leave anymore," Stan goes

on. "The digging goes on all day and all night. We work twelve hours, we get two hours' rest, and then we work twelve hours again."

And even as I watch, a woman half a dozen yards away collapses, sending up a weak cry of pain as she falls to her knees.

I start toward her, but then I stop and turn back. "The way I see it," I call to Stan, "we can die fighting, or we can die digging." And then I rush to her side.

She's middle aged, gray haired, and gasping for breath. Instinctively I reach out to take her pulse; it's racing. I place my fingers on her temples and summon my healing magic, and she's too feeble to ask me what I'm doing.

The truth is, she's dehydrated and starving. She doesn't need magic—she needs water and food and rest. But I do what I can to soothe her, to calm her speeding heart. "It's going to get better soon," I assure her.

She looks up at me with huge dark eyes. "You mean I'm going to die?" she whispers. And I swear she sounds *hopeful.*

"No," I say. "You'll be able to stand up again. And then you'll fight."

She looks at me uncomprehendingly until I tell her our plan—such as it is. She keeps staring, until eventually, weakly, she nods.

"What do I have to lose but my life?" she asks, shrugging. "It means nothing to me anyway."

I remove my fingers from her temples and take a step

back, knowing that I've been able to bring back some of her strength. I can't help her any more than that; I have to conserve my magic. I offer her what I hope is a confident smile. "We're going to win," I say. "Spread the word."

She stares at me again, her eyes searching my face, wanting to make sure I'm telling the truth. And then she holds up two fingers in a sign for victory.

When I go back to Stan, I see a small crowd has gathered in the mouth of the tunnel, hidden from the guards' view.

"Tell them," Stan commands.

I slam my shovel into the ground, and everyone jumps. "We will not dig for one single more day," I tell them. "Today is the day we fight." I look at each of them in turn. "I know you're tired. I know you're hungry. I know that what you want more than anything is for this hell to end." I take a deep breath. "And today, it does. When the sun climbs over the spire of the old church over there, our shovels and axes become weapons, and we *charge*."

The people mumble in confusion until Stan steps forward. "I'm in," he declares. Then he smiles grimly. "Death's a kind of freedom, too, isn't it?" He turns to the man standing next to him. "Are you with us?" he asks.

The man nods, and my heart seems to rise up in my throat as I watch these broken people find their last shreds of strength and vow to use them.

"We stand together," I say.

"Together," they repeat.

When I glance behind me, I see Wisty slink through the putrid muck, moving from worker to worker, also spreading the word. The hope.

She's not in disguise, because she, too, needs to conserve her magic. Now more than ever, her powers are not unlimited.

We'll conjure more weapons in the seconds before the attack. I'll be the muscle, Wisty will be the fire, and victory will be ours.

I get to enjoy that thought for another two seconds. Then I spot Darrius, and my blood seems to freeze in my veins.

He walks out onto one of the viewing platforms that the Horsemen have constructed, passing his eyes over the mass of groaning, straining slaves. He's wearing a seersucker jacket, and his hands are folded calmly behind his back—like he's just out for an innocent stroll.

But there's never *anything* innocent about Darrius.

And I know it like I know my own name: something really bad is about to go down.

Chapter 62

Wisty

I SENSE HIM before I see him. Infinitesimal sparks of electricity crackle in the air. They sting my skin like shards of ice.

Darrius is here.

Almost immediately, I'm hyperventilating, and the woman I was just convincing to join the rebellion looks at me like something's terribly wrong.

Because, of course, it is.

Trying to slow my breath, I risk a glance behind me, toward my brother on the far side of the pit—toward safety. But I see only the viewing platform in the middle, and on it, my beautiful, terrible nemesis.

Darrius hasn't seen *me* yet, though, and so I have a choice: transform into someone else, or duck into a nearby tunnel.

I think about it for about a millisecond before I start heading toward the tunnel. For now, I'll rely on stealth.

This way I can save my powers for the moment I really need them.

I'm almost to safety when out of nowhere, a giant worker steps in front of me, stopping me in my tracks. His dark hair is matted with dirt, his bearded face is scarred and sunburned, and he's wearing what looks like a raccoon skin around his shoulders—in short, he looks like a huge, lunatic caveman. With a pickaxe.

"Where you going, girlie?" he growls. "I didn't hear the quittin' bell."

I duck my head and try to dart around him, but he quickly moves to block me.

"You look like you're trying to hide," he says. His eyes narrow. "What for? Is someone lookin' for you?" He glances behind me, and a slow smile cracks his chapped lips. "I notice *Darrius* up there, lookin' pretty careful at everyone. He couldn't possibly be wantin' you, *could he*?"

I don't want to cause a scene, so I keep my voice low and light. "Me? Why on earth would Darrius be looking for little old me?" But trying to sound innocent was never my strong suit, and I don't think the overgrown troglodyte buys it.

He shrugs. "Pretty interesting how he shows up, and you make a run for it. The rest of us lookin' like model slaves so he don't turn us to ash." He puts his hand around my bicep. "So maybe I should deliver you to him. What do you think? Maybe he'll give me a day off."

"You're supposed to be on my side," I say desperately.

His grip tightens. "I'm on no one's side but my own, Red."

I can feel my skin bruising, but I don't care about that. All I care about is getting away from this guy. "I'm going to have to hurt you," I warn.

He laughs. "Girlie, you couldn't hurt a fly."

Maybe I should try to reason with him a little more. Maybe I should tell him about the uprising we're planning— he *should* be on my side. But honestly, I can't stand his kind of arrogance. I'm going to fry this guy, and I just hope Darrius is looking the other way when I do it.

"Really? Well, let me know if this hurts," I whisper. Almost immediately the heat starts rolling off me. The man gets a really confused look on his face, but he doesn't loosen his grip.

"Last chance," I warn.

And the idiot pulls me toward him, like he's going to lift me up and sling me over his shoulder. But before he can do it, I punch him in the gut with a fistful of flames. Then it's a quick uppercut to the solar plexus—no fire necessary. He goes down on his knees, sputtering and gasping for breath.

"Now pick on someone your own size," I say, and I make for the tunnel. But he whips out a hand and grabs my ankle, pulling me off balance. With a startled cry, I land on my back in the dirt and filth. My head knocks against a rock, and for an instant everything goes white, then black for a moment.

Damnit, I think.

When I can see again, I take my free foot and slam it into the guy's nose. Blood shoots out, and he rolls over away from me, shrieking. Blood is mixing in the mud and dirt, and the man's face is probably never going to look the same again.

Assuming he gets out of this pit alive.

Assuming any of us do.

Scrambling toward the tunnel again, I can hear shouting. Has Darrius finally spotted me? I brace myself for what's coming next. My fight with the caveman weakened me a little, but maybe, just *maybe*, I can electrocute Darrius before he turns me into charcoal.

But then suddenly, gray smoke starts pouring out of the tunnels, rolling toward us like a monstrous, unearthly fog. Dark clouds, borne on a rushing wind, billow up into the sky, blotting out the sun. The temperature drops twenty degrees in two seconds.

At first, everyone goes silent in shock and wonder.

What on earth is happening?

And then the panic begins. People yell in confusion as the cold reaches out its fingers and grabs them around the neck. They struggle to breathe like all the oxygen in the air has been sucked away. From deep underground I hear a terrible roaring, as if the very earth were being torn open.

Which, in a way, it is.

Now I know what we were digging toward. And I can't imagine anything worse.

Chapter 63

Whit

THE FOG'S SO BLACK I can barely see Stan standing next to me, and I've got no idea where Wisty is. From somewhere inside the new darkness, I hear the low, guttural moaning that is the sound of my worst nightmare.

It's the hellish music of Shadowland. The song of the Undead.

And it's coming from the tunnels we dug.

Open deep gate: I know what it means now. Bloom closed the portals between our world and the Underworld—and now Darrius has opened them again.

Made *us* open them again, with our own sweat and blood.

Inviting our own destruction.

The moans grow louder. I search for my sister in the mist, but I can't see her. "Wisty," I cry, but my voice is drowned out by the Lost Ones' moans and human screams.

I'm stumbling toward where I last saw her when the

Undead begin creeping up from the mouths of the tunnels. One after another, they cross the threshold into our world. Slowly, determinedly they march, the beginning of an indestructible army. In the smoke, they seem like shadows with glowing eyes.

"*What the*—" Stan says. Then he stops, his mouth hanging open in horror. He's never seen the Lost Ones.

They're figures out of a nightmare, with slimy, stringy flesh and depthless yellow eyes. Surrounding them is an overpowering stench of decay that emanates from their rotting souls. They were evil people in life, and they are paying the price after death.

I know these creatures far better than I want to, because I've been down to their world. I'll never forget the terrible, seeping cold of it—a cold that seemed *alive*, that sought out human warmth and tried to suck it dry.

In Shadowland, the trees are made of bones and the clouds are as red as blood. The Undead slink out of their skeleton forest, ravenously searching for live humans in the Underworld. They gather around them, their dead eyes flashing. They pluck at their clothes, their hair, their warm skin.

And then they devour them. Alive.

Suddenly a bone-chilling shriek pierces the air, and a body collapses to the ground just a few yards away from me. It's an old man, and even from here I can tell there's no hope for him.

A dozen Lost Ones flock around him, grunting and

gnashing their teeth. With cries of hunger, they fall upon him like hyenas. His final scream is cut off in the middle. His blood soaks the muddy floor of the pit.

I can't believe what I'm seeing. The Underworld has invaded the Overworld. And now the terror has truly begun.

Chapter 64

Wisty

"WHIT!" I SHRIEK. "WHIT!" But of course he can't hear me amid the screams of everyone else in this unimaginable hellhole.

As the Undead pour out of the tunnels, I see people trampling one another into the mud as they try to run away. I see them desperately trying to scrabble up the sheer walls of the pit. And I watch one man escape the Undead by shoving another man into their gray, grasping arms. A minute later, the unlucky slave is nothing but bones.

For far too long, I'm completely frozen. I feel like I'm witnessing the end of the world.

But what is *wrong* with me?

I have to find my brother—and I have to fight.

I step forward into the melee, hands already sparking. Can you kill something that's already dead? I'm about to find out.

I take aim at a pack of them, and I can feel the fire

burning in my blood when suddenly a voice resounds through the pit—a voice so loud it seems as if the sky itself is shouting.

"*Halt!*" it booms, sounding like a death rattle. "Stand *down!*"

And incredibly, the Undead stop in their tracks. They turn to face the center of the pit. Their moaning quiets.

One by one, the people stop their screaming. (But not their mad attempts to climb the pit walls, I note. If I didn't need to find Whit, I'd be scrabbling up with them.)

Cruel laughter echoes through the air, and the Undead tremble, cringing. Then, in the new silence, a familiar, loathed voice cuts through the mist.

"Vander," calls Darrius sternly. "It is not yet feeding time."

And incredibly, there he is, our debonair despot, striding toward a tall, imposing Lost One. Darrius steps over the bodies of collapsed workers as if they were simply piles of rock. As he nears the one he called Vander—the least dead-looking of the Undead—he begins to smile. "There will be much feasting," he says. "You can be certain of that. But not yet. And in the meantime, welcome."

Welcome? I think. *Feasting?*

And the Lost One, dressed in the rags of what once was a military uniform, gives Darrius a lipless smile back.

"It *is* good to see you again," Darrius says. "Where's Lilith?"

The Lost One bows low. "She's on her way, my lord," he

says. It was *his* voice that had commanded the Undead to stop. He must be their leader.

Then Darrius walks all around the pit, greeting the gruesome Undead *by name*.

What the *hell*?

I'm trying to wrap my mind around this, and totally failing, when Darrius turns away from the ghouls—

And looks straight at *me*.

His golden eyes light up, flashing like sunlight on a knife blade, and I shiver once again. "Well, well, well," he says. His voice is calm and smooth. "Wisteria Allgood. I've been looking for you for quite some time, you know." He steps around a pile of rubble, coming closer. His hair looks silver in the mist. He's wearing a *tie*, of all things, and my fingers itch to strangle him with it.

If only.

My hand finds the handle of a pickaxe and my fingers close around it. Crazy as it is, now's my chance. He'll expect me to use magic—not an axe. Quick as lightning, I lift the weapon and hurl it at him. It flies too quickly for me to see, heading straight and true toward his terrible golden eyes.

And then it *stops*, midair, and clatters harmlessly to the ground.

Darrius shakes his head in mock consternation. Behind him, a few of the Undead copy the gesture. "Really, Wisty," he says. "Did you honestly think you could hurt me with mere metal and wood?"

"Call me an optimist," I mutter.

"You continue to make bad choices, don't you?" he says smoothly.

"You mean like fighting you to the death, witch to wizard?" I challenge. "Would you consider that a bad choice?"

But Darrius only laughs. "I *would* consider it bad, yes. But it isn't actually a choice that you can make."

I step forward, my fists clenched. I can feel the flames in my blood. My heart roars like a bonfire. Maybe I can't kill him, but I can sure as hell hurt him. "Why not?"

Suddenly Whit's by my side, holding a shovel up like a weapon. "Or maybe *two* against one," he suggests. "How about that, Darrius?"

But Darrius ignores us both. Instead of answering, he lifts his arm into the air, and Whit and I are immediately frozen in place. My bones are stone, my skin's like ice. The chill of the Underworld fills me.

His guards immediately surround us, their weapons raised. Mingled in their ranks are the putrid Undead, their skeletal fingers already reaching for our clothes. One touches my hair, and if I could scream, I would.

"Oh, but the battle would be over too quickly," Darrius says quietly. "Me—with all my power—against a skinny little redhead and her ex-jock brother. Oh, once he might have been a worthy foe, but he has been *neutered*, hasn't he?" Darrius turns around and looks straight at Whit. "What a brilliant campaign that was! Excise yourself for the good of the City!" Then he reaches his arm out and *taps* Whit on the end of his nose—like my brother's a bad dog or something. "How stupid you are," Darrius croons. "And how *powerless*."

I'd give my right arm for a fireball right now, but I still can't move. My brother lets out a closed-mouth howl of rage.

A cruel smile plays in the corners of Darrius's lips. "No, it can't be over yet. I like to relish my victories."

As the circle of Horsemen and Undead tightens around us, Darrius begins to walk away. "Arrest them," he directs. *"Obviously."*

Whit's not nearly as powerless as you think, Darrius, I want to scream. *The minute we're unfrozen, we'll summon our powers and turn your sand cowboys into beef jerky.*

But then someone mashes chloroformed rags into our faces, and everything goes black.

Chapter 65

Whit

I WAKE TO FIND MYSELF trussed like a deer, my hands and feet bound to a pole carried on the shoulders of two striding Horsemen. Wisty, still unconscious, is flung over a Horseman's saddle, limp as a dish towel. We're flanked by the stinking Undead, who moan at us and lick their blackened gums.

I shiver when one grins at me. Wisty's probably lucky she's not awake for this part.

They carry us all the way to the City prison, parading us down the center of the street like the spoils of war. My head is pounding, like maybe they used it as a punching bag when I was unconscious.

In booking, I'm untied, but only so I can be stripped of my shoes and my belt. They handcuff me—and Wisty, too, even though she's still out like a light.

I look around in grim recognition. It's not the first time

we've been to this prison, with its floors upon floors of iron-barred cells. The One Who Is The One brought us here in the middle of the night when we were just kids, before we even knew we were magic.

Part of me wishes I were still living back then, in happy, unmagical ignorance. I was innocent, carefree. I'd never killed a man, and no man had yet tried to kill me.

The Horseman guards prod me up five flights of stairs to the top, and I can't help noticing how many rooms there are to be locked away to rot in. But we escaped before, and we'll escape now—that's what I'm telling myself. I just need Wisty to wake up so she can help.

The Horseman who's carrying Wisty over his shoulder uses a free hand to open a narrow cell. "A room with a view," he sneers. And then he drops my sister to the floor, shoves her farther into the cell with his foot, and slams the door.

Furious, I lunge toward him, but he kicks me hard in the chest, sending me spinning backward into the neighboring cell. I land hard, and before I can launch myself up again, the door slams on me with an earsplitting clang.

"Enjoy your stay," the Horseman calls as he heads back down the hall.

"Wisty," I yell as soon as he's gone. "Wisty!"

But the chloroform hasn't worn off her yet, and there's no answer.

I inspect our dreadful new digs while I wait for her

to wake up. The walls are made of cold gray stone, and there's a narrow window in one. In a nearby corner lies a small pile of dirty rags and the tattered photograph of a girl. These were probably the entire worldly possessions of the previous occupant—and now they're abandoned and covered in rat shit.

And whoever was in here? He's gone to a better place: oblivion.

Moving aside the rags, I'm surprised to notice a small hole in the wall. When I put my eye up to it, I can see part of Wisty's ankle.

It looks pale and thin and heartbreakingly fragile.

Who are we to think we can win this battle?

After what seems like hours, I hear my sister moving around on the other side of the wall. My heart leaps.

"Wisty," I call again, my face right near the hole. "Are you okay?"

"What happened?" Her voice sounds thick and groggy.

"We got captured," I say. "In case that isn't obvious."

"Damnit, Whit, we should have fought."

"We tried," I remind her. "He froze us."

From the other side of the wall comes a string of curses.

"There's a bright side, though," I tell her.

"Oh, *really.*"

I don't have to be able to see her to know the sneering, skeptical face she's making.

I stand up and look out the window, where the sunlight's glinting off the marble of the Old Palace. "We can keep an eye on Darrius's headquarters. See what he and Bloom are up to."

Now comes her muffled scoff. "*Please*. You couldn't even figure out what you were digging toward with your own two *hands*. And now you think you're going to be able to get to the bottom of Darrius's plans from your prison cell? Good freaking *luck*."

Glancing downward to the courtyard, I can see more Undead emerging from the alleyways. Scores of them—hundreds, even—slinking into the square. Then they stop and just stand there, as if they're waiting for something. I see the big one Darrius called Vander enter the palace, flanked by a dozen other Lost Ones.

"They're going in," I whisper. *But why? What could Darrius want with them?*

Other than to keep terrifying and murdering everyone left in the City.

"Who?" Wisty asks.

"The Undead." I press my forehead against the cool glass, watching the ghastly procession up the palace steps.

"Whit..." The voice is light, musical—definitely not my sister's. "Whit..."

I turn around. "Did you hear something?" I call to Wisty.

"Yeah," she says tiredly. "I hear the rats in the walls. And—wait, hold on—yes, I definitely hear something. Shrieks of terror? Howls of horror? Yes, it sounds like one of our prison neighbors begging for mercy as the Undead eat him alive."

"No, there's a voice," I insist. Although, I admit: there is a lot of screaming in the distance. I shudder, trying to ignore it.

"Whatever, dude," Wisty says dismissively.

But then, in the corner of my cell, I see a faint, delicate shimmer. Like a ray of sunlight curling around itself, dancing. The light grows brighter, and then slowly it takes shape.

It's Celia.

Or the ghost of her, anyway. I feel a smile so wide it nearly cracks my face in two. "Hey, you," I whisper.

"Hi, Whit," she says softly.

"Wait—Whit, is someone there?" Wisty calls.

"It's Celia," I say.

"Oh, great," I hear Wisty mutter. "I wonder what happy tidings she's bringing this time."

"Don't be rude, Wisty," I say.

"Oh, *sorry*. Sure, I just got chloroformed and thrown into prison by a guy who wants to murder me about as much as he wants to breathe, and you're worried about my manners," she snaps. "God, I'm so *sick* of you."

Celia doesn't seem to hear Wisty's grousing, though— or if she does, she doesn't care. She floats closer to me and says, "This is urgent, Whit. When Darrius unleashed the Undead upon the world, he gave them a power they did not have before."

"What do you mean?" I'm not liking the sound of this.

"In Shadowland, the Undead ate only flesh. In this world, they can also eat souls."

I shudder at the image. "But what does that mean?"

"Eating someone's soul doesn't simply kill them," Celia goes on. "It's much worse than that." She takes a deep breath. "When Lost Ones devour a human soul, then they live again. They're no longer Undead."

I gasp. *"What?"*

Celia nods. "They become immortal. Invincible. And more evil than ever before. Under the control of Darrius and Matthias Bloom, they will destroy the entire world."

I can't believe what I'm hearing. If what Celia's saying is true, we're talking about the end of life as we know it.

Wisty sighs in her cell. "You know, Celia," she calls, "I always liked you. But ever since you died, you're kind of a bummer."

"Celes," I say, "are you sure?"

Celia reaches for my hands, but her ghostly fingers slip through mine like the ruffling of a faint breeze. "You and Wisty need to stick together," she urges. "And you two can't fight with each other anymore. Seriously. Never again. It's important to the City that you're unified."

Wisty's over on the other side of the wall, once again whispering all the curse words she knows—some of them maybe even directed at me and Celia—and I'm thinking, *Easier said than done.*

I turn back to Celia, and her lovely blue eyes gaze deep

into mine. "Whatever you say, Celes. But what else are we supposed to do?"

"I don't know," she says sadly. "Just . . . be strong."

And then she flickers, sputtering out like a candle— and vanishes.

Chapter 66

Wisty

I FEEL BROKEN. Scared, tired, with a headache the size of the universe—and just downright *busted*. My moments of bluster (okay, some might say rudeness) were only so I didn't burst into tears.

Cry me a river, Wisteria, right? Well, I'm telling you: *I could.*

You have to understand that, waking from the chloroform, I forgot who I was. For a whole entire minute, I was nothing and nobody—I was simply a doomed and nameless girl.

I had to work to remember myself.

I think, in a way, I didn't want to.

I didn't realize it right away, but giving Whit half my powers felt like it hollowed me out. Like there's a part of me missing, and no matter how hard I search I'll never be able to find it again. Sometimes I've looked at my brother and thought, *What have you done to me?*

But I could never ask him that question.

Or maybe I'm shattered because I finally realize how tired I am of fighting. Of struggling simply to stay alive. I just want to rest.

If only the screaming in the halls would stop so I could sleep.

If only my brother would stop calling my name.

I can see his lips moving through the hole in the wall. "Wisty," he's whispering, "we have to get out of here. Now."

"I thought you were all about the cell-based recon," I mutter. "Do some more of that. I need to rest." My eyelids feel like they're made of cement.

"Listen!" he yells. "They're coming closer. Do you want your soul to be a Lost One's midnight snack?"

"I don't care," I say, closing my eyes. "I'm too tired."

"You need to wake up and smell the zombies, sis! Because I, for one, have no interest in waiting around to be killed by the Lost Ones—or Darrius, for that matter, who'll probably murder us in an even *less* enjoyable way."

I hear a scream nearby that turns my blood to ice. They're coming from outside on the street now, too.

Our City's being devoured.

Damn it all to hell: I suppose it's up to me to try to stop it.

I take a deep breath, steeling myself. "Okay, okay," I say. "So what's the plan?"

"We find Darrius and Bloom, and we defeat them," Whit says, as if this explains everything.

I put my eye up to the hole and now we're looking right at each other. "Uh—how?"

"First we disguise ourselves," he says. "As Lost Ones."

I shiver. "Ew. I'd rather be a rat. Let's try that again."

Whit shakes his head firmly. "No. In Shadowland, I watched the Undead rip animals apart with their teeth and bare hands. Nothing's safe from a Lost One—except another Lost One."

The thought of turning myself into a Lost One is beyond horrifying, but I have to admit, he's got a point.

I sigh. "All right," I say. "But I'm not doing this alone."

With effort, I get up and stand before the door to my cell. I place my cuffed hands on the lock and focus my attention on its destruction. My M builds slowly, though, haltingly, and I grow impatient. As I start to count the seconds, improbably I hear my mom's voice: *A watched pot never boils!*

I almost laugh—but thinking of her calms me a little. I focus deeper. The M grows stronger, still sluggish but steady. And a moment later, the lock melts, and the door creaks open.

On still-weak legs, I hurry to my brother's cell. His lock is easier to break. I guess I'm warmed up now—no pun intended.

Whit's standing in the middle of the tiny room, his expression a confusing mix of fear and relief. Wordlessly he holds out his hands, and I take them in mine.

"Ready?" I ask quietly.

He nods.

I'm *not* ready—but I guess it doesn't matter. I don't have a choice.

We squeeze each other's fingers, and within moments we can feel the electricity sparking. It stings like a million tiny bees. Whit's big hands grow warm, then hot. We close our eyes and try to help the power build.

I can feel Whit's pulse in his palms—that's how hard his heart's beating. Mine, too, seems to gallop in my chest, as the M rushes through us, swirling, amplifying....

But it *hurts*.

It feels like it's sucking energy from every single cell in my body. Is it because I'm trying to become a carbon copy of soulless evil? Or because I'm simply weak? I don't know, and I can't think about it. I have to fixate on the magic; I have to call it forth.

"Breathe," Whit whispers.

"Trying," I gasp.

We hold each other tighter, and then, finally, it comes: first a new, beautiful heat, and then a deep, sucking chill. I can feel myself begin to transform. I sense my blood slow, my temperature drop. The pain returns, but it's almost as if it's somewhere outside my body, floating in the air around me, only occasionally searing my skin. My bones grow thin and brittle, and my hair turns to seared, greasy strings.

It's hard to get enough air into my lungs. I almost feel like I *am* a Lost One, instead of a human imitation.

"Wow, this is unpleasant," Whit manages.

Together we stoop low, and our skin goes gray and leathery, and our clothing turns to dusty rags. When I look into Whit's eyes, I see the same terrible yellow that my own eyes must be.

I try to smile, but my face feels stiff and hard. It must look like I'm grimacing in pain. "Looking good, bro," I say.

The handcuffs slip easily over our thin, bony hands and clatter to the floor, and we step out of Whit's cell.

The halls of the prison are crawling with the ravenous Undead, all of them trying with slow but fanatical dedication to breach the cell doors and destroy the occupants inside. Judging by the nonstop, blood-curdling screams, a lot of them are succeeding. Others—the weaker ones, perhaps, the ones who've been Undead for centuries—simply press their decaying bodies against the bars and moan.

They turn their hideous eyes to us as we make our way to freedom. And then a pair of them start walking toward us with a determination that unnerves me.

They don't eat their own—I know that. But still, we start to run.

Chapter 67

Whit

WE'RE HALFWAY TO the stairs when I stop in my tracks in front of a row of cells. The people inside are yelling in terror, begging someone to free them before the Undead come. Are these people criminals, jailed rightly? Or are they innocent, like Wisty and me? I don't have any idea—all I know is that, unless I free them, they're doomed.

"We have to go," Wisty yells. She tugs on my arm and then drops it in disgust. "Don't make me drag you. Your skin's too gross."

"But they'll die," I say desperately.

"Even more people will die if we don't get to Bloom and Darrius," she retorts. "I'm going now, and so are you."

Ignoring her, I close my eyes, concentrating on the locks, imagining the pins disengaging, the cylinders rotating, and the bolts sliding open. And maybe they do, and maybe they don't—I'll never know, because Wisty grabs me again, grimacing in revulsion, and yanks me down the hall. I always forget how strong she can be when she puts her mind to it.

She's hissing something about me wasting my powers as we clatter down the staircase, winding down four flights to the main floor and freedom.

We slow down as we go through the central booking area, moaning like our Undead brethren. We just need to get outside and make it across the square to the palace without being detected.

Simple—right?

There's a herd of Horsemen guarding the door, but hey, don't we look like we're on their side? I'm thinking it's going to be easy—I mean, don't we deserve a break?—but then one of them sticks out a spear and bars our way. "No one passes," he announces.

Wisty moans a bit more in what I hope is a convincingly Undead manner. I raise my ancient, embalmed face and speak in a voice that sounds like bones rubbing together. "We must go to the palace," I creak.

The Horseman shakes his head. "Not until summoned."

"We were," I insist. Then I cough, because my larynx feels like it's made of dust. It must really *suck* to be Undead.

The Horseman frowns darkly, and two others step forward, looking more and more menacing by the second. "You weren't," the first says.

Wisty straightens up indignantly, suddenly seeming a bit too *alive*. "How do you know?" she demands.

Shhh, I'm thinking. *Don't blow our cover.*

She meets my eye, and I know she can read my thoughts. But either she can't control herself, or she doesn't care. Heat waves begin shimmering off her, scorching what little tattered clothing she's wearing. Seconds later, flames start leaping from her skin like she's a Lost One lantern.

"What the—" says the first Horseman.

The others begin to shout, raising the cry of alarm.

"Come and get it, you ugly cowpokes," Wisty taunts as bolts of lightning shoot from her hands, dropping three of the guards to their knees. They scream and beat at their burning chests.

Nothing to do now but fight.

I deliver a forearm smash to the neck of the guy nearest me, and I can feel the crunch of his windpipe collapsing. He goes down, gasping for breath. I grab a truncheon from the belt of the next guard and start bashing him with his own weapon.

Blows are raining down on my head and shoulders, and I'm trying desperately to deflect them with one arm while working offense with the other. I hear the crack of bone— mine or someone else's, I don't even know. A body shot to my ribs sends ripples of pain rushing through me. I clock one guy so hard in the mouth that my knuckles split open and a bunch of his teeth go flying. They're coming at me so fast I don't have time to work up any magic—I'm just fighting them with every ounce of strength in my body, a strength fueled by fear and rage.

None of the guards can get close to Wisty, though.

They're terrified of her fire. She lifts her arm and shrieks out words I can't understand, and the Horsemen's clubs fly right out of their hands. They hang suspended in the air, vibrating, rotating—and then they explode. Sharp, splintery bits of wood rain down on all of us.

There's a roaring in my ears and the pain in my head's more intense than it's ever been before. A Horseman charges me like a bull, slams me in the stomach, and I go pinwheeling backward and bash my skull against the wall.

Which makes the headache even *worse*.

I think I'm going down.

But then Wisty rushes at me, flames shooting out from her every cell, looking like some awful, brilliant demon. She grabs my hands and yells, "*Run*," and I feel her power surging through me, conjuring my own.

Suddenly my mind goes crystal clear, and time itself seems to slow down. The horrific din goes quiet, and then it's like the two of us are flying. We tear through the doorway and down the marble steps into the sunlight.

Freedom.

But the square is crawling with Lost Ones. One lets out a squawking cry, and the rest of them turn to us, their yellow eyes flaring. We're still in Undead form ourselves, but somehow they're not buying it anymore—maybe because Wisty's on fire and screaming like a banshee.

I leap into the middle of them, dodging the grasping arms like they're opponents on the foolball field. Wisty follows in my wake, heat and smoke rolling off her in ter-rifying waves.

A Horseman's arrow whizzes past my ear, and then an-other, but we duck our heads and keep charging through. There's a gate up ahead that leads to the City proper, and once we're through it we can hide.

We race, our breath pounding in our ears. Then comes the sound of gunfire.

We just need to make it to the gate.

The Lost Ones surge behind us, but they can't keep up. It's the Horsemen and their guns we need to worry about now.

"Wisty, hurry!" I yell.

A hundred yards from the gate, I glance back to see the nearest Horseman take a bullet in his back.

"Nice aim," Wisty yells.

Then comes another burst of gunfire—and the heart-stopping sound of my sister's scream.

She's stumbling, nearly falling, as blood streams out of a wound in her leg. I don't stop to think—I don't have time. I rush back and pick her up, throwing her over my shoulder.

"Hold on tight," I yell.

Then I run like I've never run before. Together we burst through the gate, and Wisty, thinking fast, slams it shut with her magic, buying us a precious few minutes.

I don't stop running until we're out of sight of the pal-ace. And then I set Wisty down and collapse onto the side-walk, gasping for air.

As we return to living-human form, Wisty moans and holds her thigh.

"Is it bad?" I ask urgently, pushing aside her slick, red-stained fingers.

"How the hell do I know?" she barks. "It hurts like it is."

I inspect the wound, and I'm beyond relieved to see that it's not too deep. "It's bleeding a lot, but you're going to be fine." I take off my shirt and wrap it tight around her thigh, stanching the flow of blood.

She looks into my eyes. "You got enough juice to heal it?"

I have to turn away. "Not yet," I say. I take a few deep breaths, and then face her. I reach for her hand. "I'm sorry, Wisty," I say. "If I hadn't given it away... if you hadn't had to give me half *your* power..." I trail off, as once again the stupidity of my choices hits home.

But Wisty just grits her teeth and then smiles faintly at me. "Guilt is a waste of time," she says. "Just keep going. If we live through this, you can feel guilty later. I promise to help you with that."

Chapter 68

Wisty

MY LEG IS KILLING ME. So is the look on Whit's face—like he'll never, ever forgive himself for getting Excised. And while I may not be the world's *nicest* girl, I don't believe in kicking a guy when he's down.

"I've been hurt a lot worse," I remind him as I adjust my makeshift bandage.

Whit doesn't say anything. He just nods grimly.

"Hey, we can't sit around feeling sorry for ourselves in an alleyway," I say. What I don't say: *Someone's going to find us, and probably sooner rather than later.*

"Exactly," Whit agrees. "You need medical attention."

I shake my head firmly. "We don't have time for that. I'm fine," I insist (and I'm really hoping I'm right about this). "For all we know, there are portals to the Underworld *all over the City*. What if our parents opened portals when they were dredging the river? What if the people at other work sites did, too? What if, every single second, more of the Undead are pouring into our world, Whit? *What if?*" I hear my voice rising, and I realize that my heart's begun racing. I'm starting to panic. How did I not think of this before, what the influx of Lost Ones could really mean?

It's a threat so profound, so terrifying, it's almost unimaginable. An army of the Undead means the end of any chance for freedom, or any hope for peace. It means living every single moment of our lives in fear, waiting to be devoured. With their ravenous appetites for flesh and souls, the Lost will eventually destroy everyone.

In the whole, entire world.

I'm reeling at the thought. I can barely breathe. We're looking at the *total destruction of human life*, and you can't come back from that. There's no happy ending.

"Wisty!" Whit is poking my arm. "Hello? Have you heard a word I said?"

"What? Huh? No."

"I asked if you were ready to go back to the palace," he says. "To put a stop to this."

I try not to laugh bitterly in his face. My sense of urgency has suddenly turned to fatalism. Maybe we *should* just wait here to die. Maybe we should just get it over with.

"How do we fight them? How do we kill something that's already dead?" I ask.

He shrugs. "I don't know yet. But we've got to try, don't we?"

I look down at my leg again. Whit's shirt is nearly black with my blood. "If you say so," I respond dully.

He grabs my shoulders and looks me right in the eyes. "Wisteria Allgood," he says, "don't you dare give up because the Undead creep you out and you've got a little scratch on your leg. It's time to find Darrius and Bloom and stop them, okay? We agreed on this. We made a pact."

"But not a plan," I point out.

"So we're flexible," he says. "And *fearless*."

Speak for yourself, I think. Is it the loss of blood or the sharing of power? I don't know, but I'm still not fully myself.

Whit stands up and holds out his hand. Reluctantly I reach up and let him pull me to standing. I wince when I put weight on my wounded leg.

"I'll heal it as soon as I can," he says, his voice suddenly sad. "I just need a little more time."

I nod. "I know. It's okay. It's not like I'm bursting with M right now, either."

Blood runs down my leg as we walk, and I'm feeling worse and worse about everything—until some small, bright thought occurs to me. "Wait a sec," I call. "I think I've got enough juice for *this*."

Whit turns. "For what?"

I hold up a finger, from which a hot, white flame begins to flicker and burn. I grit my teeth as I bring it down to my leg, searing the oozing flesh. Cauterizing it.

It hurts like hell. No, wait, actually it hurts worse than that.

Whit whistles low in admiration. "Wisty, you're a genius," he says. "With a high pain threshold."

The pain nearly brings me to my knees, but the wound's sealed for now. I wait until I can breathe through the agony, and then I say, "Okay. I guess we've got to do this, huh?"

Whit nods grimly.

"Remember to keep close to the buildings and be on the lookout," I say. "Who knows where the Undead are."

We pick our way down streets that are eerily deserted. An old newspaper blows into our path and Whit kicks it away. We can hear pigeons cooing in the eaves of the row houses, and their soft chirps sound like a warning. It's as if the air is tinged with menace. The hairs rise on the back of my neck.

"Where is everyone?" I whisper.

Whit says, "I don't know. If they've been released from the work sites, hopefully they're in hiding. Barricaded inside their houses."

We don't say what we're both thinking. *Where are our parents? Are they okay?*

All we can do now is hope.

I shiver and pull my sweater tighter around my shoulders. There's a strange chill in the air—a cold, stale, almost sepulchral breeze.

I stop, my stomach knotting in dread. I know that cold. I know that smell. "Whit?" I whisper.

But he doesn't answer. He has stopped in his tracks, so suddenly that I run right into the back of him.

I hear him suck in his breath. "Now we know where the Lost are," he whispers.

When I peer around him, my heart seems to vault into my throat. There's a whole pack of them slinking down the street, dark and cold as shadows. There are men, women, and even a few gray-faced, yellow-eyed children.

When she sees us, the woman in the lead smiles with sharp black teeth. "There," she croaks. "Our next meal."

And with a single cry, the pack charges. Whit and I turn on our heels and sprint back the way we came. I know the Undead aren't as fast as we are—but I also know their strength doesn't wane the way ours does.

We're not going to be able to outrun them for long.

Luckily we're in the old part of the City, where the streets curve and twist, and alleyways offer places to hide. My leg feels like it's on fire as I run. I can't think anymore. I just follow Whit blindly down a side street, knowing the Undead are close behind.

For a moment it seems like we'll lose them. But then, up ahead, we see another pack, this one led by a tall, stooped Lost One with arms like ebony sticks. He has hollows in his cheeks the size of ping-pong balls, and he leers at me hungrily.

We're caught.

"Hey, we're just a snack," I yell. "There's an all-you-can-devour buffet up there in jail." I point to the prison, looming darkly in the near distance.

But he doesn't even hear me. He just keeps coming— and so do all of them.

They're chanting something in low, sinister tones, but I can't understand what they're saying. Their eyes burn with a cold, yellow fire.

Whit and I look wildly around, but there's no doorway to duck in, no fire escape to climb.

"Can you transform?" Whit yells as the gray hordes move closer.

"No," I cry. "Not yet."

"What about fire?"

I'm trembling with the cold now. "I don't know!"

I can feel the chill of Shadowland as they lope toward us, their terrible faces grinning. There's nowhere to go. Nowhere to hide.

Whit and I are caught in the middle of their demonic circle.

"Torch 'em," he yells, lashing out with his fists to keep them at bay. "Just try!"

I try to summon my fire, but it's as if someone has poured ice water into my veins. It's a struggle even to put up my fists. It's like the cold has frozen me solid. "I can't!"

"Keep trying," Whit shouts.

Now I can hear what they're chanting. They're saying, *Hungry, hungry, hungry...*

And their fingers reach out to grab me, and all I can do is scream.

One seizes my arm and yanks it up to his lips, and I expect to feel the searing pain of his pointed yellow teeth—but instead of tearing off a chunk of my flesh, he kisses my hand. Almost *tenderly*. It's so repulsive, it takes my breath away.

Then he pulls me toward him in a deathly embrace, his expression of insatiable hunger the stuff of a thousand nightmares.

The cold surrounding me deepens to a glacial chill. Darkness blooms in my chest like some terrible frigid flower. It grows bigger and darker until it feels as huge and deep as a black hole—a vortex into which every smile, every peal of laughter, every moment of joy in my life is getting sucked away. Forever.

My lungs seize up. A giant hand of ice squeezes my heart.

There's nothing left but desolation.

Now I understand: the Lost One isn't after my flesh— he's after my soul. He's going to devour it. I feel myself fading, the bright flame of me flickering out.

But from somewhere deep inside—some tiny, buried place not yet frozen—I hear a voice. *Seek the light*, the voice cries. *Remember joy.*

And so, in my last moments of consciousness, I call up every memory of happiness and sunshine I have. I imagine sunlight on a lake, the blue of my mother's eyes, the roses we grew in front of our house, Whit laughing as he throws me a foolball...

If I have to die, I'll die with love—that's my final desperate thought. And so I reach out and pull the Undead man closer to me. In a *hug*.

The cold grows so intense that it burns. I scream in pain.

And then I realize that it really *is* burning.

I'm burning. I'm sparking. I'm *electric*!

The Undead man falls away from me, shrieking. His skeletal hands claw at his smoking skin—and then he bursts into flames. A second later, what's left of him looks like nothing but a small pile of burned paper.

Hope swells inside me, and I shout for joy.

"Whit," I cry. "I figured it out! You just have to hug them!"

"What?" he shouts. He's holding them off with his fists, but his strength is fading.

I turn toward a leathery creature that was once a young man. "Like Aunt Bea said: *only love*, Whit! Think about Mom hugging us, and Dad teaching us how to throw a foolball. Think about beautiful things, like fireflies and the ocean and sunsets. Think about Janine!"

He aims a kick at a Lost One's skull. "Huh?"

"Like this!" I seize the Lost One. His flesh is falling away in strips from his face, and I grimace in disgust as I pull him toward me. But clasping him to my chest, I call forth each and every beautiful thing that he lacks: life, light, laughter, love.

He lets up a howl that could shatter glass.

And then he's outlined in brilliant flames. He keeps

screaming until there's nothing left of him to make any noise at all.

"Holy M," Whit whispers. His blue eyes spark with hopefulness. "Only love."

And then we hold out our arms and walk into the seething mass.

Reaching for them all. Drawing them to us. Embracing them to oblivion.

Chapter 69

Whit

"I SAW YOU," calls a high, tremulous voice. "That was *incredible*."

The Undead we didn't destroy have fled, terrified by our shocking (literally) death-hugs—but now I'm so beat, I can barely look up to locate the source of the compliment.

"Really, how did you *do* that?" it asks.

I manage to lift my head up. Twenty feet above us, there's a young blond girl leaning out of a window, her gray eyes wide with amazement.

Wisty wipes the sweat from her brow and smiles. "Easy as pie," she says. "You just gotta love 'em to death." But her pale, damp face and gasping breaths belie her breezy words. It's *not* easy as pie—not by a long shot.

The girl peers appraisingly at us. "You're magic, though. I can tell," she says. "I'm not."

"Which is even more reason you need to stay where

you are," I tell her. "Be safe. You don't want to mess around with these people. They—"

"They're not actually people," she interrupts. "Right?"

"Well, they were once," I say.

She leans out the window even more, so far that I'm worried she'll lose her balance and tumble down into the street. "Why do they want to kill us?" she wonders.

"They're hungry," I say gruffly. "Now please, go back inside." I don't have time to play twenty questions with this kid.

But Wisty looks thoughtfully up at her. "I think they want to be people again," she says.

The girl thinks about this for a moment, and then she says solemnly, "That's sad."

Wisty smiles again. "Wow—compassion for the things that would eat you faster than a french fry? That's impressive."

The girl blinks down at us. Her clear pale eyes suddenly remind me of Pearl Marie Neederman's, and my stomach twists in remembered grief.

"So they're not alive, but they're not dead, either," the girl says. "Is that what you call a paradox? That was one of my vocabulary words. I mean, before Darrius sent my teacher to a work site."

"Yes, kiddo," my sister says. "It's a paradox."

I can't take it anymore; I start walking away. "Listen, it's been nice talking to you, but we have to go."

Wisty pushes herself off the wall she's been leaning

against. "Yeah. Basically we have to go try to kill Darrius right now."

The girl nods calmly, like this is the most normal thing in the world. And considering the tyrannical leaders this City's known in these last few years, maybe it is. "I hope you win," she says.

"Me too," I say. *For the sake of all of us.*

She waves at us as we head down the alley. We move slowly—partly because we're being cautious about finding more of the Undead, but more because we're exhausted. I'm dizzy and weak from our battle, and my emotions feel like they've been scooped out of me with a giant spoon.

We make it only a quarter mile before Wisty declares she has to rest. "Hugging those things was disgusting," she says as she collapses on a cracked concrete stoop.

I nod as I sit down beside her. "Like making out with a corpse."

"But it *worked*," she adds. She turns to me, eyes suddenly bright. "We need to spread the word, Whit. Find the Resistance and tell them how it's done! Train them in the art of killing what's already dead!"

I'm glad to see she's got some of her spunk back, even if she's still too tired to stand up. But finding the Resistance? Between the slave camps and the Lost Ones, I doubt there's much of the Resistance left.

I don't say that, though. I say, "Let's just gather our strength for a bit."

Still, I feel a surge of optimism. Maybe we *can* train

people to fight the Undead. Maybe there's a chance to turn the tide.

"Right," Wisty agrees. "Five minutes of rest. Then we'll go."

But we don't even get those five minutes. Because suddenly the air's full of the thunder of hoofbeats and the ringing of swords drawn from their sheaths. A dozen Horsemen have rounded the corner and are bearing down on us.

I leap up and haul Wisty to her feet as the Horsemen sound their guttural battle cry. "Run," I shout, shoving her away as a dark-bearded rider lassoes me around the waist like I'm livestock. He laughs as he expertly tightens the rope with a flick of his hairy wrist, cinching it around me like a torturous belt.

"Wisty," I yell—but the only answer is her piercing scream.

Then the Horseman whoops and digs his spurs into the flank of his mount. The horse rears up on its hind legs, nearly yanking me off my feet. When it drops back down to all four feet, it surges forward, breaking into a canter and wrenching me forward.

I have to sprint madly to keep up, but my legs are still weak from fighting and my feet trip over each other. As much as I try to stay upright, I'm practically being dragged out of the alley.

"Whit!" Wisty screams. "Help!"

I crane my neck to catch sight of my sister, knowing

already there's no way for me to help. Still, when I sense the Horseman's grip on the rope loosening as he adjusts the reins, I yank my body hard to the left, trying to break free. But another Horseman comes galloping up and lassoes me from the other side. Now I'm caught between two enormous barbarians, and it's all I can do to stay on my feet, to not be dragged through the streets.

Buildings go by in a blur as we race back toward the center of the City. The Horsemen whip their mounts into a frenzy, and my lungs feel like they're going to explode. Just when I think I might pass out from the strain, we crash through the tall iron gates of the Old Palace grounds and the Horsemen jerk their mounts to a stop.

I take in air with great, gasping breaths. The Horsemen who'd been pulling me let me go, and I fall to my knees and vomit.

Sweat stings my eyes and knives of pain stab my chest. I lift my head to see Wisty crawling toward me over the cobblestones, weaving her way between the horses' legs. Tears streak her cheeks.

Her shoes are gone, and her toes are shredded and bloody. "Oh, sis," I whisper, knowing exactly what happened. When she couldn't run fast enough, they pulled her along like a bundle of rags.

I want to murder them all for doing this to her.

"I'm okay," she assures me, wiping away her tears. But she doesn't look okay.

"Stand up." The words are thrown at us, sharp as rocks.

Wisty's eyes widen.

We know that voice.

Slowly, we struggle to our feet. The Horsemen who've surrounded us take a few steps back, and now we can see everything.

We're in the middle of the vast courtyard. All around the perimeter stand the Horsemen and the Undead, poised to attack at any moment. And just a dozen yards away stands Darrius. And Bloom.

Our smirking, loathed enemies. Yes, we wanted to face them. But not like this. Not like captured animals.

Darrius holds out his arms, as if he's glad to see us. "Welcome to the palace," he says, his voice smug and saccharine. "And welcome"—he pauses, licking his lips in anticipation—"to the Allgood family reunion!"

I look in confusion at Wisty—what is Darrius talking about? We were never separated!

But then Bloom and the Horsemen on either side of him step aside. And they reveal a small iron cage.

Containing my parents.

And Janine.

The cry feels like it's ripped from my throat.

He's got all of us now.

Chapter 70

Wisty

"HOSTAGES," DARRIUS CROONS. "Just in case you were hoping to stage a coup."

Even from twenty feet away, I can feel his golden eyes burning into mine. The air between us crackles with energy, the way it always has.

I can't look away from him, even if I want to. He's so familiar, so mesmerizing, so evil.

He smiles slyly, revealing his perfect white teeth. Slowly and deliberately, he approaches, almost floating across the cobblestones. He stops mere inches away from me, and then he lifts his hand—and touches me on the cheek.

The pain is instantaneous, a stunning electric shock. But I stifle my scream. I won't give him the satisfaction of knowing he's hurt me.

"Now I have you," he says softly. "For good."

I throw my head back, my eyes blazing. "I highly doubt that, Darrius."

His eyebrows lift in surprise. "Really, Wisteria. Such misplaced confidence! Honestly, it's almost embarrassing." Darrius turns, takes a few steps away. His eyes sweep the square, counting his soldiers—and his prisoners—in cruel satisfaction.

"Who says it's misplaced?" I demand. "You don't know who you're messing with."

"Actually, I do," he says. "I know you far better than you think." He gestures to the gilded Old Palace, with the blue flags of our former government still flying as if nothing bad had ever happened. "Remember when you came to see me at the old toy factory? Remember the Family? We had so much fun, Wisty. You should have joined us when you had the chance."

"I'm not into torture and murder," I say through clenched teeth.

"Oh, but we were so much more than that," he says. "As I told you that night: the world is a vexed and chaotic place. Our souls are dark and troubled. Is it so wrong to act on that darkness?" He comes toward me again, so close I can feel the deep, pulsing thrum of his magic. The power of his magnetism. His eyes look like topaz. *He is so terrible, so terribly beautiful.* "Surely," he whispers, "there is a place where desire and darkness meet."

I step backward, breathing hard, my body weakened by his presence. I manage to look away from those jewel-colored eyes. "You couldn't be more wrong," I say. "Every-body's soul is both light and dark. We can choose between the two, Darrius, and it's that choice that determines everything."

He shakes his head. "Oh my dear, such charming naiveté. How long, I wonder, will it take me to win you over to my side?"

"You won't," I vow. "Not ever."

His brow furrows, as if he'd expected a different answer. "So you're going to make it hard on yourself, then. That's too bad."

"Why are you even doing this?" I demand. "You're already in power! Why are you calling up the Undead? Why are your Horsemen murdering us? Why destroy the world you rule?"

Darrius only chuckles. "If you don't believe in the essential darkness of the human soul, Wisteria, how can I explain myself?"

I grit my teeth in anger. "Why don't you try me. I'd like to get inside the mind of a psychopath."

He frowns now. "Psychopath? I'm insulted."

I hold his gaze as I speak. "Right. You're not a psychopath. That's giving you too much credit, actually."

"Wisty," my brother hisses. "Enough."

I ignore him. I can't stop. I *won't* stop. I need to keep Darrius angry until our powers—or at least part of them—return. "You're just a selfish, narcissistic, megalomaniacal, post-adolescent *freak*."

"That's enough!" Darrius shouts. His eyes blaze fiercely and his fists clench.

"Oh, really?" I sneer. It's a delicate balance: he's got to be mad enough to keep toying with me, but not mad enough to lash out and kill me on the spot.

And he can't know that Whit's got magic again—not yet.

I glance over to my parents, caught in their cage. My dad's gripping the bars; my mom's gripping Janine's hand. Their expressions—of panic and terror and love, all mixed up together—are like nothing I've ever seen before. It hurts me to look at them.

I turn back to Darrius. "I know all about you," I seethe. "You're just a depraved and vicious runt whose parents never loved him."

A dark shadow passes over Darrius's face and his cheeks go pale.

"You *will* be quiet now." He points a long finger at me, and suddenly it's as if my jaw's been wired shut.

I scream, close-mouthed, in frustration. The rest of me still works, though, so I flip him off.

Flushed in anger, Darrius calls out to his army. "Shall we kill her right now? Or shall we torture her a little first?"

My mother lets out a stifled cry.

Something tells me he's not ready to hurt me, though. He, too, wants to play a mind game. I flip him off with my other hand.

A few of the Undead surge forward, but sure enough, Darrius motions them back. "I promise you," he calls to them, "you may feast on her flesh. And on her brother's flesh as well. But for now, hold still. *I* will do the killing."

Then he faces me again. "With all your powers, here you are. Helpless as a child. It's so *exciting* to be able to show you how wrong you were about everything! You've been trying to stop me, and failing so *spectacularly*, for so much more of your sad, stupid lives than you ever realized!"

Whit and I look at each other: *What is he talking about?*

Darrius is working himself into a frenzy. "I've been waiting for this moment for so long!" He points to a lamp-post, with its antique flickering gaslight. "We are going to string you up there, Wisteria, and flay you until your flesh falls from your bones. Do you think your mommy will like watching that?"

The image flashes before my eyes and my knees almost give way beneath me. Is this really going to happen? I still can't speak. My M's still low. And if I make a move toward Darrius, he'll kill my family.

Darrius smiles a murderer's smile. "Or maybe I'll burn both of you to death. Roast you slowly, like a marshmallow. We'll see how it goes. But before you die, in terror and agony, there's something I'd like to show you."

Darrius takes another step back. He's in the exact center of the square now, standing on the gold porcelain tiles that long-ago City dwellers arranged in the shape of the sun.

He takes a deep breath and raises his arms to the sky, and his mouth forms the words of a dark and unknown language. I expect thunder and lightning, or knife-sharp hail, or a shower of bombs—but nothing at all happens above us.

Instead, something is happening to Darrius himself.

As I watch in horror, his skin darkens and shrivels. His shoulders hunch as his body bends lower. His hair falls out in clumps, and his eyes begin to glow a terrible yellow.

Darrius has become a Lost One.

What the—

The creature that was once Darrius holds up a single gnarled finger, as if to say, *Wait!*

My brother, standing by my side, whispers, "This is not good."

And then the air begins to shimmer all around Darrius, blurring his dark body. A breeze swirls through the square as he begins to shift again. The Lost One straightens up, grows tall again. His hair turns as pale as moonlight, becoming a helmet of gold. His eyes fade to an icy, merciless blue.

My whole body begins to tremble.

No.

Freaking.

Way.

Not again.

Chapter 71

Wisty

PEARCE IS NOW STANDING in the center of the court-yard, sunlight blazing on his cruel, narrow face.

It can't be him—and yet it *is*.

Pearce: the son of The One Who Is The One; the boy who, disguised as a wizard named Heath, tricked me into loving him.

My stomach churns and I feel like I might throw up. I can't understand why—or how—this is happening. I want to scream all the curses in the world, but my jaw's stuck shut. My head feels like it's going to explode.

My parents are shouting from their cage, but the buzzing in my stunned brain drowns out what they're saying.

Pearce's thin lips curl back in a smile. "Aren't you glad to see me again, Wisteria?" He turns to my brother. "And Whitford, I trust you remember me fondly."

"We should have killed you when we had the chance," Whit rages.

Pearce nods curtly. "Yes, no doubt you should have. But that's the problem with you two. You believe in that ridiculous thing called *mercy*."

My hands clench into fists and adrenaline floods my veins. I don't care if I'm not magic yet, I'm just going to freaking *destroy him*—

Suddenly two Horsemen grab my arms, and though I fight them with all my strength, they easily carry me to Pearce and drop me right in front of him. And then they step back, like they don't want to be anywhere near what's about to happen.

I can hear my mother screaming and my father shouting one word, over and over: *No!*

They don't want to see their baby girl die.

Face-to-face, Pearce and I stare into each other's eyes. Hate fills mine, but his icy orbs seem almost bemused. He loves how he's surprised us, it's obvious.

And he surprises me again when, quick as a snake, he leans in and kisses me on the mouth. His tongue slithers its way between my teeth. His lips are cold and slimy.

Instantly the spell is broken, and I begin to sputter and choke. "Don't you ever do that again," I scream.

"I don't plan to," he says calmly. "That was my good-bye kiss." He smiles and brushes a lock of pale hair from his forehead. "Yes, you and your wizard brother *almost* killed me that day on the battlefield. I came so close to dying that my mother made a deal: I would share my soul with one of the Undead; in return, he would share his deathless strength with me."

"So that would explain the hideous transformation we witnessed," Whit mumbles.

"I didn't think you *had* a soul," I say to Pearce.

Pearce sighs. "You always underestimated me, Wisty." He shakes his head. "Sometimes I don't know what I ever saw in you."

"You're not going to win this, Pearce," my brother challenges.

"Oh, really? Is that what you think?" Pearce asks mockingly. "Soon the two of you will be gone, and the City will truly belong to me. Unlike my father's rule, mine will have no end. My Undead friends make a rather invincible army, don't you think? Devourers of flesh and souls, and oh so grateful to trade their world for ours. They will faithfully serve me *forever*."

He turns around to face the knot of Bloom and his henchmen. "That reminds me. Now that my greatest enemies are powerless before me, it's time for my second-in-command"—and here he points to Bloom, who steps forward eagerly—"to *die*," Pearce finishes.

Bloom doesn't even have time to scream.

Pearce throws up his hands, and a white light flares from his palms. An instant later, Bloom is a pile of ash. The swirling breeze blows what's left of him away.

Chapter 72

Whit

PEARCE TURNS BACK to us triumphantly. "I don't think you ever liked him, either," he confides.

"You're a monster," Wisty says.

Pearce nods as he begins pacing back and forth. "Yes, I suppose I am now. Alive and Undead at the same time. Instead of a true soul, I carry a piece of the Shadowland inside me."

"No wonder you always felt like ice," my sister whispers.

Pearce frowns thoughtfully at us. "But you—you two are really unbelievable. You were on your way to the palace, weren't you? Even before my men *thoughtfully* gave you a ride. Surely you must've had some plan to defeat me."

Neither Wisty nor I answer him.

Pearce's cold eyes spark with disbelief. "No? You *didn't*? Did you come here planning to improvise or beg for mercy? Oh, wait—I get it! This is a suicide mission!"

And his laughter peals out across the square.

I'm *dying* to throttle this guy. I'd practically give up my powers again for the chance to wring his skinny white neck with my bare hands.

I take a step toward Pearce, and I note how the Horsemen tense up. They'll happily bludgeon me to death before I get too close to their leader.

"Actually, we did have a plan," I announce.

Wisty looks at me sharply: *We did not*, her eyes say.

Okay, no, not exactly. Not if you're talking about a plan with clear steps to follow. Unfortunately we never got that far.

"It was a simple idea," I say. "With a high degree of difficulty."

I look around at the gathered forces, enemies from this world and the next. There are hundreds of them, if not thousands. They've got guns and swords and flesh-ripping teeth. Let's face it: if I were a betting man, I'd probably have to bet against us. The odds are just too long.

But I banish that thought as quickly as I can. I've got to focus. I'm following what I think is Wisty's lead: keeping this crazed wizard talking while waiting for our powers to build.

Then maybe, just *maybe*, we might have a chance.

"You would probably call our plan pitiful," I go on.

"No doubt," Pearce interjects.

I ignore this. "See, our plan was to cut off your head, Pearce. Or is it Darrius? Mr. Lost One? Whoever or *whatever* you are, it doesn't matter. The point is, we were going to take you out. Then see what happens to a headless beast."

Pearce halts his pacing as he considers this. He seems honestly surprised. "Really? That's it? That's all you had?"

"We were going to sacrifice ourselves to do it," I say. "So yeah, I guess you could call it a suicide mission."

Pearce looks delighted. "I'm so pleased to hear that we have the same goals: *your deaths*. I wonder, though—if I murder you both, would it still be considered suicide? Now, there's a question worthy of *The Book of Truths*."

My sister can't hold her tongue anymore. "It's already in *The Book of Truths*," she shouts. "You should read your scripture more closely. This has all been foretold, Pearce. *'From ashes and exile, vital leaders rise.'* You know what that means, don't you?"

I look at my sister in surprise. *I* don't know what it means—does she?

Pearce grins wildly. "A pre-death lesson in scripture?" he dares. "Let's hear it."

Then Wisty turns to me, and her fierce blue eyes meet mine. "*You* were exiled, Whit," she says softly. "When you gave up your powers."

"That's only half of the prophecy!"

"It's time," she whispers.

She flexes her fingers, and sparks shoot out.

"My powers," I protest. "I'm not ready—"

But Wisty never did know how to listen. The fireball shoots from her hands anyway, a huge, glowing star, and it goes flying straight toward Pearce's heart.

Chapter 73

Whit

PEARCE QUICKLY LIFTS an arm and shoots a beam of cold blue light that disintegrates the fireball in midair. He laughs madly. "No, no, no! That's too easy! *Wisteria*, you can do better than that!"

Beside me, Wisty curses as she starts to burn inferno-bright. I have to step away from the heat. She ducks her head, and I can tell she's not thinking clearly anymore. She's letting anger take her over. She's going to charge Pearce, flames and all.

It's all happening way too fast. She launches herself forward. The Horsemen are running at her, trying to grab her without being burned, and she's sprinting toward Pearce now, her mouth open in a shriek of rage.

I'm summoning the juice to transform when I see a Horseman's club fly out and connect with the side of Wisty's head with a sharp, sickening crack.

She goes down immediately. Her flames flicker, sputter—and go out.

I race to her side, calling her name. I can hear Pearce laughing.

"Isn't this fun?" he howls.

I turn Wisty over. Her eyes are closed and her hair's already matted with dark blood. Her pulse is faint and fast.

"Wisty!" But of course she can't hear me.

It wasn't supposed to happen this way.

Pearce watches with curiosity as I put my hands on Wisty's cheeks and summon my healing powers. I pray they're ready by now. This has to work.

I can't do this without her.

But I don't feel a single jolt of magic. Desperately, I reach back to the very first time I learned I could bring someone back from the brink of death—and how that someone was Wisty. It took days, and now I have only moments.

Concentrate, Whit, concentrate.

The whole world is hushed, like it's holding its breath. Come on, magic: *heal.*

"Is it bad?" Pearce calls. "I certainly hope so."

I grit my teeth and hunch over her, whispering how everything's going to be okay. As if that's not about the biggest lie I've ever told.

Then—slowly, achingly—I can feel the magic begin to build. It flows through my veins like my own blood, sluggish at first, but then circulating faster until I can feel myself heating up. As if I, too, have the power of fire.

"Everything's going to be fine," I keep saying, "everything's going to be fine." And I can feel how my magic leaves my fingertips like warm beams of light and pours into her thin, limp body. I sense how it finds the swelling in her brain and soothes it. How it stops the flow of blood. How it calms her labored breathing.

Bit by bit, the color returns to Wisty's face. The blood stops staining the cobblestones. Eventually, she opens her eyes. Focuses them on my worried face.

"My head hurts," she whispers.

"So does mine," I tell her. I'm feeling drained. Shaky. Scared as hell.

From Pearce's direction I hear confused muttering. Then he calls out, "So *this* is interesting! Either she wasn't hurt as badly as I thought, or you've got a little magic in you. I thought we'd *neutralized* you, Whitford! You didn't actually get your powers back, did you?"

My brain feels like it's been beaten with a shovel. I don't answer Pearce.

"Fine," he says. "You don't want to talk. So let's just do a little experiment." And with that, he points a finger at Janine. "*Bang*," he says—like a kid with a toy gun. Janine's eyes go wide in horror, and then she gives one earsplitting shriek and *collapses*.

Before I even have time to think, I'm by her side, reaching through the bars of the cage and screaming her name to her unhearing ears. My fingers dig into her neck; I can't find a pulse.

"No!" I shout. She can't be gone—not that quickly. That's what I tell myself as I frantically try to bring my healing powers back. I've already had enough people I love die in my arms, and I'm not going to let it happen again.

And if I can't save Janine, then what else matters?

"Whit, I'm *fine*," says a familiar voice.

I whirl around and see—*Janine?*

My eyes dart back and forth between the girl on the ground and the girl standing before me. Each one has the shiny curls I loved to twirl around my finger, those tiny ears I loved to kiss, and those damn combat boots I would have loved to throw out. Am I going insane?

The conscious Janine smiles at me. "Whit, stop messing with that thing on the ground," she says. "It's nothing. An illusion. Let it die."

Suddenly I have no idea what's going on. It's like a spell has been cast over me, and I'm frozen in indecision.

Janine beckons me forward. "Whit, come here. I've missed you so much." She holds out her arms to embrace me.

Helplessly I'm drawn to her. I start to stand. It's been so long since I've kissed her....

"It's a trick," Wisty shouts. "Pearce can transform into anyone!"

It takes me a moment to understand what she's saying. My mind's clouded with confusion and longing.

"Heal her, Whit," Wisty screams. "The *real* Janine needs you!"

The panic in her voice is enough to make me stop and turn back to the body on the ground. *Janine, is that you?* I put my hand on her cheek. It's cool as marble. My heart feels like it's breaking open.

"Heal her!" Wisty yells again.

I give one last look to the standing Janine. And I watch as she shimmers, melts—and then Pearce reappears. Laughing.

"Just playing around," he says. "Isn't this *fun*?"

"You're sick," I spit.

I grab Janine's hands and hold them to my chest. I will all the strength of my heart to surge into hers. Mine pounds harder and harder. It feels like it's going to jump out of the cage of my ribs and explode like a firework in front of me. I'm burning up; I have to clench my teeth so I don't shriek in pain.

Behind me, Pearce watches closely. Gauging how much of my powers I've gotten back, no doubt. Reconsidering his plans for my demise.

The magic streams through my body, flowing into the girl I love.

When I finally feel Janine's pulse beating lightly under my hand, I drop my hands in relief. She's not conscious yet, but I know she'll be okay.

And then I hear clapping.

"There you go with that *mercy* business again," Pearce

says. "Wasting your strength to save someone else. Making it so much easier for me to kill you."

I struggle to my feet, and Wisty comes to stand by my side. We're both breathing hard. Trembling.

We reach behind us through the bars of the iron cage and meet the clutching hands of our parents. "We love you so much," my mother sobs.

I don't have the strength to speak.

"Anyway," Pearce says, "I'm bored of this. It's time to say good-bye. First to you, and then to your parents." He laughs ruthlessly. "What's *The Book of Truths* say? 'Ashes to ashes, dust to dust.'"

And he points his fingers at us, and a corona of light surrounds his body. Inside it, he shakes and convulses as lightning shoots toward the sky. He bends down, as if summoning his strength—and when he stands up, shrieking, and flings out his arms, a huge wave of invisible fire comes roaring our way.

Our skin immediately dries, shrivels, crackles. In one moment, we are flesh; in the next, nothing but air and heat.

And *ash*.

Chapter 74

Pearce

HE'S DONE IT. He's *actually* done it, and he wants to scream in triumph.

The raging power still courses through him, sucking energy from every single nerve, every single cell. Pearce's heart pounds in his chest like a drum, and white noise roars in his ears.

He raises his fist in the air, and the Horsemen lift their clanging spears and shout in victory. The Lost Ones merely leer and grin. They're hungry, and soon, they know, it will be time to feast.

Pearce walks toward the small pile of cinders that was once a boy and a girl, a witch and a wizard. How puny it is! He almost kicks at the ashes with his foot, but then he stops, out of a spontaneous—and uncharacteristic—sense of respect.

How strange to think that some of these minute gray particles were once his greatest love and his greatest enemy. He will never forget when, as Heath, he kissed Wisteria Allgood with a passion hotter than fire.

Pearce turns to her parents now. The father's screams sound from the cage, and so do the mother's sobs. Janine, now conscious, only weeps silently. The scene could melt a heart of ice. But Pearce's heart is made of stone.

With a wave of his hand, the cage around them vanishes. Why not? They're too broken to run. They have only a few moments of life left anyway.

The battle's over. The war has been won. And though he's weakened now, Pearce knows his full powers will return soon enough.

He shivers with pleasure.

Though, he must admit, he feels a minuscule shred of regret. Yes, he'll miss Wisteria Allgood a little. The girl had *fire*.

With her wild red hair and her ocean-blue eyes, she was a sight to see. An image of her comes to him so clearly, it's almost as if she's standing before him again. Glowing. Shimmering. She's so real, he could almost reach out and touch her—

Chapter 75

Wisty

YES, IT WAS THAT EASY. We explode into cinders.

I'm everywhere and nowhere at once. I am myself, and I am also the whole great, spinning world. There is no pain. No fear. There is only light and wind and a thrilling, dizzying sense of weightlessness.

Where is Whit? Is he feeling what I feel?

Peace?

Believe me when I say there is a part of me that doesn't want to come back. Ever.

But I have to. We both have to. Because it was our trick, you see: shape-shifting of the highest order.

Pearce didn't turn us to ash—we did it to ourselves. And now it's time to return.

It isn't easy to revert to my body, to this skinny, wounded assemblage of blood and guts. It takes power. It *hurts*.

But as I flex my restored limbs and straighten my spine, rising up from a pile of ash, I feel energized somehow.

Stronger. Maybe it's the look of joy on our parents' faces as they rush to our sides. Or maybe it's the look of shock on Pearce's. The way his jaw falls wide open when we materialize in front of him again, smiling triumphantly at our illusion. He stumbles backward, knocking into one of the Horsemen, who reaches out an enormous arm and steadies him.

Enraged by our ruse, Pearce rewards the Horseman for his help by turning toward him and putting his hands on either side of his rough, chiseled face. At first it's tender, almost like a caress—until the man's skin begins to melt away.

The Horseman bears the agony without a sound. At first. But then he starts to scream. And soon he's just a bare, eyeless skull with grinning, jagged teeth.

Just like the bad old days.

The other Horsemen let out frenzied cries of betrayal, and Pearce turns on them viciously. His voice booms across the square. "Enough!" he thunders. "You have served your purpose. I have no more need of you!"

Whit looks at me in astonishment. "He's not going to—" he begins.

But Pearce's voice cuts through the air again. "Devour them!" Pearce shrieks to Vander and his Lost Ones. "My Shadowland comrades, *feast!*"

The pandemonium is instantaneous and deafening. It's the definition of *all hell breaking loose.* Whit and I watch, stunned, as the howling Undead turn and lurch toward the Horsemen, their terrible eyes glowing in anticipation of warm, red blood.

The Horsemen reach for their swords, their guns. They're skilled at violence; they can trample a man to death without a second thought. But they have no idea how to kill the Undead.

A bullet can't stop a corpse.

The Horsemen try to beat them back, but they're out-numbered. It's one thing to escape a single enemy—it's another thing entirely to escape a starving, cunning swarm of them.

The air is pierced by screams. Something comes flying toward me and crashes down at my feet. I jump back in horror: it's a Horseman's boot, with a severed foot inside.

In little more than an instant, the Horsemen have lost a tenth of their men.

This is what will happen to the whole entire world if Whit and I can't stop it.

I flex my fingers, and I can feel the M running hot. The crazy shape-shift should have drained all my power, but sharing my M with Whit has somehow made it stronger for both of us. It's just a matter of the right moment to use it.

Cut off the head of the beast.

In the center of the mayhem, Pearce smiles cruelly. "Do you see what the Undead are capable of?" he asks us, his voice full of awe. "They're like a plague of locusts.

'They will cover the face of the ground so that it cannot be seen'—isn't that in *The Book of Truths*?"

By now I've got a fireball burning behind my back. "I don't remember that part," I say. And then I launch it at Pearce's chest.

He ducks, and it misses him just barely, exploding on the cobblestones and taking out another unlucky Horseman. I can't say I feel too bad about that.

Pearce cackles. "Missed me, missed me, now you have to kiss me," he says tauntingly.

"Kiss *this*," I murmur. Another fireball hits Pearce in the shoulder, spinning him around like a left hook.

"Ow," he says. But he's *grinning* at me. "I always did love chaos," he barks. "It's so much more interesting than order."

He still thinks this is a *game*.

But I'm deadly serious. When I look at him, my mind's flooded with every terrible thing he did—each lie he whispered, every child he hurt, all the innocent lives he stole—and the fire burns so hot inside me that I feel like a shooting star. I feel like my fury could consume him.

Or consume us both.

My brother launches himself into the air, taking the shape of an enormous white bird that dive-bombs Pearce's head, raking its talons along the side of Pearce's skull and opening up deep, bloody gashes.

Pearce falters as the blood runs down his face. How

fortunate that half-Undead wizards feel pain just like everybody else! Pearce wipes the gore from his eyes and flings bright-red splatters to the ground. In the air, my brother turns and wheels, his great wings shining in the sun. Then he tucks them in as he plummets down behind Pearce, slamming into him from behind.

Pearce is flung forward to his hands and knees. I aim another burning sphere that connects with the side of his head. I swear I can hear a crunching sound—as if, by the time it reached him, my flames had become solid as stones.

Pearce struggles to stand. Just as he gets nearly vertical, my brother the bird crashes into him again. This time I *know* I hear a crunching sound.

I'm floating up in the air now, sparks showering off me. Pearce falls down, tears flowing down his cheeks and blood streaming from his wounds. He summons another wave of invisible heat, but I can sense it now, and I move out of its way.

All around us the Undead keep howling, and I pray there are enough Horsemen for them to eat so they don't start coming for us. Not until we finish with Pearce.

The magic's running through me stronger than I've ever felt it before. And I wonder if Aunt Bea was right— that power willingly given away returns in greater force, exactly when you need it most.

My brother and I come at Pearce from all sides, flame and feathers and fury. "Surrender now," I shout.

Pearce is pale from blood loss, from using his dark powers, but he shakes his head defiantly. "You'll have to kill me," he says.

From the mouth of the bird comes my brother's voice. *"Gladly."*

Chapter 76

Wisty

I SEND STREAMS of searing magic Pearce's way and he doesn't block them anymore. He cringes, cowering against the ground, but for some reason he doesn't try to flee.

It's almost as if he really wants to die.

Whit lands beside me, then flashes back to human form. He's breathing hard, but I sense his power's not exhausted yet. We look at each other—at our parents, at Janine—and we grimly nod. We're ready. *Time to end this thing.* We're going to set this City free.

The next second, we're both running toward Pearce, me with fire and Whit with fists. Until something...*crazy* happens. Something unimaginable. And it stops us in our tracks.

Pearce's crumpled body begins to shudder and convulse, as if something's tearing him up from the inside. And then, like lava bursting from a volcano, a brilliant red cascade of sparks shoots out from his chest. The sparks turn yellow, then white—and there's a great hissing sound as the sparks begin to come together. First, they form the shape of a torso . . . and then limbs. . . .

We watch, stunned, as the magic light coalesces into the spirit of a man.

A man with a familiar, cruel face and the Technicolor eyes that have haunted my dreams since the day I last saw them.

The dreadful spirit stares down at the broken, weeping body of Pearce below him. Then it turns its terrible gaze on us. "My son was always such a disappointment," says none other than—honestly it feels like my mind's melting to even think it—*The One Who Is The One.*

I can barely form the words. "But I—I killed you," I stammer.

The One smiles. "You killed my body, witch," he allows. His voice doesn't come from the spirit's glowing mouth; it comes from inside my mind, and I feel each of his words like a hammer in my brain. "So I used my boy's." He glances down at Pearce again. "I had higher hopes for it than it—than *he*—delivered." He hovers menacingly above his sobbing son, oblivious to the battle between the Horsemen and the Lost that rages all around him. "I was tired of waiting. Stuck inside the last shred of his soul. Held tight like a captive."

Whit gasps. "*You're* the Lost One he shared his soul with!"

This . . . *creature* disgusts me almost more than he terrifies me. "Like a parasite," I hiss. "A tapeworm."

333

The One's light flares alarmingly. "Call it what you will. I thought I could trust him to carry out my bidding. I believed I could count on him to destroy you. But when I realized that he could not, my strategy changed." He pauses, his attention shifting upward. "In Shadowland, I grew unused to sunshine," he says—as if he's just making conversation. But then he turns his face to the sky, which immediately darkens. Clouds rush in overhead, great gray billows like the toxic smoke of the Underworld. The temperature drops immediately.

Then he turns back to us. "Much better," he says. He gestures to his son, who slowly lifts himself up—or maybe *is lifted up*—from the ground. Pearce stands before us, enveloped in the harsh, cold light of his father's ghostly power. His shoulders are shaking. He looks scared and broken.

Like a little boy whose daddy never loved him.

"We are connected, you see, but now *I* am in charge," The One says. His voice inside my head grows louder. "And I will have my revenge. It has been a long time in coming."

The sky goes all the way to black now, ripped through by lightning. In the brilliant flashes, the half-eaten corpses of the Horsemen stand out in sharp relief against the cobblestones.

"How nice to see that my Undead friends are having a picnic," The One says, and his laughter slices through my thoughts like a blade.

Then the air fills with a terrible roaring, and Pearce

straightens up, as if he's been yanked by puppet strings, and he begins stalking toward us, the spirit of his father glowing around him like a hellish aura.

I can't tell where Pearce ends and his father begins. Their hands reach out for us, burning with blue incandescence. They're pulling me forward, as if by a new and irresistible gravitational force.

I send a stream of white-hot fire toward this half-human, half-Undead monster, but it has no effect. Pearce's lips move quickly as he recites a dark spell. His phantom father grows larger and larger. His cold light is swallowing up everything.

They advance, and I am sucked toward them. My limbs are burning and frozen at the same time. My legs move me forward even when I want them to stop—they don't even seem to belong to me anymore. I feel my arms opening against my will, as if I'm welcoming death's oblivion.

I hear my mother screaming.

I feel The One's words inside my head, and I wonder if Whit hears them, too.

Life ends, but death does not. Just surrender. Give yourself over to eternity.

I don't know why I can barely breathe. I open my mouth as wide as it can go, trying to draw oxygen into my lungs. I try to summon my M again, but it's not coming—

The light from The One is blinding.

I feel the monster's touch, and a devastating pain shoots through me. I don't know if I'm being ripped to shreds or if it just feels like it. I don't know who I'm fighting. I don't know anything anymore.

My eyesight begins to blur and everything wavers in front of me.

I can't breathe at all now. My mind feels like it's shutting down.

There's that small voice inside me again. This time it doesn't encourage me, though. This time it says, *So this is what dying's like.*

And no, I don't see a white, reassuring light. My life doesn't flash before my eyes. I see only fire. I feel only fear. I hear the sounds of battle, and above it all, the screams of my parents as they're forced to watch me be killed. This time it's not a trick. This time it's for real.

Pearce is whispering something, but I don't know what it is. The One is laughing, a sound like screeching hellhounds.

Then suddenly, like a curtain pulled across my face, the numbness comes. It's almost a relief. I'm going to die.

I am actually going to die.

I fall down to the ground, gasping. And that's when I see the dark shape racing toward us, shrieking madly, brandishing a terrible, shining sword.

It's a demon from hell, coming for me. And I welcome it.

Chapter 77

Wisty

BUT JUST BEFORE it reaches me, the demon swerves off course and races toward the mighty monster that is Pearce and The One.

"You said you wouldn't hurt her!" it's screaming. "You promised!"

The bright sword swings down in a crazy flash of metal, and Pearce's right hand, severed in an instant, crashes to the ground. Its fingers still twitch, as if grasping for something to hold on to.

Pearce arches his back and howls toward the black sky. The One's spirit roils and darkens.

The shadowy figure turns to me, smiling triumphantly. I can*not* believe it. It's not a demon—it's *Byron Swain*.

Then a sudden blow from Pearce's other hand knocks Byron to the ground. He lands hard on the cobblestones, and I scream, "Byron, run!"

Pearce staggers forward, blood pouring from his stump. The One's spirit burns blistering hot, then icy cold.

"You will pay for that, you stinking, rat-faced traitor."

I don't even know who says it—The One or Pearce. But what does it matter? They both want to kill us. *All* of us.

Byron flinches in fear. He's trying to get to his feet, and he's brandishing his sword, like he expects his luck to hold. But he knows as well as I do the extent of these wizards' powers.

Which means he must know he's going to die.

"Byron," I scream again. I can finally move again, but alone I'm too weak to help him. I can't even turn him into a weasel that would be smart enough to run away.

Quickly I grab my brother's hand, and together we stagger toward Byron. We lift him up and hold him, swaying, between us. He's badly hurt: his skin is burned from The One's cold fire, and he's bleeding. He must have had to fight his way through the Undead to get to us. It's a miracle he even made it.

The One's voice resounds. "I will kill all of you together!"

And that's when it hits me. When I realize exactly what I need to do. "Mom! Dad! Janine!" I scream. *"Come here!"*

My mom's eyes spark in fear. Janine hesitates, and doubt crosses my father's face. They know I don't have the powers to face The One. Each of them must be wondering, *What can I possibly do?* They just have to trust that I'm not asking them to die with me.

They have to believe that I know what I'm doing.

Because I think—I *think*—I do.

I once channeled my magic through Byron and it grew stronger. It's like Aunt Bea said: *Power willingly shared can grow even stronger. Power given is power gained.*

You just have to trust me, I think *at* my parents. *Trust me, trust me, trust me.*

I send it out like a prayer.

And then, as if they can indeed hear my thoughts, they run forward, until they're standing by my side. I can almost hear their hearts pounding. Mom takes my hand; Dad takes hers; Janine grasps Whit's. And here we are: six people trying to stop the end of the world.

Remember, only love.

"Take us all at once," I shout to The One—to Pearce. "We'll make it easy for you!"

"*As you wish!*" roars the monster.

The One's outlines blur. Pearce's face goes dark with rage.

But I'm not afraid. I can feel the energy around us changing. It's even bigger than the six of us, and for a second, I'm at a loss—what strange and mighty magic do I feel?

And then Whit says, awed, "*Look!*"

We turn toward the square, toward the carnage of the Horsemen. There aren't any left that I can see. Not alive, anyway. But the Undead haven't turned on us yet, because striding into the square is an army of kids.

Led by the blond-haired, gray-eyed girl who we told how to kill the Undead.

Shockingly fearless, this mob of kids rushes toward the Undead, their arms outstretched. I close my eyes; I can't bear to see them die.

Soon I hear the screaming, and I'd give anything to make it stop.

But then Whit gives a shout of triumph. "They're doing it," he cries.

And I look, and I see that it's the Undead who are screaming. Who are running. Fleeing. Who are being destroyed by love, by *children*.

The One howls in rage, his spirit rocking skyward. Pearce is dragged into the air with him and hangs like a rag doll in midair.

"My brothers, retreat!" shouts The One. And he points a giant glowing arm at the center of the square, where the tiles were laid in the shape of a many-rayed sun. There's a terrible shattering, cracking sound, and then the porcelain sun breaks open, disintegrating, and its pieces plunge down into what is now a huge black hole in the earth.

Ashen smoke billows out from it, and I smell the cold rot of Shadowland.

But instead of more Lost Ones crawling out of the hole, the Lost are diving in, returning to the nightmarish land where they cannot be killed.

Chapter 78

Wisty

THE KIDS IN the square cheer, but for us, the fight's far from over. The One's blazing ghost sinks back down to face us, and Pearce drops to the ground with him.

"They will be back later," The One says. "With reinforcements. No need to worry, however...." He smiles. "You'll be dead by then."

"I'm not so sure about that," I challenge. I squeeze the hands of Byron and my mother, and I can feel the power coursing through us.

We are juiced, we are electric, we are freaking *radioactive*.

Goaded by his father, Pearce suddenly lunges, grabbing for Byron's face like he's going to melt his skin off. But Whit blocks it, smashing his big arm down like a gate in front of the wizard. The One, though unable to break his connection to Pearce, veers to send a stream of blue fire at me from his fingertips.

It bounces away, as if there's a force field around us.

Only love.

Not hate or greed or longing.

The six of us stand together, blazing like suns.

The One conjures hail that crashes down from the black clouds, but not even that can touch us. He howls.

I don't know how to kill a spirit, but I know how to kill a body.

"*Now,*" I shout, and the electricity shoots out of all of us with the force of a rocket, careering toward Pearce, who isn't fast enough to move away. When it strikes him in the sternum, he's lit up from within. I swear I can see his thin, pale bones, glowing like fluorescent lights.

He screams and screams and screams.

And I can feel his pain. His terror.

It's the worst thing I've ever felt.

I close my eyes and clench my teeth. I won't stop. Beside me, Byron shakes and sobs. With all that power coursing through him, he must feel like he's about to explode.

And I do, too. My blood boils in my veins. There's a white-hot energy searing through me, a feeling that no longer has anything to do with mercy or love.

I keep the power coming. And I can feel Pearce's heart the instant it stops.

Lightning explodes from the sky, tearing the black clouds to tattered shreds. The ground beneath our feet begins to rumble and shake. A pillar from the Old Palace comes crashing down, splintering into shards of white marble. Two others teeter like they're going to fall any minute.

The One screams in agony, the sound so loud it feels like it will split my head apart. He turns on us, raving, and then he looks back at his son. With all the power of his deathless spirit, he shoots crackling white electricity at Pearce's heart. The lifeless body writhes and jumps, ripped through by an incredible force.

Whit gasps. "He's making a defibrillator," he says.

"A *what*?" I yell.

The electricity flows into Pearce, wave after pulsing wave. His clothes burn away from his chest. Smoke rises from his skin.

"He's going to start his heart again!" Whit cries. "With electricity. Just like we do in the hospital!"

I stare at my brother in amazement. *It can't be.*

But sure enough, a moment later, Pearce's eyes open. They are as cold and icy blue as they ever were. He's alive.

And I want to just crumple to the ground right there. How do I find the mental strength to keep fighting?

And, more practically: how much longer can we run this protective circuit of magic through us? I don't think Byron can stand it much longer. I can feel him weakening. He's not used to so much energy.

Pearce blinks at us as he sits up and manages to get to his knees. He's panting. His cheeks are pale. He opens his mouth to speak. For a minute, nothing comes out but gasping breaths.

Until he says something I never thought I'd hear.

He raises his fist at the incandescent shape of his father. "When I was wounded on the mountainside, you just *pretended* to give me back my life," he shouts. "And now you've done it again. But you don't know how to give! *All you ever do is take.*"

The One's light flickers. "Silence, idiot," he snarls.

"You can't keep stealing from me," Pearce yells. "My power. My will. My body. They aren't yours! I'm *done.*" As he screams this, he begins to crawl. But not toward us.

Toward the pit that leads to Shadowland.

And The One, his parasitic father, must follow him; they are connected. "Don't you dare," he shrieks. His phantom fingers claw at his son's back.

But Pearce is inching closer to the ground's gaping maw. "I will!" The fingers on his one remaining hand scrabble at the edge. He's going to pull himself over into it.

The One burns bright as a supernova. His howl scissors through the air. "We'll return! With an army of the Lost!"

Pearce smiles ferociously at the raging ghost. *"We won't."* Then he turns to us. "But you have to make sure of that!"

I start, as if jolted by a shock—I'd been mesmerized by the battle between father and son. *"How?"*

"You have to close the portals," Pearce cries. He's halfway into the hole now.

But his father is raising a cyclone above the square. He's blazing in fury. And his ghostly hands are trying to close his son's mouth.

Close all the portals that we, as slaves, opened? "They're everywhere in the City! How do we find them?" I cry.

"*This* is the only one that matters!" Pearce says. "The sun in the center of the City. The founders marked it—because it's the mother of all portals. Close it, and you close them all!"

I'm at the end of my strength. The end of my powers. "But *how*?"

"Shut up!" The One screams.

But Pearce, for once in his life, will not be controlled by his father. His pale, desperate eyes bore into mine. "You have to close it—from the inside."

It takes me a minute to figure out what he means. And then I understand. One of us must follow them to Shadowland.

And lock ourselves in.

Watching me, The One begins to roar with laughter. "Ah! She understands!" he yells. His Technicolor eyes flash and burn. "So, Wisteria, the choice is yours. Will you do it? Do you love your world enough to die for it?"

And I remember what Whit asked me, long ago, in Shadowland, right before what I'd thought was our final showdown with The One. *Are you ready for your own end?*

Yes, I'd said then.

I toss my head back, and the cyclonic wind whips around my face. This might be one of the last things I ever feel. "The answer was always yes!" I shout defiantly.

And Pearce's face lights up—in joy or triumph or

malevolence, I have no idea. But what does it matter? Because a second later, he leans his body out over the black hole, and then, with a thin and haunting cry, he plummets down into it.

He's gone.

Gone.

The blinding awful spirit of his father rockets up to the sky. The One's arms now grasp at the roiling clouds, as if they could hold him up in this world. Their black forms explode in color: blood red, bile green, bone white.

The One's shrieks ring in my ears. Thunder explodes in the heavens.

And then, with a stunning gravitational force, The One is sucked down. Back into the earth, and beneath it, to the Underworld, right on the heels of his dying, unbeloved son.

I let go of Byron's hand.

I pry my mother's grip from mine.

Let's end this thing.

It's time to close the portal. I grit my teeth as I march forward. At the lip of the portal pit, I look around me, taking in the world one last time.

The square. The marble palace. The faces of my family. The hint of blue sky, like a promise, at the very edge of the horizon.

And then I step forward, and my foot touches only air.

Good-bye.

But then I'm hit with a tremendous force from my left—

so hard I go flying sideways and stars explode in front of my eyes.

I land facedown on the cobblestones. Blood streams from my brow. But quickly I lift myself up and turn—only to see Byron, my friend, my nemesis, at the edge of the hole, smiling at me.

"I always did love you," he says softly.

And then he leaps into the void.

"Byron!" I scream, but it's too late.

A brilliant blue light erupts from the pit. Azure flames reach higher and higher into the sky, shooting up to the clouds. When it makes contact with them, they explode into tiny crystals of ice that fall like diamonds.

Inside the blazing light, I see the faint, swirling ghosts of The One Who Is The One, of Izbella, and of Pearce. A family united in death.

And then I see the faint, shimmering outline of Byron, who paid for our freedom with his life.

The roaring wind grows louder and stronger. It rushes through the square with blistering force, snapping the flags on their poles, ripping plants from the ground, knocking the army of kids to their knees.

And then, suddenly, it's gone.

The world is silent. The sun comes out in a blaze of new gold, warming the corpses and the ashes.

It's over.

And I can't stop screaming.

EPILOGUE

WITCH & WIZARD

Chapter 79

Whit

IT'S BEEN A WEEK since we defeated Pearce and The One—or, as the newspapers put it, "wrenched our City from the hands of evil."

We spent the days lying low. Being with our family. Recovering.

Because, you know, saving mankind kind of takes it out of a person.

Janine walks into the room where I'm doodling on the margins of a newspaper while Wisty tries to comb her wild red hair into some kind of order. (It's not working that well.) Janine comes over to me and sits on my lap, wrapping her arms around my neck. "Ready?" she asks.

I bury my face in her sweet-smelling curls. "No," I mumble.

Wisty frowns in the mirror. "I swear, one of these days, I'm just going to shave this mop off," she mutters.

"You'll start a new fashion trend," I warn her.

Wisty considers this for a moment, then says, "Never mind."

She gives up on the brush and slips her hair into a shining ponytail. However she wears her hair on the upcoming broadcast—when we address the citizens of the City we saved—will be how all the girls wear it tomorrow. Wisty's basically a superhero these days.

And, okay, I've got something of a fan club, too.

Wisty straightens her shoulders and gives me an expression that's part smile, part grimace. Her smiles, her laughter, are so rare ever since we lost Byron that seeing one now feels like the sun shining for an instant from behind gray clouds. "All right," she says. "Let's get this show on the road."

I hug Janine tight around the waist. "Are you sure you don't want to do the public speaking for me? You're so good at it."

She shakes her head. "The people need to see *you*," she says. "You and Wisty. Together. 'From ashes and exile, vital leaders rise.' We understand now: that's you two."

I sigh; I know she's right.

She straightens my collar. "You both look great."

Wisty grins at Janine, then sticks her tongue out at me. Typical.

Together my sister and I leave the backstage greenroom and step onto the platform high above the palace courtyard. The crowd gathered below begins to shout and cheer, fists pumping in the air. The red lights on the cameras blink on, and when I raise my hand, the noise quiets. All over town, video screens flash our faces, larger than life. We're in the streets, the schoolyards, the living rooms—everywhere.

For a moment I stand there, blinking in the lights. "Go on," Wisty whispers. "You wrote the speech, didn't you?"

I shrug. Not really. I had a simple plan, with a high degree of difficulty. The plan was: *wing it*.

Heck, it worked the last time.

I gaze out on the square, and when I see all the hopeful faces, my heart fills with joy and relief. I clear my throat. *Time to do this thing.*

"Friends and fellow citizens," I begin. "Together we mark the end of a hellish journey. We have fought a long battle and defeated a terrible tyrant so that we may gather here, in peace and freedom." I pause, my eyes searching the audience for familiar, magic faces: Aunt Bea, Mrs. Highsmith, my parents. When I spot them, gathered in a little group, I stand up straighter. "But for some of us, the battle began first inside ourselves. We were told—and, more importantly, we let ourselves believe—that magic was something to be feared. That because it was complicated and occasionally unpredictable, it was dangerous and we should not have it. My friends, how wrong we were." I take a deep breath. I'm finally saying what I know to be true. "What I want to tell you today is that we are *all* magic, whether or not we can transform or heal or burst into flames. We are magic because we are *alive*. We are magic because we feel joy. Because we make art and music and... hell, even babies." I blush when I say that last part. But my parents are beaming at me, and Aunt Bea makes a hot-pink rose bloom in the air over her head. "And for those of us with more obvious powers? Well, we are going to try to share them with you. Because sharing magic is what makes it—and all of us—stronger."

Applause ripples through the audience, but I raise my hand. We're not done.

Wisty steps forward to the microphone, her eyes bright with happiness and unshed tears. "We stand here before you triumphant and humbled. For all the magic that my brother and I share, The One's demise was brought about by a regular boy. A teenager. A *friend*." Now she stifles a sob as she looks toward the side of the stage, where Byron's girlfriend, Elise, watches, her face a heart-wrenching mix of pride and grief.

"You know he's going to come back and haunt you," she'd told Wisty through her tears. *"Be on the lookout for ferrets."*

Wisty and Elise smile at each other now. "This friend gave his life for me, and for all of us," Wisty tells the crowd. "And so, when you look at the people around you today, think of Byron Swain, and remember this: ordinary people can have depths of courage you couldn't even fathom." She has to stop for a second to blow her nose. Then she goes on. "Byron said to me once, 'We have to stick together.' And so when I stand up here, I think of Byron Swain. I think, *We have to stick together.* We have to do what's *best* for each other. That's the secret to running a City, or a world."

I put my arm around Wisty. She's spoken the truth, and I've never been more proud of her. "Today the legacy of cruelty is finally over," I declare. "My sister and I stand here before you, ready to serve."

But then Wisty interjects, "No, that's not exactly right." Her voice wavers at first, but quickly grows strong and firm. "We're finally ready . . . to *lead*."

The sound of applause is deafening. Cannons fire at the edge of the square as confetti falls down from the sky like snow.

Like ashes of the lost.

I turn to Wisty and gather her up in a huge bear hug. Here we are, sister and brother, witch and wizard. *Free.*

Janine rushes from the wings and joins in, and then my parents come up onstage and so does crazy old Aunt Bea. We're all hugging one another and crying and clapping and Wisty can't help it: she starts shooting off sparks.

The cheering grows even louder. Then Wisty turns and flings up an enormous rainbow that arcs magnificently over the square, its colors glittering like heavenly, electric jewels.

What can heal a broken City? Magic is definitely part of it.

But in the end, it comes down to love.

Love.

I hope you can feel it, too.

MAX
IS
BACK!

MAXIMUM RIDE FOREVER
COMING IN 2015

TURN THE PAGE FOR A SNEAK PEEK.

Prologue

One

Hey, you!

This is important. What you're holding in your hands is the only written record of the new history of the world. Don't freak out—I know I'm making it sound like a textbook, and believe me, I hated school more than anyone. But this much I can promise: It's not like any textbook you've read before. See, this chunk of pages tells the story of the apocalypse and all that came after—some pretty heavy stuff, for sure, and I don't blame you for being nervous. We all know that history tends to repeat itself, though, so for your sake and the sake of the future, I hope you'll read it . . . when you're ready.

Max

Two

I KNOW WHY you're here, and I know what you want.

You want to know what *really* happened.

You want the truth.

I get it. I've wanted the same thing my whole life.

But now I'm convinced the only real truth is the one you find out for yourself. *Not* what some grown-up or CNN tells you. The problem is, the truth isn't always kittens and rainbows. It can be harsh. It can be extremely hard to believe. In fact, the truth can be the very last thing you *want* to believe.

But if you're like me, you'd rather put on your big-girl pants than dwell on things—and truths—beyond your control.

Like the fact that I was a test-tube baby whose DNA was grafted with a bird's, so rather than your typical childhood filled with cartoons and tricycles, I spent my most adorable years in a dog crate, poked and prodded by men in white coats.

Cowardly jerks.

And how my flock and I escaped and spent our entire lives after that being hunted down by Erasers—human-wolf mutants with truly eye-watering dogbreath.

While rolling with the punches (and bites and kicks), I had a mountain of personal crap to deal with, too. I was betrayed by my own father, who also turned my half brother, Ari, into an Eraser to kill me. Family fun!

Then Fang left us—left *me*, heartbroken—to start a new flock with my freaking *clone*. I won't lie—that one stung.

And I can't forget the crazies.... There are a lot of bad people out there who want to do a *lot* of bad things. From the suicidal Doomsday cult to the population-cleansing nutcases, we've fought them all.

And the icing on the cake? Something happened—a meteor? A nuclear bomb? We might never know—that caused all hell to break loose...and destroyed the world.

Yep.

But you want to know what *really* happened after the apocalypse. Fair enough. The story belongs to all of us, especially *you*. Our history is your future.

Disclaimer: This is a story of perseverance and hope, but it's also one of grief. I've seen things—terrible things—that no one should even know exist. I've witnessed the world's darkest days and humanity's ugliest moments. I've watched cities collapse, friends die. This is the hardest story I've ever had to tell.

Still think you can handle it?

Let's go back, then. Our journey starts on an island somewhere in the South Pacific, not long after the sky first caught fire. You'll want to make sure your seat is in a locked, upright position, and prepare for some turbulence.

After all, we're talking about the end of the world.

Book One
APOCALYPSE

1

BREATHE, MAX. FORCE the air in and out.

The air was heavy, and the rotten-egg stench burned the inside of my nose, but I focused on inhaling and exhaling as I ran. The earth shook violently and my feet slid over loose rocks as I raced down the slope. Red-hot coals pelted the earth around us as volcanic ash set our hair on fire and ate tiny, stinging holes in our clothes.

"Our backpacks!" I yelled, stumbling to a stop. I couldn't believe I'd forgotten them. "They're all we have left. Tools, knives—the crossbow!"

"We left them in the field!" Nudge cried.

I shaded my eyes and looked up—the air was thick with spewing magma, ash, and glowing rock belched up from deep beneath the earth. "I'm going for them," I decided. As the leader of the flock, responsible for everyone's survival, I didn't have much choice. "You guys get to that rock outcropping by the southern beach. It's the only protection we'll find."

"You have five minutes, tops," warned Gazzy, our nine-year-old explosives expert. "This whole part of the island's gonna blow."

"Right," I said, but I was already sprinting up the hill through the hailstorm of fiery pebbles. I might have flown faster, but I couldn't risk singeing my flight feathers right now. I grabbed the backpacks and raced back.

The ground shuddered again—a churning quake this time that felt like it was shifting my organs around. I lost my balance and catapulted forward, the provisions we needed torn from my arms as I face-planted hard.

Sprawled in the dirt, I focused through the dizziness just in time to see a smoking boulder the size of a refrigerator bouncing toward my head. I tucked my chin and rolled, saying a silent prayer.

Then I heard the sound—*BOOM!* It was like a rocket had been set off inside my brain. I may have blacked out, I don't know.

Shaking my head, I opened my eyes and gasped. The boulder had obliterated the space where I had just been lying, but beyond that, the top of the volcano was now shooting off a thousand-foot column of liquid fire and smoke.

I gaped, mesmerized, as bright orange lava oozed over the cliff we'd called home for the last three months.

Then the sky started to rain blazing rocks, *big* ones, and I snapped back to attention.

Craaaaap.

I leaped to my feet, frantically grabbing backpacks and scooping up the scattered tools that were all we had left. The ground around me was being covered with hot ash, and as I reached for Gazzy's pack, it went up in flames. I snatched my burned hand back, swearing as the nerves convulsed with pain.

"*Max, hurry!*" My ears were ringing, but Angel's voice was clear inside my head. Ordinarily, I would be annoyed at being bossed around by a mind-reading seven-year-old, but the terror behind her words made my throat dry up.

I looked back at the volcano. Considering the size of the boulders it was hurling out of its crater, conditions could be even deadlier farther down the mountain.

What was I *thinking*, leaving my family? Forget the tools—I had to run!

My mouth filled with the taste of deadly sulfurous gas, and as it tore at my lungs I wheezed, choking on my own phlegm while glowing bombs fell all around me. I stumbled through the ash and rubble, tripping again and again, but I kept going.

I had to get back to my flock.

Another hundred yards and I would be at the meeting place. Pumping my legs, I took the turn onto the rock outcropping at top speed . . .

And sailed toward a river of boiling lava.

2

WHOAAA—

I windmilled my arms as momentum propelled me out into midair, with nothing but red-hot death below. As gravity took hold and I felt myself starting to drop, my avian survival instinct kicked in automatically. A pair of huge speckled wings snapped out from my back and caught the air, swooping me aloft on a hot, acrid updraft. I quickly wheeled back to the outcropping and closed my highly flammable wings.

"Wow!" Total's voice reached me over the sounds of the eruption, and then I saw his small, black Scottie-like head peer out from a shallow cave beneath the boulders. He came and stood next to me, his paws stepping gingerly on the hot ground. His small black wings were tucked neatly along his back. Did I mention that everyone in my mutant flock had wings? Yup, even our talking dog.

"I thought you were a goner," he said, nose wrinkling from the horrible smell.

"Your faith in me is touching, Total." I tried to steady my voice, but it sounded hollow and shaky.

Gazzy came out and nodded up at the volcano with seriously misplaced admiration. "She's a feisty one. This is just the start of it." With his love of fire and explosions, this eruption was the best thing that had ever happened to him.

"The lava's, what? Fifty feet wide?" I backed up as the edge of the outcropping began to get swallowed up by the tar-like river—a thick black goo with brilliant flashes of orange where molten stone glowed with heat. "We'll fly across, find a safer place on the northern side."

Gazzy nodded. "Right now we can. But see that molten mudslide rolling toward us? It's about two thousand degrees Fahrenheit. If we don't get to high ground fast, we're cooked."

It already felt like my clothes were melting onto my body—clearly Gazzy knew what he was talking about.

"Let's move!" I yelled.

Fang was already grabbing up the backpacks. Always calm and always competent, he was the steady rock to my whirling tornado. I rushed to join him, trying not to wince as my burned hand throbbed. We didn't have much, but what we had we couldn't replace: Besides our few weapons, we had some clothing stripped from the dead, cans of food that had washed up on shore, medicinal herbs plucked from now-extinct trees.

"Okay," I panted. "Have we got everything?"

Nudge shook her head, her lovely face smudged with soot. "But if the lava reaches the lake..."

Then the water supply we've stored there will be obliterated.

"I'll go back for the jugs," Dylan and I said at the same time.

"The sulfur levels just tripled!" Iggy shouted. "Smells like acid rain!"

"I'll go," Dylan repeated firmly.

Fang was my true love, but Dylan had literally been *created* to be a perfect partner for me: It would be against his nature not to protect me if he could. It was both endearing and maddening, because, *hello?* I'm not so much a damsel in distress as I am an ass-kicking mutant bird kid.

Now Dylan touched my burned hand so tenderly that for a second I forgot about being tough and was just grateful for his help during the chaos. He nodded at the other kids. "They need you here. Just work on getting everyone to the northern beaches, and I'll be back in a minute."

I frowned. "Yeah. But be careful, okay?"

"You're not actually worried about me, are you, Max?" His turquoise eyes twinkled playfully.

"No," I said, making an *ew* face at him.

He laughed. "I'll catch up."

I turned, smiling and shaking my head, and of course there was Fang, standing behind me silent as a shadow. He cocked an eyebrow and I flushed. I opened my mouth to say something, but he was already reaching past me for the backpack Dylan had left.

"Hover chain?" Fang asked brusquely. He knew me better than anyone, so he knew when to leave things alone. When I nodded, he unfurled his huge black wings, then leaned down and picked up Akila. A big, beautiful malamute, she was the only non-mutant among us—and the love of Total's life. Trying not to breathe the poisonous air, Fang leaped up and took off across the steaming river of molten rock.

"Okay, Iggy," I ordered. "You're up next! Nudge, get ready. Total, wings out. Gazzy and Angel, I'll be right behind you. Let's go, go, go!"

When I was sure my flock was airborne, I shook out my wings and followed, pushing down hard with each stroke as I struggled through the swirling ash. Burning and smoking debris pelted me from above, and waves of lava roiled below. The air was so toxic I could actually feel my lungs shriveling.

It was a short, hard flight. There was a fierce swirling wind from above that pushed us down almost as hard as we pushed up against it. The lava below us burned a deep red-orange, and as it took in more oxygen, it crackled loudly and started to spit. It took all my strength to stay aloft as my flight feathers curled up in embers. I blinked away tears, trying to spot my flock through the sizzling smoke and steam. The skin on my ankles started to blister—I was literally being slow-roasted, and I prayed that the others had made it across.

You are in a cool place. You are in Alaska. It's freezing. Cool air in your lungs... I saw Fang emerge from the steam, a dark figure carrying a large dog. Everyone else was across now, but I veered back over the river of lava to do one final sweep, make sure we had everything....

My neck snapped sideways as a red-hot rock smacked into my head, and before I knew it I was careening down again toward the smoking, burping mouth of hell. I managed a strangled scream and then felt my whole body jerk as a hand yanked me upward.

"Gotcha." Fang smirked at me with that crooked smile of his and held me in his arms. "What do you say we get outta here?" Even with the chaos swirling around us, my heart skipped a beat at that smile.

Our feet sank into the far bank *just* before the mudslide surged into the river. It sent lava shooting up hundreds of feet like a fizzy explosion of orange soda, but we were already out of its reach. And even though my feathers were smoking and my eyebrows were singed and I was gagging on ash, I was grinning as I ran.

We made it. We've all—

"Wait." I skidded to a stop and turned around.

"What is it?" Fang asked, still tugging at my hand.

The hot air pressed in and sweat dripped down my face, but cold horror gripped my stomach like a fist.

"Where's Dylan?"

About the Authors

James Patterson is the #1 bestselling author of the Maximum Ride, Witch & Wizard, and Confessions novels, as well as *Homeroom Diaries*. His blockbuster fiction for adults, featuring enduring characters such as Alex Cross—in addition to his many books for younger readers, including the Middle School series—have sold more than 300 million copies worldwide, making him the bestselling author of the decade. He lives in Florida.

Emily Raymond worked with James Patterson on *First Love* and is the ghostwriter of six young adult novels, one of which was a #1 *New York Times* bestseller. She lives with her family in Portland, Oregon.